RARE SINGLES

●

Benjamin Myers

RARE SINGLES

Benjamin Myers

BLOOMSBURY CIRCUS
LONDON · OXFORD · NEW YORK · NEW DELHI · SYDNEY

BLOOMSBURY CIRCUS
Bloomsbury Publishing Plc
50 Bedford Square, London, WC1B 3DP, UK
29 Earlsfort Terrace, Dublin 2, Ireland

BLOOMSBURY, BLOOMSBURY CIRCUS and the Circus logo
are trademarks of Bloomsbury Publishing Plc

First published in Great Britain 2024

A catalogue record for this book is available from the British Library

ISBN: HB: 978-1-5266-7190-5; TPB: 978-1-5266-7189-9; WATERSTONES: 978-1-5266-8320-5;
EBOOK: 978-1-5266-7188-2; EPDF: 978-1-5266-7187-5

2 4 6 8 10 9 7 5 3 1

Typeset by Integra Software Services Pvt. Ltd.
Printed and bound in Great Britain by CPI Group (UK) Ltd, Croydon CR0 4YY

To find out more about our authors and books visit www.bloomsbury.com
and sign up for our newsletters

This one
is for
Jessica Woollard.

The rhythm of memory
puts time ahead of itself and we're pulled to miss
a coast that is not yet home. The tide. It's an
oxygen machine, still going. Its constant hum.

'Scarborough' by Zaffar Kunial

Ripples of energy run through the crowd like those from a stone cast into the sea's shallows.

He is hot, overheating. Skin prickles and adrenaline. Hollow legs.

There is electricity all around him, and in him. The room feels airless, a vacuum. All the clocks are melting. He feels like he is drowning in himself.

The glare of the lights trained to the stage obscure his view but if he squints from the wings, he thinks he can see familiar faces in the front row. Faces from the past, faces of those he has loved and lost. All ghosts gathered.

Am I dead already? he wonders. Or am I just dreaming?

PART ONE

The Golden Hour

The early white sun shone through the crooked blinds, the cold light of morning crawling across the worn carpet to wake him.

Bucky lay on his back and his hips hurt. Hurt like Hades. There was fire in the sockets almost all the time now, especially the right one. A terrible, torturous burning that was bad at night and even worse in the morning.

The pain only worsened when he rolled onto his better side, so he lay still. The screaming sensation in his joints was barbaric and he took it personally. If the thought of getting up and about seemed monumental, then the idea of travelling halfway across the world was an abstraction he didn't want to consider until he had at least eaten his breakfast, drunk his first coffee, taken a long, slow shower, swallowed his pills and then sunk a second coffee. Then, and only then, might he entertain the notion of shifting his lumber beyond the four walls of the small sagging house he had called home for forty years.

He was on a waiting list. They called it a procedure and apparently the *procedure* involved sawing your leg off and then reattaching it. Both of them, sometimes.

Hell.

The mind boggled.

The hip pain at least distracted from the aches and ailments in his right knee, the throb of his crooked knuckles and the troubles in his lower back, which seized up with frustrating regularity. At its worst though, the fire in his hip joints relegated all his other long-standing gripes to miserable but minor spasms and manageable twinges, each a memory of tough times. Whichever way he cut it, one pain or another dominated his every waking moment.

The UK was a long way away, an almost incomprehensible distance. He saw it as an ancient kingdom, swirling in mists. Fair maidens and knights on horseback, maybe. A deep and ancient ocean sat between him and it.

And then there was the whole medical insurance business to consider; the business being there wasn't any. He couldn't afford it. Couldn't afford travel insurance either, though he had been told it was a different medical set-up over there. In England, Bucky had read, rich and poor alike were all allowed in the same hospitals, for free. *For free.* Here in the States they called that socialism, and such even-handed fairness was branded evil, its exponents branded traitorous, un-American enemies of the state. Here if you couldn't take care of your own business, you were close to worthless, but the good thing was anyone could rise up the ranks if they buckled down, made enough cheddar. That was the homespun myth that they called the American Dream. Bucky called it straight up bull scat.

Meantime, he had to get a prescription filled.

Sweet relief from the pain was only ever achieved in that short window when the last pill was wearing off and the next one was taking effect, and even then it was only fleeting, a brief respite from the constant blaze that burned to the core of his bones. He called this period the golden hour.

In the golden hour everything was like it used to be, back when he was young and strong, when hope hadn't corroded entirely and he needed nothing more that the love of a good woman to get him through the rough patches. He had learned long ago that was more important than food or money or status or music or possessions, and with Maybellene, he had found it. It had been a privilege knowing her and being with her, all the way to the end, until the wheels fell off, just as the song said. His hip pain was nothing compared to the loss of his wife and the complete absence of love that had opened up like a swirling black vortex in her wake these past months. The disappearance of someone who had understood and accepted him diminished Bucky, as if, without her eyes to see him or her laughter to chide him, he was somehow less visible now. Shrunk down, and aged too. Some days it felt he was slowly fading from view.

It was nearly a year since she'd passed and it was not getting any easier. If anything, life felt harder as fall came around again to remind him of those dark final days, the calendar a cursed reminder of Maybellene's rapid decline.

'Hell,' he said to the ceiling.

★

At the pharmacy he waited in line and felt the painful downward drag of gravity. Sometimes it all just gets to you, he thought, no matter how much you try and train your mind otherwise. Sometimes it just weighs you down. Ageing was certainly some grade-A, forlorn BS. Layer in grief and some days a man could get to wondering what the point of it all was. A positive mental attitude was always harder when it felt like the sun had been extinguished.

There was an old-time jar of liquorice root sticks on the counter. Raymond was serving and Bucky plucked one. Raymond was the son of a woman he went to school with. A good football player when he was younger, Ray, and built like a refrigerator from the age of fifteen, but not quite good enough for it to define him. Every town has a few failed college-level quarterbacks, but Raymond had had the good sense and parenting to not let that failure put him on the wrong track towards bitterness and regret – the *coulda-woulda-shoulda* crew, with which he, Earlon 'Bucky' Bronco, was more than a little familiar. He slid the stick into his mouth and sucked it. No, Ray had gone into academia, into pharmaceuticals. He'd done it right. Smart kid, Ray. Straight. Had a plan. Got his degree.

Ray had been the pharmaceutical assistant at Walgreens for as long as Bucky had been hobbling in on his degenerating bones.

Must be some seven years since. Polite too. He had always asked after Maybell when he was picking up her drugs – and always calling her 'Miss' too. Respectful.

'And how's Miss Maybell?' he'd ask.

'Fine, son. She's doing fine.'

'Tell her I'm asking after her.'

Bucky worked some spittle into the liquorice stick. Lately the tone had shifted in Walgreens. The queues had got longer, the clientele more furtive. Younger too. A different energy prevailed most mornings. Some of the kids you saw, they practically rattled when they walked.

Hell.

He passed them out here, rat-scratching and speed-scurrying between places, perpetually on the make, hunting out new pills with new names. A few of them always seemed to be carrying flat-screen TVs or suitcases full of old CDs or wheeling a child's tiny pink bicycle. The thing that a lot of people didn't understand was that getting high and staying high was a full-time occupation; junkies *work*.

Bucky rolled the liquorice stick from one side of his mouth to the other. He couldn't judge them; one or two of these kids had been his salvation when he had hit a few bumps in the road and found himself in short supply. Everyone round here was carrying their silent traumas like sacks of rocks across their backs; that was just how it was. It was all part of surviving this endless trip they called America, and it seemed like everybody was hooked on one damn thing or another. That some were legal and others not rarely mattered.

In some ways it was probably tougher than when he was a young greenhorn. Life was faster, the stakes higher. The prisons fit to bursting. He had heard a news report the other day that said a high percentage of his countrymen believed there could be another civil war in the US within the next decade or two. Bucky couldn't argue.

Back in the day, street life was more covert, you dug in deep below the radar. A few drinks, a nice smoke and *dancing*. Dancing was everything. Not much of the hard stuff. No one danced on that. Some pills, perhaps. Pills fit in with the soul scene; they'd lift you up to where you needed to be. And cocaine back when he was coming up? Forget it. Cocaine was uptown, celebrity stuff. Cocaine was gone. Might as well have been snorting caviar. Later in the seventies, sure. But not before that, not in the sixties. Powders were out. The point was, back in the salad days, these things rarely defined a person. It was just something you did on a weekend; it was no reason to go pawning your mother's pearls.

At least today his pills served a purpose. They got him up upright and mobile, yes, sir. Got him moving, yes. Functional. They afforded him a golden hour or two. A shimmering oasis in the endless desolate desert of pain. A little bit of something was usually better than a little bit of nothing.

★

When it was Bucky's turn he handed Raymond the prescription, who took it out back, then returned to the counter a minute later to square up at the register. He passed the paper bag over the counter.

'Here you are, Bucky,' he said. 'This'll get you where you're going.'

'Reckon I'm going to England.'

'The what now?'

'I'm talking about England.'

Raymond wound his neck in with surprise. He flattened his chin down into itself and feigned a face of exaggerated disbelief.

'En-gland?'

'Yes, you know. Kings and queens. Country houses and cucumber sandwiches on the lawn. Cups of tea. I had an invite.'

'You had an invite to meet the King?'

Bucky shook his head.

'Uh-nuh. No, man.'

Raymond whistled through his teeth and reached for the prescription and reread it again, this time in a fresh context that was shaped by this casual and unexpected revelation. He looked up.

'You feeling alright, Bucky?'

'Surviving rather than thriving, but apart from the hips and the rest of it, fine enough, fine enough. But I *am* going to England.'

'Well, why do you want to go and do a thing like that at your age?'

'At my age?'

'I don't mean any offence, Buck.'

'Don't we all just keep going until we don't? Like I said, I've had an invite. To sing.'

'To sing?'

'Yes.'

'To *sing*, Bucky?'

'Saying it twice doesn't make any difference, Raymond. Yes, to sing a couple of my old cuts from back in the day. Seems like they've an ear for it over there. They've got me on at this music festival or some such. A whole weekend of music, as it transpires.'

From behind him he heard restless mutterings in the queue, but Raymond shot them a glance and then carried on regardless. Bucky knew the boy was no pushover; he worked to his own clock.

'Well now, Bucky Bronco at a festival in London: *watch out*.'

'Not London.'

'No? Where then?'

'They say it's a town called Scarborough.'

'Scar-boro? Are you sure about that? I've never heard of a *Scarboro*, England, though I believe there's a Scarboro, Illinois, as you head west, halfway to nowhere. Do you know it?'

'I don't believe I do, Raymond.'

'Farming country, as I recall. Corn and swine. Out past Shabbona. You know Shabbona?'

'I don't believe I do,' Bucky said again.

'Yeah,' the younger man continued, unmoved by the mutterings of discontent from a restlessly clucking clientele over who he wielded a certain degree of power. 'It's over in DeKalb County. From memory I believe it's somewhere between Sterling and Aurora, just off the 30.'

'Scarboro?'

'I'm talking about Shabbona now, Bucky. Shabbona's in DeKalb County. Not much to it but flat fields and big skies. I only know it because I had a cousin work two summers out at Amboy, and weekends we'd go driving the backcountry roads, and I remember seeing the signs for all these places.'

Bucky heard more murmurs of impatience and disapproval, and flat tongues clacking against the roofs of dry mouths. There was a cough and the shuffling of feet. A curse word.

'Of course,' sniffed Raymond, 'Amboy itself is in Lee County, not DeKalb. You know who lived in Amboy? Charles Dickens's brother, and that's the truth of it.'

'Don't know Shabbona, don't know Amboy,' said Bucky. 'And I don't know Scarboro, Illinois either. Dickens I know a little about. But it's stone cold fact that I'm headed to Scarborough, England tomorrow, and I suspect it's a different spelling to the one you're thinking of anyway, Raymond.'

The drugstore assistant leaned in and, with one eye closed, said in a conspiratorial voice: 'Are they paying you?'

'They're paying me *good*.'

'Tell me what qualifies as good these days, Buck?'

Bucky looked over his shoulder, then back again.

'More than I've had in my hand for a long godly while. Plus travel expenses. *And* a hotel room.'

'Oh, a hotel now is it, Bucky?'

'Yes, sir, indeed.'

'Like some Four Seasons or Hilton business?'

'I reckon it must be something like that, yes.'

Even Bucky was getting restless to leave now, but Raymond always had a way of wandering off on conversational tangents when the mood took him. Fascinated by the sudden possibility of vicarious contact with the wider world, he leaned further forward on the counter. His wide frame had gained a few pounds since he'd traded his football days for a more sedentary life, but he was still an imposing figure. It was perhaps this as much as his education that got him the job in this neighbourhood. As sweet as he was, Raymond did not look like the type of person who any would-be jacker, stick-up artist or back-door drugstore cowboy might want to mess with. Aware of the area's reputation as one of the city's edgier projects, his appointment by Walgreens was a strategic one.

'Are you sure you're feeling OK, Buck?'

'As sure as your name is Raymond Burke.'

Raymond narrowed his eyes a little. Bucky did the same in jest.

'Is the food fine out there?'

'Now that I don't know,' Bucky conceded. 'They invented the sandwich though, so I reckon I'll make it through. I could do with dropping a few pounds anyway.'

Raymond lowered his voice a level.

'Do they let you order in on room service?'

Bucky raised his hands in supplication, and shrugged.

Behind him someone said, 'Excuse me, excuse me,' but Ray ignored them. The impatience of his customers was a constant. He'd seen fist fights in here. Knives pulled. Such distraction was nothing; it was expected. Another day at the coalface.

'This wouldn't be one of those Internet scammers now, would it, Bucky?'

Bucky shook his head.

'Hell, no. I spoke to some cat on the telephone. A woman. Truth be told, the accent was a little chewy to fully fathom, but I think I got the measure of it. Besides, they're transferring half the payment up front and whoever heard of an Internet scammer that pays *you*.'

Behind him, someone urged: 'Come *on*, G.'

With his brow furrowed and lips pursed, Raymond flashed the customer a more serious silencing glance. It worked.

'Did you give them your bank account details?'

'Sure did.'

Now it was Raymond who shook his head as he leaned back and exhaled long and slow, and Bucky sensed a spark of satisfied vindication in the young man's eyes, but before Raymond could admonish him, he cut him off at the pass.

'It hit my account this morning,' he said, casually brushing a piece of imaginary fluff from his collar with the back of his hand.

Now it was Bucky who leaned in and lowered his voice.
'Two-and-a-half-thousand bucks.'

Raymond's eyes widened. His voice was too loud:

'They're paying you two-and-a-half-thousand *dollars*?'

Bucky felt the unseen ears of a dozen hopeless addicts prick up in unison.

'Sweet Jesus, dial it down a notch,' whispered Bucky. 'Actually they're paying me five.'

'Five thousand dollars to hear Bucky Bronco sing? Hell, if this is legit, I'm pleased for you, I really am. Me, I'd do it for the cucumber sandwiches, man.'

'Well now, I've no doubt you would. But you've never had an international hit across the water now, have you, Ray?'

'And you have?'

From the queue, more mutterings, then a voice: 'Yo, we're *dying* back here.'

'Well, it turns out yes, in a way, as it goes,' he said with a smile. 'Seems old Bucky Bronco might have a surprise or two left in him after all.'

★

It was his first time in O'Hare. It smelled of sugar and perfume, oil and salt. It smelled of anticipation. Bodies brushed against him and the whole place hummed with a palpable tension. Outside, the planes were stacked in an endless holding pattern of departures.

Bucky sat with his coffee and watched them roar along the runway and then rise, their pointed noses striking skywards, each dependent on the skill of those who flew them. The thought that a pilot might have just that morning been served divorce papers or maybe had one too many cocktails the night before made him nervous. Hell. Trusting your life in a stranger's hands that way wasn't normal.

The air inside the plane was different. It felt heavier somehow. He was seated near the toilet and he could smell its acrid chemicals. He watched the clouds swirl around the tips of the wings and wondered how many of his fellow passengers understood the mechanics that enabled flight; he knew that he certainly didn't, never would.

The light in the plane was soft too, and the seats reclined in an agreeable fashion. Small screens on the headrests offered a selection of movies, though Bucky couldn't work out how to use them, so thumbed through the airline's magazine instead. It was full of articles about hotels with infinity pools, German beer festivals and the best places to buy chorizo in Catalonia. Mainly though he looked out the window and watched first Illinois, and then the Midwest, slip away beneath him.

He was offered a small bottle of wine by a flight attendant with a smile that he thought could deliver a death sentence and you'd still gladly accept it. He declined, but then when he saw other passengers were drinking for free, Bucky called her back and took some. 'Thanks, sweetie.'

With a wink, she even gave him an extra one: 'For later, just in case.'

His hips hurt from all the standing around at check-in and having to walk too far in the airport, so he pushed a pill from its packet and washed it down with the rest of the wine and waited for the gentle benumbed hum of the golden hour. He was in the clouds now, then he was above them, and everything was white, all light. The wine was warm but it slipped down easily, and Bucky settled in. His eyes became heavy and the hum of the engines made a strange mechanical music of sorts.

Here I am, he thought. Closer to heaven than hell for once.

Bucky must have slept for a while because when he opened his eyes and looked down, they had left the land mass of everything he knew – America – and on which he had spent his entire seventy-some years, behind, and in its place was nothing but infinite darkness. A map on the small screen in front of him charted the plane's progress across the Atlantic, and below him there was nothing but a dark void of water so vast and indifferent that he felt his heart flutter in fear. In that water lay another world of deep existence, so much of it still unexplored.

He had seen enough National Geographic shows about it. Down there were myopic fish that existed in absolute darkness and spineless alien-looking creatures that emanated electrical charges. And also down there were oil spills and seabeds dredged to ruination and tiny pieces of plastic that were invisible to the eye but which were irreversibly embedded in the ecosystems of aquatic- and bird-life alike. He had seen shows about that too. The place was polluted and corrupted by man before it had even been fully understood.

Hell.

And here he was, Bucky Bronco, up above the birds, higher than those clouds that he had spent a lifetime gazing at, higher than any man should really be, with a bellyful of wine and pills and peanuts on top of it, and feeling as alone as an astronaut adrift as the plane followed the curve of an earth. He just wished Bell was by his side to witness this unexpected turn of events. She never did get to experience flight.

Then it was dark in the plane too, then it was night, and the hum of the engines, and the combination of the wine and the pills together, and also the altitude and the soft night light, sent him right back down into the rough, cloying quicksand of a second strange sleep.

They changed planes at Dublin, Ireland, a short layover, but Bucky was too tired to do anything and, despite the opioids, his hip sockets were burning as if molten metal had been poured into them, a base form of agony to which he could never grow accustomed. Instead he shuffled sleepily to the gate and took the seat nearest to the entrance, drank some water and waited for his connection to be called. When it was, he queued his way onto another plane, into another seat, took another tablet and drifted in and out of consciousness, waking twice in turbulence with a start, the second time saying, *'Oh, mercy,'* in what he thought was a loud voice, but when he looked around none of his fellow passengers seemed to have noticed from behind their eye masks, or they were too distracted themselves by the brief plunging of the plane, so perhaps the plea had been internal, part of his wandering dream-state.

He had departed in darkness and arrived in darkness and somewhere in between lay 3,820 miles of stupefied uncertainty. Bucky was spaced out and thirsty. He was also a little fearful. He was entering another country, another continent, for the first time.

★

England.

He followed his fellow passengers off the plane through customs to the luggage carousel. The airport was grey and the roof was low. Outside he could see that the breaking day was shaping up to be grey too, and the English sky was also low. It bore down, oppressive. It was hard to believe it was the same sky that hung over his little house; that hung over Chicago and Illinois and America and all countries everywhere, but it was a comforting thought too.

One wheel on his new suitcase kept jamming as he dragged it past the sign that said *Welcome to Leeds Bradford – Yorkshire's Airport*, and only then did he realise he was in Yorkshire, a place that he knew was famous for its desserts.

Bucky walked slowly through the arrivals lounge, and then he was out into the main lobby of the airport, where a small crescent of people still wearing the look of sleep – or perhaps a lack of it – were waiting to meet their loved ones off his early flight, and another one that had just come in from Reykjavik, Iceland.

A woman stood to one side, nervously scanning the slow trickle of yawning businessmen, solo flyers and parents carrying pyjama-clad children floppy with fatigue. She was carefully holding a piece of paper in front of her with both hands, on which was written: EARLON 'BUCKY' BRONCO: KING OF SOUL. She spotted him first. She saw a big old man with a limp that he disguised as an easy-going rolling shamble, and mournful eyes. His tall frame was holding too much weight, most of which was gathered around his midriff. Yet still there was an air of dignity in the way in which he carried himself. Regal, almost. Bucky's dry eyes fell upon the sign, then her. She smiled.

She was younger then him by a stretch, twenty years maybe. Around fifty, he judged, though his ability to guess people's ages was diminishing with the passing of time. Now there was only young, middle-aged – which seemed to range from about thirty to sixty these days – and old; the woman meeting him was still in that broad central bracket. She had lived some, he could see that, but she had not been worn down by life. He could see a strength to her, and as he moved closer he noticed that her eyes were a deep beautiful green, and that beneath the harsh white lights, her dark hair was in fact a deeply radiant auburn, while her nose was large and noble. She was striking. Then, as she casually shifted from one foot to another, he couldn't help noticing that she had a nice thick figure beneath her coat. Bucky smiled back as he walked towards her.

'Dinah?' he asked.

'Welcome to Yorkshire, Mr Bronco.'

'Well, amen to that. Thanks, sweetie. But, you know, you can call me Bucky, or Earlon if you like. But no one good has called me mister in a long-ass time. Bucky's best, I reckon.'

'OK then.'

He extended a hand. They shook. He registered her surprise at the largeness of his hand as it enveloped hers, and the crooked line of his large knuckles too. It was as if the everyday transaction felt odd and awkward to her, though he hoped she sensed a warmth to it too. As they stood there in the airport, Dinah couldn't remember the last time a man had formally shaken her hand; it just wasn't done much round her way. Hugs and kisses or shoves and slaps were more commonplace than such chivalry, whereas handshakes were for job interviews and being turned down for loans and thanks-but-no-thanks and not much else.

'How was the flight?'

How *was* the flight, he wondered to himself.

'Well now. It was long, but just fine. There was wine. And a little turbulence, I guess. It feels strange to fly right on through from daytime to daytime again.'

'I can't tell you how excited we are to have you visit. To have *the* Bucky Bronco, here in the flesh.'

'In the flesh indeed. It's my pleasure, honey. What time are we on now?'

She looked at her phone.

'It's just after seven.'

Bucky shook his head, baffled and bemused.

'Seven in the morning feels like seven in the evening right about now.'

She smiled.

'I bet.'

'So it's Friday?'

'It is.'

She nodded to his small suitcase. 'Would you like me to grab your case, Bucky?'

'Now what kind of a gentleman would that make me if I had a lady haul my luggage? No, I'm good, thanks, Dinah.'

She found herself flushing at the compliment of being called a lady, even if it was in jest. Another first. She covered her embarrassment with conversation.

'Are you hungry? Have you eaten? We could get you something to tide you over. A bacon sarnie or a pasty or something.'

Bucky's hips were howling now. The golden hour had passed too quickly and all the standing around at the baggage carousel was sending shooting pains down both legs.

'I reckon they must have fed us about half a dozen times over the Atlantic, and once more on the hop from Dublin. I'm good. I could do with taking a load off though. Are we far, Dinah?'

'I'm parked just outside.'

They walked towards the door together.

'Funny how sitting doing nothing but watching your own eyelids can be so tiring,' he remarked.

The door opened before them and closed behind them, and as the temperature dropped and the cool air greeted him, Bucky felt as if he were passing from one realm to another. In a brief moment his life leaped forward. He had stepped into the unknown.

★

Outside, oily drizzle fell in the still and discomfiting darkness, and behind it the sky threatened violence. Beyond the tall lights of the distant car park, there was nothing but the sluggish autumn morning laid dormant against the waking day. A taxi drew away from the kerb with a plume of synthetic cherry vape smoke trailing from the driver's side window.

Dinah stopped for a moment.

'Look, I hope you don't mind, but I just need to say this now and get it out of the way: "Until the Wheels Fall Off" is just about my favourite song of all time.'

Bucky raised an eyebrow.

'Just about?'

'OK, it's definitely my favourite.'

'I'm just playing. That makes an old man happy to be told that. And surprised.'

'But you must hear that all the time.'

Bucky frowned. The rain was falling and resting in their hair, the drops momentarily glistening like tiny ornaments, shimmering jewels. The day was still deciding what to do with itself.

'Well, I'd say just about almost never.'

When they reached Dinah's car, she helped lift his case into the boot, then cleared the cluttered passenger seat of a dog blanket, a half-empty Coke bottle, some scratched CD cases. She brushed away crumbs, sand.

'You must be jet-lagged.'

'Not having had it before, it's hard for me to say. But I guess I do feel a little ... discombobulated, if that's a word?'

'We've booked you in the Majestic. It's the oldest hotel in town.'

'Any place called the Majestic sounds like somewhere I could lay my head.'

'Well, names can be deceptive. But it was majestic once, so that counts for something. Plus, I believe you said something about wanting to experience a flavour of old England?'

'Sounds about right. We got far to go?'

'At this time of day, an hour or so.'

Dinah started the engine and the car stereo loudly burst into life. It was 'Until the Wheels Fall Off'.

'Christ—' She reached for the dial. 'Embarrassing.'

Not knowing how to respond, Bucky chose silence – and a small smile.

She struggled with the gearstick, accidentally revved the engine excessively and then they pulled out into the northern morning.

Soon they were in the countryside, heading east towards York. Even though it was early, Dinah explained, she still favoured the back roads over the motorways that caused her anxiety at any time of day. The motorway had a habit of making her sleepy when it was dark or drizzling, and she preferred the alertness that the winding lanes, railway crossings and minor bypasses required. Bucky listened, nodding silently.

Tiny villages and even smaller hamlets flitted by. Many were little more than clusters containing a few houses clinging to a narrow road, with perhaps a solitary squat farm sitting low in the damp landscape, a ploughed field or two away. Others had a village green, a shop and a pub, and most that they drove through on the arcane roads were dormant and looked as if they had always been there, and always would.

Time peeled back its layers and Bucky felt a flicker of delight when he saw his first red phone box.

'Look at that,' he said. 'Just like in Mary Poppins or something.'

'What's that?' said Dinah.

'That phone booth. It's just like in the movies.'

'Oh yes. Most of them aren't in use these days. Most get more use as urinals, though some of them have been turned into libraries.'

'Libraries?'

'Well, yes, little ones.'

'I heard the English were eccentric, but that's crazy.'

Towards York the commuter traffic was beginning to thicken on the ring road for the final working day of the week, so they bypassed it and continued east. The sky before them was streaked with fiery fingers of extending sunlight.

'Lord Jesus, this is some beautiful green country,' Bucky said quietly.

'This is the Wolds.'

'Wolds?'

'Don't ask me what it means. All I know is, it's old country. Ancient England. The Vikings settled around these parts.'

'I can see why. There's so much space. Back home, so close to an airport or a city, they'd be filling it with strip malls and projects, drive-throughs and billboards.'

'I guess you're not in America anymore.'

'Well, hell, I guess I'm not.'

They fell silent, but to both Dinah and Bucky it didn't feel like an awkward silence, rather a prolonged comfortable moment that befitted the time of day and the end stage in the latter's long journey. A few minutes passed before Dinah finally cleared her throat.

'Look, I've tried to be cool about this, and Graham Carmichael – he's the one who is putting on the Weekender, looks like a bit of a homunculus, his head's too big for his body, do you know what I mean, but a nice enough lad – well, anyway, he pleaded with me not to embarrass myself when I said that I'd be your chaperone, so to speak, but I'm just so excited that you're here. Honestly, *Bucky Bronco, for God's sake.*'

Catching herself, Dinah flushed.

'Sorry, but, come on, there's an actual legend of soul sitting in my crappy little banger.'

Dinah took a ready rolled cigarette from a packet down by the handbrake and lit it. She offered one to Bucky.

'No thanks. Used to, but not anymore. Or not cigarettes anyway, though most other things are fine.'

'Saving your voice?'

'Something like that.'

She opened the window an inch and attempted to blow a lungful of smoke through the gap, but it just folded itself back into the car.

'It's actually my last and only vice,' she said. 'Apart from the booze and the odd spliff.'

'Spliff?'

'Joint. Weed.'

'Oh, now you're talking my language.'

'Bucky Bronco,' Dinah said again, shaking her head in disbelief. '"Until the Wheels Fall Off". I can't even truly tell you how much that song means to me.'

'That's crazy.'

'I mean…'

She inhaled, shook her head again, then exhaled from the corner of her mouth, then flapped a hand at the cloud that in front of her.

'It's not often I'm lost for words, ask anyone, but, my God. That one song has been the soundtrack of my life since I first heard it when I was fourteen or fifteen, and I bet there's not a week has gone by when I haven't played it. Not a single week. Sometimes daily.'

'Are you putting me on?'

Dinah looked at Bucky, surprised.

'Of course not. *Of course not.* Why would I? But like I said, you must get this all the time.'

'About once every half-century.'

She laughed.

'Sweetie, I'm not even joking,' said Bucky. 'Back home that song has been d-e-a-d, *dead* for decades.'

'What? Now it's you who's having me on.'

'Nuh-uh. I mean, I'm told there's been the odd email over the years, usually asking me if I'm *the* Earlon "Bucky" Bronco, singer of "Until the Wheels Fall Off", but I never did mess with computers much, and who knows who these folk are or what they want. In my experience, when strangers get in touch it's usually bad news, so I don't reply. Most people from the past are best left there. But then you peeps get in touch asking me to come over and sing, and there is talk of money, a hotel, expenses, the whole nine yards. Hell, he even said something about *fans* – well, then I just had to come and see what was up for myself.'

'Everyone knows you fell off the radar for a while, and things in the soul scene aren't what they used to be, but you still make a living from gigging though, right?'

'Make a living?' said Bucky, astonished. '*Still* make a living? Oh, I hate to break it to you, sweetie, but I've never made a penny from singing that song, or any song for that matter. Not a single red cent.'

'But it's a classic Bucky, a dance floor filler.'

'Not at home, it isn't. Not anywhere.'

'Bollocks,' she said. 'Sorry, but that is bollocks.'

Bucky repeated the word, smiling to himself: '*Bollocks.*'

'It was huge on the northern soul scene when I started out,' Dinah continued. 'And it still is for some of us. I've heard it played at several weddings and at Colin Coverdale's funeral after he got flattened by an ambulance near Driffield. Imagine being killed by an ambulance.'

Bucky's sigh was deep and doleful. His eyes were trained to the stubbled fields and farmsteads that flashed by.

'I mean, this is great to hear, apart from the ambulance bit obviously, poor Colin—?'

'Coverdale.'

'Yeah, commiserations to Colin Coverdale, but you know I cut that track in the spring of sixty-seven and then a follow-up later that year—'

'"All the Way Through to the Morning".'

Bucky shot Dinah a look as she carefully ground out her cigarette, then squeezed it through the gap in the window. It bounced on the damp road, trailing a brief flicker of glowing ash behind them.

'Oh, Jesus, you have done your homework,' he said. 'You know it?'

'Of course I bloody do. It's like the holy grail of northern, a single that people can barely ever find, much less afford. It's rarer than pressings of "Until the Wheels Fall Off", even. It's only really existed in our imaginations for twenty years until the Internet came along, and then it appeared online, which was great, but not the same as having the test pressing, *the* original historic artefact. Not that I go in for that side of things – I leave that to the obsessives. The men with their carrier bags and their dandruff, bless them.'

'Heck,' said Bucky. 'This is all news to me, sweet pea. And all for a bit of plastic that wasn't even officially released.'

'But you do know that original copies of "Wheels" aren't exactly easy to find either?'

'That's because it bombed like Dresden, honey. Unlike its creator, that song could not get arrested. Now I'm wishing I had a copy.'

'You don't even own a copy of your own single?'

'Nuh-uh. Just out of interest, how much does one of those things go for?'

'Hard to say, really. It's got to be up there with a mint edition of "Do I Love You" by Frank Wilson though. I remember a copy of that going for over ten grand a few years back. Or was it a hundred? I forget. Either way: silly money.'

'Wait, what? Please tell me that a grand isn't a thousand bucks like it is back home?'

'Pounds, Bucky,' said Dinah. 'But, yes.'

'Damn,' he said, then again: '*Damn.* I don't believe it. Ten G's for a little slice of scratched-up plastic? You know how many hours I'd have to work to make that kind of bacon?'

'It's nuts, isn't it?'

'Especially as I sold my only copy back in the day.'

'How much did you get for it?'

'I don't recall, but most likely a hot dog and a beer. A lid of weed maybe.'

'Jesus, Bucky. You only got one copy?'

'Hell, I don't remember.'

'But what about royalties?'

'Like king and queens, you mean?'

'Royalties on sales. And airplay. At least you earn off it now?'

'Yeah, I know what you mean, honey,' Bucky sighed again. 'But the thing you've got to understand, Dinah, is that I got paid seventy-five dollars to cut that track in one afternoon when I was seventeen years old, and that might well have included signing over the rights to it and the B-side too. I don't fully recall.'

'"The Bees & the Birds".'

'There you go again with your research. I'm impressed.'

'Seventy-five dollars though, Bucky. That's hardly proportionate remuneration, given the sheer staying power of that track.'

'Well, at least I got seventy-five more for "All the Way Through to the Morning", as I recall.'

'That's exploitation, is that.'

'Sure it is, but that's also America, what are you going to do? I was seventeen. Seventy-five dollars was decent scratch when you're young and hungry. Still is. Back then seventy-five bucks got you a room for a month, maybe two. Or a suit and some shoes. Or maybe a good long weekend so memorable you'd have forgotten it by the time you woke up with a sloppy grin on Monday afternoon.'

'So what did you spend it on?'

'I don't recall. One or all of the above, I expect. Nothing lasting but a vague memory.'

'Bucky, that's a tragedy.'

He shrugged.

'Maybe. Or maybe not. A hundred-fifty dollars for two afternoons' work isn't so bad.'

'It is when someone else is making hundreds of thousands of pounds off that work. Millions, for all we know.'

Bucky felt wired and tired in a way he hadn't felt since the days of holding down three jobs on four hours' sleep. The motion of the car and new thoughts of the long-forgotten past were making his eyes heavy and his teeth itch.

'That's life, sweetie. It's best to learn these lessons when you're young. And the lesson was: the odds are stacked against people like me since the moment our mothers birth us. I've never sung that damn single ever since.'

Dinah took her eyes from the road and studied Bucky's face for a moment.

'Wait – you're telling me you've never sung "Until the Wheels Fall Off" since it was released? *Ever?*'

'Nope. Neither that nor any other song, except maybe to the moon when I overindulged and no one else was looking.'

'Are you saying you've never gigged?'

He shook his head.

'There's never been no call for it.'

Dinah was incredulous.

'So – hang on – this is you first performance since then? Here in Scarborough?'

Bucky turned and looked at Dinah. He made a face that spoke of reluctance and apology. She waited for him to smile or laugh and tell her that he was, of course, joking. But he didn't. He wasn't.

'Except for church, yes. That's where I was first spotted. Got pulled into the studio the week after. Cut "Wheels" and a couple of other tunes there and then. Besides all that, no one else ever asked until now.'

★

By the time that the undulant farmlands of the countryside had given way to roundabouts and retail parks, and then, further east towards the coast, clusters of new-build housing estates encroaching upon the fields and suburban streets where tall, thin red-brick guest houses sat shoulder to shoulder, it was light and the young day's morning traffic clogged the road into town. They stopped and started and stopped again. Bucky saw the pallid faces of people driving to their jobs and thought about how all across the world people were going to places they didn't want to go to, just to eat and survive and maybe buy themselves a little breathing space from the constant war of it all.

'Welcome to Scarbados,' said Dinah.

'Scarbados,' Bucky laughed. 'I like that.'

'That's northern humour: why celebrate something when you can mock it? So there's also Ches Vegas for Chesterfield and Pontefract is Ponte Carlo. And don't forget Maccapulco – Macclesfield – oh, and Hullywood for Hull.'

They cruised through green traffic lights and Dinah took a right turn, then suddenly there below them, at the end of a sloping street, was the sea, brown-grey and broad, steady in the soft morning light.

'Whoah,' said Bucky. 'Been a long time since I saw the ocean. A long, long time.'

'It's more of a sea really.'

'There's a difference?'

'Well, I reckon there must be, otherwise why have two particular words for it?'

'And what do they call it?'

'Call it? The North Sea, of course.'

'That makes sense. And what's waiting at the other side of it?'

Dinah hesitated for a moment.

'Denmark maybe. Or Norway. Sweden? One of those places. You probably think I'm thick as mince for not knowing. Anyway, we'll be just in time for a morning dip.'

'Dip?'

'Yes, a swim.'

'The hotel has a pool?'

'In a manner of speaking. It's not heated, but it is right on the doorstep.'

'I'm not sure I quite follow, sweetie.'

'You're looking at it,' said Dinah. 'The North Sea. That's the pool. It's entirely free for everyone.'

'People swim in that sorry-looking soup?'

'They do indeed, me included, for most of my long and illustrious life.'

'In October though? Isn't it…'

'Freezing? No, it's fully heated.'

Bucky looked at Dinah.

'What the hell?'

'I'm pulling your pisser, Bucky. Of course it's freezing. As cold as the proverbial witch's tit.'

'Then you Scarbados folk must be three pickles shy of a quart.'

'I don't know what means, but possibly. It's good for you though.'

'Now that I very much doubt. Anything that they say is good for you usually hurts like hell one way or another.'

'Really, it is. It's been proven. The cold water eats up some of the fatty cells, strengthens the heart and gives your skin a good scrub too. It deals with the aches and pains, or maybe it's just so cold it makes you forget about them. But it works, and that's what matters. It's a real test of anyone's mettle. Do you have any ailments, Bucky?'

'Ailments? How long have you got? I reckon this battered old warship of a body is only just about held together by skin and pills and hope, and not much else. Hell. Getting old sucks like a hungry calf.'

'Well, maybe you should try it. Sea swimming doesn't reverse the ageing process, but the feeling you get afterwards is the best. There's something about the motion of the tide running through you too, do you know what I mean? You get a kind of glow. It's like you've been magnetised.'

'And that's what folk in England do for kicks, is it?'

'Don't knock it until you try it. It could be just the tonic after a long-haul flight.'

'I reckon I'd prefer a real tonic, with a dash of Scottish whisky. That'll get me glowing. Yeah, I think maybe I'll take a rain check on that for now.'

★

They fell into another silence as the traffic thickened and they edged ever closer to the town's centre, closer to the sea. The silence was that shared by two people further acquainted than they were an hour ago. Below them a mile-long strip of sand formed a honey-coloured crescent along which was dotted the first early morning dog walkers and the occasional swimmer peeling on a wetsuit or launching a paddle board.

'Nice beach,' Bucky mumbled.

'Yes, the South Bay. It's one of two. Over there, past the headland, that's the North Bay. Obviously. The town is split. See the castle, up there?'

Dinah pointed across the town, northwards, to the stone building that was perched, vulture-like as it ominously watched the horizon.

'Oh, look at that,' said Bucky. 'That's like some real Robin Hood shit. Some Harry Potter shit. How old is that place?'

'I'm not sure. Probably about a thousand years. But I think there was a hill fort there before it.'

Bucky whistled through his teeth.

'I reckon the oldest place in my neighbourhood is Phat Phil's friendly chicken joint, established nineteen twenty-who-knows-when.'

'I'll take you up there if you like. You've got plenty of spare time.'

'Honey, with these hips of mine I reckon you're going to have to airlift me up or parachute me down. Either way it's a saga.'

They stopped at a junction. Bucky saw a sign that read *Never Feed the Gulls* as an abundance of fearless seagulls circled overhead. A truck with colourful advertising hoarding hoisted on the back announced that *The Circus Is Coming to Town!* as it glided past. Then they were there.

Dinah turned off the engine, yanked the handbrake.

'Your home for the weekend.'

Before them loomed a vast stone citadel with an ornate and weathered façade. Its appearance was imposing, Gothic almost. Bucky thought it resembled a great ship set to sail across an empire, its chains just moments away from being unanchored from the bedrock and cast off with the smashing of a champagne bottle and an almighty yawping splash. Rounded towers rose at its four corners and, below them, greasy green smears of seagull excrement ran down the side of the building to gather in voluminous powdery heaps stacked on the stone shelves of its many ledges. Bucky could see that there were also ragged bird nests up there: little untidy baskets made from marram grass, twigs and, in some cases, plastic straws, sweet wrappers, shredded bits of nautical rope and all manner of other discarded items. Beyond the hotel's clifftop position was nothing but the vapid vastness of the sea, which was softly belching creamy breakers onto the beach below.

'The Majestic Hotel,' said Dinah.

'It certainly is.'

They left the car and walked towards the front entrance. Bucky noticed a couple of fluffy feathers float by on the breeze.

'You should see it from the other side,' Dinah said. 'It's more impressive. It drops down several storeys. There's ballrooms, terraces, all sorts. The Majestic used to be *the* place in Scarborough. In the whole of the North, even.'

'"Used to be". I sense a "but" coming.'

'Well, it's not now – obviously. It's been left to rot a bit, I'm afraid. It's not what it once was. It's just about held together by memories of past glories. That would be a good motto for half the towns up here actually. Or maybe just England in general. *It's not what it once was.* Or perhaps, *managed decline.* Maybe its great past was just an illusion all along.'

'Hell, none of us are what we were,' smiled Bucky. 'Seems like maybe England and America aren't so different after all. Me? So long as there's a bed and some running water, I'll lay my head anywhere. I'm just about fixing to drop.'

'I bet you are. And I'm running late for work. Are you OK to get yourself checked-in?'

'Sure, honey.'

'I thought maybe you'd want to ease out of the jet-lag and then I could come back this evening and take you out for tea. Say, around six?'

'Sounds good, Dinah. Will we be eating at all?'

'Of course. Tea means dinner.'

'My bad. Just checking. And thanks for the ride, I appreciate it.'

Bucky looked around him – to the sea, then south along the coastline and finally straight up above at the rounded dome of the Majestic's nearside corner turret.

'What a life,' he said. 'What a life.'

He shook his head in disbelief, then dragged his suitcase, and himself, into the hotel lobby.

★

Dinah hurried home. There was just enough time to change into her work clothes – jeans, branded blue jumper, matching blue name-tag – and then fill the slow cooker with a packet of Richmond sausages, a tin of baked beans and a tin of tomatoes. A stock cube.

'Been to see him then, have you?'

His monotonous voice startled her.

'Christ, Russell.'

Her husband was swaying in the doorway, dressed only in his boxer shorts; boxer shorts she bought for him four Prime Ministers ago. His distended stomach was hanging heavy over the waistband. She noticed, as she always did, the nub of his belly button sticking out, and not for the first time it repulsed her to the point of anger, though of course she did not show this. She never did. Internalisation was her speciality, low simmering rage her natural marital state.

'He's here then, is he,' he said again. 'The septic?'

'If you mean Earlon Bronco then, yes, he is. Now, look – your tea's on already. If you want spuds you'll have to do them yourself, or there's tinned in the cupboard.'

Russell scratched his belly and lifted his leg. He farted. Dinah made sure not to flinch or show any reaction; she refused to grant him the satisfaction.

'What is it?'

'Stew.'

'What kind?'

'Sausage.'

'I was thinking of going vegan,' he said.

'Well, you can pick the sausages out then. Where's Lee?'

'In his pit, tugging himself half-blind presumably. Got any baccy?'

'No.'

'Liar.'

Dinah sighed and then pulled a tobacco pouch from her back pocket and threw it across the kitchen. Russell caught it and rolled five cigarettes in quick succession, then threw it back to her – 'Here, you're nearly out' – but her back was turned and it fell to the floor. What few flecks of string and dust were left spilled out of the packet and onto the lino. She ignored it, ignored him, and busied herself with tying her hair back and checking her appearance in the mirror. To her reflection she said, 'Is one of those for me?'

'They've to last me all day.'

'You could consider buying your own.'

'With what? Tobacco doesn't grow on trees, you know.'

'It sort of does,' she replied, but in a voice so low her husband didn't hear her.

He lit his cigarette from the stove, exhaled then turned the kettle on.

'What's he like then, the septic? Septic tank, Yank.'

'Yes, I got the joke the first time, Russell. He's nice. Not quite what I expected, but nice.'

'Why, what did you expect, some young stud who was going to sweep you off your tired feet?'

'Like you did, you mean?'

'Exactly.'

'And I've been sweeping up after you ever since. Anyway, I'm late and I'll be late back tonight too.'

'Maybe *I'll* be late. Maybe I have a hot date with a mysterious Sherman. Sherman tank, Yank.'

'Saying it three times doesn't make it any funnier, you know.'

Russell leaned against the sink and idly rooted around in his shorts. It was another micro-provocation that Dinah didn't have time for.

'You love me really,' he said.

She unplugged her phone from its charger, pocketed it and then left.

★

The hotel lobby was busy and Bucky's hips were screaming with pain. His right leg in particular felt as if an electrical current was running up and down it, and no matter how much he tried to recalibrate his thinking towards it, the silent agony was not something that he could grow accustomed to. It never went, only dissipated, and then returned with a vengeance. Lying, sitting or standing for any length of time only exacerbated it, and then his mood soured. He had never been a good patient, but robbed of Maybell's sympathetic ear this past year, he had struggled to control the debilitating sense of despair that followed the pain as sure as night follows day. He lived only for the golden hours.

As he waited in line he shifted from one foot to the other. The sweeping stairway before him suggested an opulence and grandeur to the hotel that was at odds with the ambience and the current clientele. Bucky wasn't passing judgement on them – he was a guest too – but desperation has a scent, and he could detect it. It was more than familiar. This place was once stunning, that was obvious, and its walls held within them so many stories, but it had surely seen better days. Something was off about the building; as if, Bucky suspected, it was haunted by its own sense of absence.

Outside the front entrance several people milled around smoking cigarettes and sucking on vapes beside a large coach that had an A4 printout Blu-tacked to the inside of its windscreen with 'Mystery Tour' written on it in Comic Sans. On the pavement were two tall towers of conference suite chairs, several tables and an old mattress with a large red stain in the centre of it, stacked against the wall.

In front of him, a man wearing shorts, a vest and flip-flops and with one arm amputated just below the elbow was loudly remonstrating with the woman at the reception desk. When did life, Bucky wondered, become reduced to nothing but a series of queues? Lately he was always waiting in line, and usually for something he didn't even want to do in the first place. Sometimes it seemed like the entire world was waiting impatiently: everything thwarted, everything delayed. Society was held together by such fine threads. The one-armed man was becomingly increasingly angry. He pointed his arm at the receptionist and wiggled his nub. Many minutes passed before Bucky finally got checked-in.

The lift was out of order, so on rigid legs, and with his dry eyes prickling with tiredness, he dragged his suitcase up the sweeping staircase beneath dramatic arches whose faux-gold leaf patina must have once represented the British Empire's wealth and almighty power, but now showed nothing but neglect. Two more stairways followed and Bucky had to steel himself while he caught his breath. He leaned against the handrail, thinking only of his pills, his beautifully reliable painkillers, and the brief respite from decrepitude that they would soon bring him. Perhaps, he thought, a hot bath and a little whisky chaser might also help him acclimatise further.

As he rested a set of doors were suddenly flung open and two boys came charging down the hallway towards him. One of them was on foot and deftly dribbling a ball in front of him, while the other rode a scooter, its small wheels wearing a groove into the tread of the hotel's tired carpet. They were young, seven or eight, brothers perhaps, or cousins. They had dark olive skin and as they came closer Bucky heard their chatter in a tongue foreign to him that he guessed – but only guessed – was Middle Eastern. Their wide brown eyes appeared to widen further still when they saw Bucky, big and breathless against the banister, his swollen feet bursting out of an old pair of Nike Air Jordans like doughy loaves in two bread tins.

The boy on the scooter braked to a halt and stared, silently blinking before the other joined him by his side. Neither said anything. The football was half-deflated. Bucky nodded towards it.

'I'd offer you fellas a game, but I'm afraid I'm not quite fully fit at the moment. Truth is, I'm dead on my feet right about now.'

Still the two boys remained silent. Their stares were neither rude nor intrusive, but curious, as if they were at an art gallery and he was the exhibit – an old classic by one of the masters of course, he thought.

'Hey, if one of you guys could help an old man with his luggage, I could give you...'

Bucky patted the many pockets of his old hunting gilet that he had worn for years precisely because in it he could carry everything he needed, and then checked his trousers. He had keys, a few loose coins – quarters, pennies, naturally: what little cash he had exchanged was in a tight roll somewhere at the bottom of his hand luggage – alongside his wallet, Maybell's old mobile phone, a Chicago Bulls key ring, a Q-tip and a plastic strip of Tylenol. Then he remembered his inside pocket, where there was a roll of Life Savers – someone had told him that sucking them on a plane would prevent his ears popping when they came into land, but he had slept right through the descent.

'Half a roll each?'

Implicitly understanding the international language of confectionary, the boys eyed the sweets and conferred with one another for a moment, but as they hesitated a woman reversed out of a hotel room behind them. She was hauling a large trolley containing cleaning products, toilet paper and a laundry bag. Seeing the boys, she spoke in a low voice that was calm but emphatic. They rolled their eyes and she repeated the words again, more forcefully this time, until they reluctantly turned and left, their feet and wheels moving silently across the landing, then through another set of double doors and into another corridor lined with rooms, all part of a vast network of floors and back stairways that appeared labyrinthine and endless to Bucky.

'Sorry if they were troubling you,' the cleaner said.

She too was of Middle Eastern complexion, Arabic probably, though Bucky was suddenly aware that his sense of geography and understanding of ethnic diversity beyond America, and certainly beyond Europe, was pathetically limited. He noticed that her eyes were a piercing green in colour. They looked right at him – through him, almost – from beneath a brightly coloured scarf that was wrapped around her head. Her complexion was smooth and vital, radiant, and there was something classical about her mouth, but it was those eyes that Bucky found most striking. They fixed upon him, almost defiantly, in a way that suggested they had seen things that he could never comprehend.

'Oh, they were no trouble,' he replied. He checked his key fob. 'Hey, could you tell me where room 333 is?'

She offered the faintest of smiles.

'Of course. Room 333 is just along here. Please, allow me to show you.'

He followed her to the far end of the corridor and as he did he caught passing glimpses into other recently vacated rooms that were awaiting cleaning. They were small, dingy spaces and those on one side did not have a single window. Bucky saw piles of matted towels and bedding, empty beer and wine bottles, and, in one, a splatter of something wet on the carpet below a cracked flat-screen television.

'You are lucky,' she said blithely. 'You have a view. Freshly cleaned also.'

With her own key she opened the door of room 333 and stood aside to let him enter. His room was similarly small but it was saved by a large window that looked right out across a sea that appeared infinite. Dinah was right: from this side he had a much better perspective of the hotel's perilous position perched on the clifftop, a huge stone eyrie watchful over the turbid waters. Directly below was a terrace containing tables, chairs and one small solitary man grasping what looked like a morning pint of beer.

Beyond that, there was the sea wall, a thin strip of high-tide beach and then nothing else but the water, gossamer-grey and moody.

'You are not from here.'

The cleaner's voice came from behind him. It was a statement rather than a question.

'No,' replied Bucky. 'No, I'm not. America.'

Her face flickered with interest.

'America?'

For the first time in years – perhaps ever – Bucky felt aware of a certain sense of privilege posited by that one simple word and all that it represented. America. The mythology of it. *America*.

'Yes.'

'New York? The Big Apple?'

'Chicago. Chi-town aka The Windy City. What about you?'

'My parents were from Afghanistan.'

Now it was his countenance that registered a change.

'Afghanistan, oh, man.'

She nodded.

'I'm from Afghanistan also. But I was mainly raised here in England.'

'I'm Bucky,' he said, extending his hand. She looked at it as if it was something unexpected, like a cauliflower or a telescope or a discarded shoe. Nonetheless she shook it.

'And what's your name, sweetie?'

'Shabana.'

'Sha—?'

'*Bana.*'

'Funny, there's a place near to where I come from called Shabbona. Yes, Shabbona, Illinois. Similar. I was just talking about it the other day. Shabana is a nice name though.'

'It means "belonging to night".'

'Seems about right. I like it.'

'And your name – Bucky? That sounds like an American cartoon name. What does it mean?'

Bucky laughed.

'Yes, ma'am. I'm not sure it means anything, but my real name is Earlon. When I hear that it usually means I'm in trouble because it was only ever my mother or my wife who called me that – or the police when I was younger. Bucky's just fine with me.'

Again he patted his pockets.

'I'm sorry, Shabana, but I've not had a chance to get any of your British coins.'

He rooted around for his money roll, and when he found it he peeled off a £10 note.

Shabana shook her head.

'No, no, please. That's too much. In England there is no need.'

'Well, I appreciate the honesty you've shown to a stranger in a strange land. But here…'

Again she refused the tip and instead awkwardly backed out of the room and returned to her trolley.

'I hope you enjoy your holiday here, very much.'

'Thanks. I hope I do too.'

★

There was no whisky and no bath. Just tap water and a feeble shower that dribbled like a leaking catheter.

But worse than that, there were no pills either. Bucky couldn't find them.

'Hell,' he said out loud. '*Hell.*'

He checked everywhere – his suitcase, his backpack, his pockets – and then he checked again. He stood in the middle of the room, mentally retracing his steps, his actions, all the way back to the plane, to his seat by the window, to a couple of bottles of warm wine at the beginning of the golden hour, and as he did his heart turned to a cold stone sinking to the sunless depths of a deep, dark lake when he realised he had left an entire month's prescription of painkillers in the elasticated flap of the airplane seat in front of him. Sixty tablets in all, minus the few he had taken over the past couple of days. All gone.

'Oh, sweet Jesus, have mercy.'

He felt his breath shortening as a quickening sense of mania took hold and sweat gathered on his brow. His blood slumped. Bucky sat on the edge of the bed with his head in his hands, and groaned, loud and long like a wounded animal. Did they have opioids in England? Yes, probably – but over the counter, and without a prescription?

Some called it hillbilly heroin, others called them blues or berries. Back home the country was gripped by an epidemic. On the streets they were known as percs or rims, tires or wheels. Others called the little pill kickers or ozone. But whatever their name, they were the giver of gold. These painkillers on which he was hooked were the provider of succour and sunlight. Problem solvers, dream weavers. Mute lovers. Their initial effect was like bathing in lava, sinking in silk. Waking in a womb. A loving embrace. They were the starship pilots steering him all the way out to the celestial constellations. At least, that's how it used to be. Now though, it was just about feeding the need and maintaining some sort of equilibrium, and if he couldn't locate any pills, and soon, he was screwed. Totally banjaxed sideways. Without them, Bucky had to face pain management alone, not to mention the foreboding horrors of instant withdrawal. There would be no carefully managed dosage reduction here, no slow petering out – just cold clucking, like in the junk days of old, or what he saw in the young walking dead around the neighbourhood today.

Then he remembered.

He reached for his wallet and there in the internal zip-up pocket was the scissored-off corner of a sheet of tablets. One of the pill placement holders was empty, its foil exterior long-since stripped away, but in the other one tablet remained. One solitary emergency tablet, whose value now did not have a price. A thousand dollars would not convince him to part with it.

But Bucky knew it wasn't enough. This last pill was the little boy's finger stuck in the hole of the dyke, a temporary delay of impending disaster. He knew the egg timer had already been flipped and the grains of sand were rapidly falling, but it was at least something. A tiny, bitter, green delay tactic of precisely eighty mgs, the highest dose. He peeled back the foil and snapped the pill in two, then without delay washed one half down with some dusty-tasting water from the bathroom tap that sputtered into a washbasin ringed by a faint brown tidal line.

He looked around for a phone with which to call room service for some whisky, some ice and maybe some soda, all of which might at least hasten the onset of the golden hour, if indeed there was to be one at all, but there was no phone, no room service. Just the walls, the window, the choppy sea slapping sadly against autumnal sand.

Bucky kicked off his old Nikes, undid his belt and lay back on the bed. Beneath him a coiled spring twanged, its sharply pointed end digging into his back. Something more deeply painful snagged at his heart too.

'Oh, Maybell,' he said. 'My Maybell.'

★

Dinah supressed a deeply rooted yawn, swallowed it down and then continued to scan the items lined up in front of her.

A bottle of multivitamins. Bleach. Nesquik. Tampons.

The red lines of the barcode's scanner flashed a matrix across three tins of mackerel in turn. A pig's ear from the pets' aisle. Noodles.

'£11.47 please, love.'

The customer, a young goth woman with an undercut, studs in her cheeks and a map of silver razor scars up her forearm, packed her items, paid and then left without a word. The next customer lined up their purchases and Dinah resumed the scanning.

Aspirin. Bombay mix. Oxtail soup – twenty-four cans of. Fat balls. A Wispa.

A song was playing over the PA. It was a song she knew intimately, and despised. It was one of the *live-your-best-life-babe-you-got-this-festival-moment-phone-advert* songs. She heard it ten times a day, every day, minimum. Why did they never play the music she liked, songs which said something, and which wasn't infused with the cynical aftertaste of focus-grouped marketing ploys? Why was it never 'Stoned Love' or 'Knock on Wood'? Why was it never 'Every Time I See You, I Go Wild' by J. J. Barnes or 'Until the Wheels Fall Off' by Earlon 'Bucky' Bronco, who right this moment was alone in a hotel room across town, hopefully enjoying a deeply satisfying sleep after his long and arduous journey across the Atlantic. Dinah couldn't wait for the shift to end so that she could get back to the Majestic, back to Bucky.

Monster Energy drink. Fairy liquid. Fairy lights. Marshmallows.

'£18.49 please, love.'

The song ended and was replaced by another recent hit that she was also regrettably familiar with. Maybe the store did a deal with record labels and bulk-bought a batch of pop songs, which they would play on rotation for three months, music that Dinah imagined was deemed 'motivational and uplifting' and 'conducive to spending' by a committee of neatly bearded marketing consultants who selected them for all their branches across the country in order to maximise sales. The chorus to this one didn't even have lyrics; any attempt to articulate and convey emotional meaning or resonance had instead been replaced by a gutsy, wordless wail delivered at full volume and with little subtlety by a female singer whose high-octane vocal range had been squeezed through an auto-tune effect like meat through a mincer. Lazy, really. Was this song rubbish, wondered Dinah, or was she just getting old? She loved music too much to readily dismiss it, but the pop music they played in-store felt particularly cynical and anaemic. She refused to be emotionally manipulated in such a callous way. There was enough of that in her life already.

Perhaps, she idly wondered, the music was rubbish *and* she was getting old. Perhaps it didn't have to be one or the other.

Her phone vibrated and though employees weren't allowed to use them while working, she sneaked a look anyway. It was a message from Lee, her son: *bring rizlas*. It was followed immediately by another message: *& choc milk*. And another: *the cabrees*.

Ten seconds later, there followed a fourth message: *not the cheap shit*. But instead of typing the last word, he had used an emoji instead, that of a small steaming pile of excrement with oversized eyes and a smile. He couldn't even be bothered to type the four characters required to form an entry-level curse word; instead he sent his mother a personified digital turd. Thousands of years of human evolution, she sniffed, had led to this point. What a world. What a life.

Dinah knew that even though it was early afternoon her son was messaging from either his bed or the sofa after a long night of talking and gaming online with his Filipino fiancée, a young lady who seemingly had a thing for unemployed, under-qualified twenty-something stoners with porn addictions who still lived with their parents.

She turned her phone off.

One customer left the queue, another joined it, and the beeping of barcodes could be heard right across the shop floor in the all-too-brief respite between the pumping pop songs. A movement over by the front entrance caught her eye, a melee. Royston Wisdom, the shop's sole overworked security guard and local MMA coach, was in a scuffle with someone, a shoplifter most likely. It was a daily occurrence. They were both bent double and temporarily tied in one knotted tangle of limbs but only when they straightened up did Dinah see the man who was in the vice grip of Roy's headlock: it was her husband Russell.

'Oh, Christ,' she said, rising from her chair and slapping a LANE CLOSED sign down on the conveyor belt, much to the chagrin of the customers waiting in line. 'Not again.'

She hurried over in the hope that she could diffuse the situation before Wet Stephen, the by-the-book branch manager, got involved.

'He's at it again, Dinah,' said Roy, raising a bottle of vodka in his free hand. She noted it wasn't even the semi-decent stuff, but the cheapest on offer. The silly sod didn't even have the good sense to steal a better brand, or from a more upmarket shop. And to try and get one over Roy Wisdom – a nice guy who she had been to school with, but also a traveller by birth, a high-born gypsy who would happily use Russell as a toothpick were he in a less charitable mood – well, that was just stupid.

'I was going to pay,' Russell pleaded half-heartedly, pathetically.

Dinah looked around to see who was watching – half the shop's clientele, as it turned out, but thankfully not Stephen – then she stepped in close.

'You bloody idiot,' she hissed. 'You're an embarrassment.'

Then to Roy, who still had one beefy, kettlebell-pumped arm locked around her husband's neck, she said, 'Anything broken, Roy?'

'Hardly,' said the security guard, assuming she meant bones rather than bottles.

'Anyone hurt?'

'Hey, come on,' Russell croaked. 'I'm a bloody pacifist, me.'

Roy shook his head.

Dinah saw the map of burst capillaries on her husband's cheek, each strand part of a diagram that marked a life devoted to drinking, and noted how pale, unkempt and feeble he looked locked in Roy's muscular embrace. One of them smelled of the subtle tones of an expensive cologne, and it wasn't Russell. She looked around again and when there appeared to be no one from management forthcoming, which was unusual as Wet Stephen had something of the voyeur about him the way he stayed glued to the monitors of the store's closed-circuit system, she moved in even closer.

'It's just sometimes he forgets to take his medication. You know how it is.'

'No, I don't,' Russell protested.

'Yes, you do. And you've been told you're not supposed to drink on it.'

'It's the third time, Dinah,' said Roy.

'And it's the last time,' she replied.

In the grip of Roy's arm Russell looked from his wife and then up to the guard and back to his wife again. He appeared sanguine, expectant.

'Last time it was sixty-four batteries,' said Roy. 'Duracell triple A's. Who needs sixty-four batteries anyway? No one but a petty thief, that's who.'

'You'd be surprised,' said Russell. 'Round the—'

'Shut up, you,' Dinah whispered. 'Really, it's the last time, Roy, he promises – don't you? We both know the police will do nothing anyway, even if they bother to turn up, which they won't.'

Squirming, Russell looked up to the security guard who rolled his eyes and released the armlock.

Russell adjusted the collar of his top and smoothed the sleeves into place, then began to head into the store. Roy stopped him with a hand slapped emphatically on his shoulder.

'What?' said Russell. 'I just need to buy some baccy.'

'Obviously you're banned, you bonehead.'

Russell stepped back and straightened himself out.

'So? I was banned anyway.'

'Next time I'll twist your head off like a chicken in an abattoir, you mug.'

'At least mugs serve a purpose, unlike you.'

'You've got his word,' said Dinah, to both Russell and Roy.

'Unfortunately we both know that's worthless,' said the latter.

'That's fair. But there won't be a next time. And if there is I'll be doing the twisting myself.'

'I am here, you know,' said a petulant Russell, affronted by the conversation from which he was excluded.

Roy deftly spun Russell around and gently but forcefully shoved him out into the street.

'Pick some baccy up for us, will you, love?' he called back over his shoulder.

Dinah looked at the clock. An Ed Sheeran song started playing and she thought of all the ways she would like to kill Russell. Then she noticed Wet Stephen, the branch manager, crossing the shop floor, with a grimace on his face. She thought of all the ways she would like to kill him too. And Ed Sheeran. It would be a glorious mass slaughter, a beautiful massacre to quell the boredom. She briefly pictured slipping about in their collective blood, entrails dripping between her fingers as customers and staff looked on. Maybe some of them would even applaud her.

There were two hours of the shift still to go.

★

The sound of a seagull woke him, and kept him awake. The throaty welp of it was at his window – urgent, insistent, entitled.

Bucky stood and his hips howled in a room that felt designed to depress. He parted the curtains and looked straight down into a mess of twigs, moss and feathers, a raggedy crusted bowl in which there sat the gull. It looked at him with indolent eyes, as if he were the trespasser here, as if he were the interloper. His head was throbbing. He went to open the old sash window but it was nailed shut, fresh air being of lesser importance to the hotel than what he assumed was suicide prevention. Certainly the Majestic had an end-of-the-line feel of finality about it. It was deeply ingrained, a place haunted by its own decline, where someone might feel compelled to extinguish everything. Some windows, he thought, are just more inviting than others that way.

Again he saw several figures making their way along the promenade and down to the beach directly below. The late afternoon sea was still and flat now, eerily so, a dirty old mirror mottled with a patina of salt and grit reflecting a similarly dejected-looking sky. It was high tide; the sea had retreated and returned again while he had lain on a creaking mattress, the waning light shining through the threadbare curtains.

At the slipway there were men, women and a girl in a wheelchair. Here they changed first into dry robes and then, beneath those, into wetsuits.

The daylight was beginning to soften and the beach was reduced to a small strip of sand, a ribbon of golden grit pressed between land and water. From high up at Bucky's window the swimmers were small shapes clad in black Lycra as they waded out, waist-deep. As a meek sun shone, the girl was lifted up out of the wheelchair by one of the men and gently laid into the water and held there, in a movement that looked to Bucky like a ritual. Holy almost.

A full flock of seagulls high above the hotel sounded like sirens cutting through the sanctity of the moment. Bucky leaned and twisted to get a better look at them but they flew higher still on an updraft and departed – all except the roosting gull that sat eyeing him with contempt from his windowsill, plump, arrogant and squat in its squalid nest. He closed one curtain against it. It was a feathered fiend, a beaked monster. He couldn't stand to see its probing eyes a moment longer.

Bucky barely heard the meek tapping of a knuckle on his hotel room door. He had dozed the afternoon away in fitful, disturbed spurts and now still felt foggy. The half tablet had eased the pain in his joints only very slightly and he had swallowed three Tylenol on top of it, which had then made his stomach ache, so he had swigged a dose of Pepto-Bismol, which had made him feel constipated and a little bloated, so he had got up again and taken a Wind-eze, before lying down for the last half hour of restless dosing.

He was exhausted, but also suddenly famished. There had been no golden hour, no lush oasis in the endless desert of physical torment, and, well aware that he was down to his last half a tablet, already his mind was craving more opioids. And where his mind went, Bucky's body was sure to follow. It was the psychology of a special kind of addiction manufactured for the capitalist

43

age. That he was aware of this only made his predicament all the more humiliating.

The performance was still forty-eight hours away and deep down he already felt uncertainty as to whether he could make it to then without having a complete mental and physical landslide. He felt too long in the tooth to face life clean.

He opened the door.

'Room 333,' said Dinah. 'A most numerically significant number to have. Hi, Bucky.'

'Hi,' he said, his voice raspy with tiredness and dehydration. 'Come in.'

She walked into the room smelling of perfume and cigarette smoke.

'Yes, if I remember rightly, 333 is an indication that angels are helping you on your journey.'

'My journey – to here?'

'To self-acceptance, apparently. I'm quite interested in numbers, as it happens. *I think* 333 also refers to an important verse in the Bible.'

'You're a believer, Dinah?'

'In soul music, yes. But in religion, no, I can't say I have that type of faith. What about you?'

Before Bucky could answer Dinah pulled out her phone and searched on Google, then was talking again.

'Here we go, verse 3:33 refers to the land of milk and honey which, as everyone knows, is North Yorkshire, also known as God's own county, and specifically Scarborough. I mean this room's a bit of a hole but at least the number has meaning and the view is practically panoramic. Look at that. Have you slept?'

Bucky felt swept up by Dinah's conversational tornado.

'Barely. Kind of. I'm not sure.'

'Is it jet-lag?'

'Seagulls, among other things.'

'Oh, them.'

'And the light. And this goddamn hip pain.'

'I've got some aspirin you could take?'

He shook his head.

'It's a bit beyond that, sweetie. Tell me about these gulls though. How do you sleep with the racket that these creepy monsters make?'

'Oh, usually just with earplugs and an eye mask. And wine. I stick the earplugs in Russell's nostrils to stop him snoring, put on the eye mask so I don't have to see his soppy face, and the wine is the knockout cure for consciousness. Touch my wine without an invitation and I'll have your hands off.'

'They've been driving me crazy for hours.'

'You get used to them, though I'd be lying if I said I hadn't spent many a long hour laid in the dark concocting imaginative ways to slaughter the whole bloody lot of them. Don't get me wrong, I love all God's creatures and all that, but some I love a little less than others. I've been there, trust me. I've been where you are.'

'I was definitely harbouring the same genocidal fantasies as I lay on my gnarly mattress,' said Bucky. 'What was your favoured method, just out of interest?'

'Just out of interest, there were many. Rat poison being one. Crossbow another. Fire hose.'

'Oh,' said Bucky. 'That's brutal.'

'Tiny grenades secreted in Scotch eggs and razor blades in battered sausages – that sort of thing. Waterboarding was one idea, though there's no need to torture them and also they're seabirds, so I'm not sure if that would even work. Or perhaps just trapping them humanely and driving them far inland, and then releasing them there to confuse the buggers. Somewhere like Harrogate.'

'What's at *Harrowgate*?'

'Retired rich people who don't need to get up early. I've got to admit though, I think I'd probably miss the meddling little bastards if they were gone. I mean, what's a seaside town without a soundtrack of seagulls all squawking as if the sky were on fire?'

'Well, maybe,' said Bucky, though he felt sceptical and distracted.

'You'll sleep better tonight, I'm sure. Are you hungry?'

'As a racehorse.'

'I thought perhaps I could take you to a local institution.'

'Is it far?'

She pointed across to the harbour below, where amusement arcades lined the coastal road in a strip of flashing lights. He saw signs for places called Coney Island, Gilly's Leisure Centre and Henry Marshall's Fun Time.

Out in the hotel corridor a group of raucous men barrelled by, the boom and baritone of their voices carrying down the narrow passage.

'Are you up for it?' Dinah said behind him.

Bucky hesitated.

'It's just these old pins of mine, sweetie. Like an old racehorse I'm fine on the flat for a while, but it's the hills that get me. Climbing up to this room earlier damn near finished me off. They'll be sending me off to the glue factory soon enough.'

'Oh, Bucky, I'm sorry. But why didn't you take the lift?'

'Out of order.'

'But there's two.'

'God *damn*.'

'But don't worry, we can take the funicular down the hill.'

'The what?'

'The funicular. It's a tramway, right next door.'

'Like a streetcar, you mean?'

'A bit, only this one moves diagonally down the hill. The town used to have five of them, though there's only two left now. They were built to ferry tourists from the town up-top down to the beach and foreshore below. The Victorians knew a thing or two about engineering.'

'Well, hell. Lead me to it, Dinah. Just give me one minute to freshen up.'

In the bathroom Bucky quickly washed his face, which appeared sullen and jaundiced in the dull light, then he brushed his teeth and checked his hair. He patted it down with his palms. He should shave, but that could wait. He sprayed deodorant then pulled out the final half tablet from his pocket and held it in his hand. He looked at his reflection again and saw a tired old man trapped in a funk of his own making. He saw rheumy sour-milk eyes staring back at him, dejected and run through with tiny bloodshot bolts. Once that man was young, he thought. Once that man was fearless and powerful and had everything ahead of him, and now here he was in the future, with a lot less ahead of him. But it wasn't over yet. Not until his heart stopped beating or the wheels came off. He swallowed the pill down with water, worry and regret; he couldn't think beyond it. He needed it now. Later could wait.

Bucky turned off the bathroom light behind him.

'We're good,' he said.

★

The day dropped to full darkness as they walked slowly along the foreshore road. Neon lights lit the puddles that remained from a briefly urgent afternoon downpour that had fallen while Bucky was restlessly turning in his bed. The air was cool and clean now, and sounds rang out across the water from the arcades as they passed by: sirens and klaxons, music and machinery, the clatter of coin drops. Automated laughter, real laughter.

The pavement was cast in hues of electric pink and flashing yellow, and Bucky was experiencing a second wind of sorts. As they walked crowds flowed around them like water circumventing obtrusive rocks in a river. The daytime visitors with their oversized bags of candy floss and strips of coupons, a mixture of the very old and very young, were being replaced by a Friday night crowd now, all in search of a release from the week through physical connection, sweet derangement, possible violence and certain oblivion. Bucky could feel the energy changing from the bodies that brushed against him and detected also the spicy fragrances of perfume and aftershave that cut through the lingering smells of hot oil, salt and sugar – all underpinned by a foundational fishy base note of decay that wafted over from the stacked creels and rinsed buckets of the working harbour.

The same truck that Bucky had seen circulating that morning that promised – threatened, almost – that *The Circus Is Coming to Town!* passed by again. He couldn't see who was driving it, and so its appearance felt spectral. It glided by as if he were the only person to see it.

'Here we are.'

They stopped outside a brightly decorated ice-cream parlour designed with a distinctly American-influenced aesthetic.

'This place is a Scarborough institution,' Dinah added. 'Don't be fooled by the exterior – it might look like one of your burger joints, but the menu is very English. I thought some local cuisine might be of interest.'

'When in Rome,' said Bucky, following her.

Inside, it was brightly lit. Its yellow walls, buffed mirrors and polished chrome surfaces radiated a warm and nostalgic cosiness against the chill of the October evening. Dinah and Bucky hoisted themselves up onto red leather stools at the semicircular diner-style counter.

Bucky surveyed the illuminated old signage that hung from the walls, advertising Banana Delight, Fresh Farm Egg Milkshake and Knickerbocker Glory, then turned around on his stool to take in the rest of the parlour. He whistled through his teeth.

'I'd say I've travelled four thousand miles only to wind up in America in the fifties – or I would if I knew what in the hell it was this place was serving. I must have entered a new dimension or some such. This place is a straight-up trip.'

The waitress, wearing a starched yellow pinafore, chatted with Dinah while Bucky read a menu offering Bovril with buttered crackers, Eton Mess, Ovaltine, Peach Melba and chocolate Horlicks. The words swam before him. He gripped the Formica surface to steady himself and to quell the tremor that was in his hands. Hunger or jet-lag? he wondered, even though he knew the honest answer: withdrawal. Bucky took a breath and looked up. The mirrors that framed and reflected his face were decorated with slogans: *Get your vitamins the easy way* and *Eat ice cream every day*.

'What do you reckon, Bucky?'

'Huh?' He could feel himself fading. 'I reckon I need to learn a whole new vocabulary to understand this food – oh, wait, I know what a Peach Melba is. But have they got anything, you know, savoury?"

'Of course. And order anything you like. The Weekender is paying.'

'Honey, you're going to have to take the lead here. I'm at your mercy.'

'OK, leave it to me, Bucky.'

Dinah ordered and they were soon faced with an array of plates. There were cheese sandwiches and tuna sandwiches, toasted teacakes, crumpets, salad, a Cherie Amour sundae followed by a Bananarama sundae, whose colour exactly matched that of the walls and the staff's uniforms, a pot of tea for two, and a cup of Bovril that would sit untouched.

'Are you trying to kill me with calories?' Bucky said.

'Just stay alive until Sunday. Actually, Monday would be even better as I have to get you back to the airport for your night flight.'

As he picked up a white bread sandwich and bit into it, Bucky wondered just how real that request might become. They tucked in.

★

'Are you married, Bucky?'

Empty plates sat before them. Despite the oddly exotic names, the food wasn't that different to what Bucky ate back home – lots of sugar, salt and unnatural colours – and as he placed his long sundae spoon into the small pool of molten-yellow ice cream, he belched quietly – 'Oh, pardon me' – and slumped on his stool.

Again the benumbed buzz of the golden hour had not come, only a mild alleviation of the pain in his joints. Already his system was beginning to protest at the irregularity of his diminishing opioid intake. Soon, he knew, it would be protesting at such a volume, and with a greater sense of rancour, that it would be impossible to silence with ice cream, crumpets and over-the-counter painkillers, which he was routinely popping like peanut M&M's. He could feel the cruel mechanics of forced abstention crunching and grinding into action within him. And despite the food, he could taste the oncoming withdrawal working at a deeper register – a suggestion of rust, dust and desperation. His mood was turning. His mind was crumbling into darkness.

Not for the first time he wondered if a prescription for his pills could be located in this town, and if not, whether some comparable temporary stopgap measure could be scored instead. Street drugs? Though he was loathe to consciously admit it to himself, the fact of the matter was that he knew that he would consider anything to get him through the weekend, anything at all. A short-term solution was all he sought.

'Bucky?' Dinah said again.

'Sorry, sweetie, I was miles away. All this food's sent me into a good old slump, for sure. Call it a sugar coma.'

'Oh, no problem. I was just thinking about how, even though it feels like I've known your music for years, I don't really know much about you. And obviously I'm a bit of a nosey bugger, so I was just worrying if you're married.'

Hot Bovril, he thought. *Nosey bugger.* These Brits.

'Yes,' he replied, though Dinah noted the slight hesitation before he answered. It was a conversational gap in which she knew there sat another story.

'Is she back in Chicago, your wife?'

Again he hesitated, and this this time his brow furrowed into a stack of deep-set wrinkles that made her think of a pile of pancakes.

'She passed.'

'I'm so sorry.' The silence hung between them for a moment, and was on the verge of sprouting into something awkward when Dinah asked Bucky, 'How long has it been?'

'Coming up a year or so,' he replied, even though he knew it was exactly a year this weekend. Sunday, in fact. The day of his show. Is that why he was here? he wondered, startled to find himself only just asking this question for the first time, even though it had been lurking within him unacknowledged for the several weeks since he'd received the invitation. Of course, was the answer. *Of course* that was why he was here, on the other side of the world, embarking on this foolish escapade. Because here

– or anywhere – was better than back *there*, alone on a Sunday in the house they had shared, and where Maybell's shadow was still laid across everything like a wet grey blanket, like a sheet of lead. Or so he had thought until he lost his pills and now already found himself flailing within mere hours of arrival. Stupid, he thought. So stupid to put yourself in this position. He was a stupid old man, lost without his wife, eating ice cream in an English coastal town off-season, where a handful of well-meaning people had the misguided notion that he would be able to entertain them, when in fact he could barely tie his shoes without chemical assistance.

Hell.

'What was she called?'

'Maybell,' replied Bucky, pulling himself back from the brink of total disassociation. 'Or Maybellene, like the song. But pretty much everyone around and about called her Miss Maybell.'

'You must really miss her.'

Bucky slowly nodded.

'I do. I miss her like…'

Bucky reached for the right word, but couldn't find it. Not for the first time it evaded him as the feeling was just too expansive to cover with a simple, singular descriptive image. Vocabulary, he thought, had not yet caught up with death. It was too limited. Death evaded description. Or not even death, but the sense of loss that follows it. Grief, mourning, whatever – none of the words had the crushing power of the icy black whirlpool that spun in his chest at four in the morning when he was utterly consumed by both her absence and the notion that he was already beginning to forget the sound of her laughter, the sound of her voice as she asked a simple question, or gently admonished him for not feeding the cat, or when she called him the Bucky Monster because of his love of all things sweet. It was this forgetting that he feared most, this erosion of the fringes of memory.

'Like…'

He shook his head.

'Yes,' he said. 'Yes, I do.'

'It's a terrible thing, grief. When it's on you, it's all encompassing.'

'It is. It is.'

'It's like a planet crossing the sun, casting everything in shadow.'

Impressed by the poetry of her observation, Bucky nodded.

'And you're in that shadow space now, aren't you?' said Dinah. 'I can see it.'

Again he nodded, but dared not reply in case the sob that had taken seed in his stomach and was now rising up through his chest escaped involuntarily.

'Grief is the price of love,' she said. 'Think of it that way if it helps: grief is the price of love.'

Bucky's eyes washed over with wetness, but he fought it. He turned back the tide of tears that had never truly been allowed to flow, not since that first diagnosis.

Another long moment's silence passed before Bucky felt compelled to fill it.

'You know that song – "Maybellene"?'

'Chuck Berry, isn't it?'

'Sure is. Chess Records of Chicago, 1955. Great city, great time, the birth of rock 'n' roll, near enough. One million copies sold in its first year. Maybell claimed that Mr Berry had written it about her, but seeing as they never met, and she must have been a little rug rat when it came out, I'm not so sure. But she never let the fact get in the way of a good tale. Not once.'

Dinah smiled.

'How long were you together?'

Bucky exhaled a long slow whistle.

'Hoo-ee. Damn near fifty years, give or take a few little, um, hiatuses, mainly of my own making. A whole half century, and married for a good chunk of it.'

'That's amazing. What an achievement.'

'My greatest,' he smiled sadly. 'It wasn't always smooth, and there were plenty of breaks and mistakes, but my wife's love for me is, or was, without a doubt, the high point of my life. I mean, this woman was angelic, Dinah. She'd had to have been to tolerate a lifetime of old Bucky Bronco's BS. Had to.'

'I'm sure she was very proud of you.'

'I don't know. Maybe. Maybe.'

'Of course she was. And if not, she will be now.'

'You think?'

'Of course – look at you, over here, out on the road for the first time ever, performing music that you wrote, for people who are willing to pay good money to hear it. That's something special, is that.'

'I wish I could feel that way about it.'

'It's just pre-show nerves, Bucky.'

'Perhaps,' he said absently, though he knew the truth of the situation.

'Your music and your talent brought you here. Think about that for a moment. Like I told you before, there are people who are obsessed with "Until the Wheels Fall Off". Utterly infatuated. I mean, I'm talking about folk who play it multiple times every single day. In the car, in the kitchen, on their headphones. And – yes – when I say *they*, I mean *I*. But it's not just me. There are others who would remortgage their houses to get their hands on one of those unreleased test pressings of "All the Way Through to the Morning".'

'That's crazy,' he replied. 'And it's certainly nice to hear this, but I guess I'm being reminded now of all the mistakes and missed opportunities over the years – and not all of them my fault. Things were a whole lot different then when I started out, and I'm still not sure they're even a whole lot different now.'

Dinah gestured to the waitress for her to bring the bill.

'How do you mean?'

Bucky waited until it had been placed on a yellow plastic platter in front of them.

'If you're born poor in American, or raised in the wrong neighbourhood, you expect some shit. Everyone knows "the dream" that anyone can make it is just a myth and that the game is rigged from day one. Those cards are stacked. Most don't make it; out on the street or down at the bottom, it's all just a case of surviving. That's all. Surviving. If that shit doesn't come, you're one of the lucky ones.'

'What happened to you?'

Bucky slid off his stool onto swollen feet and pain bolted up his legs. They felt hollow, barely able to support the bulk of his hefty body. He was light-headed.

'Shit came.'

★

Over the road from the diner, the pier was casting long shadows. The bait and tackle shop and seafood wholesalers' were all closed and the fleet of small trawlers were now far out at sea, the twinkling lights of Scarborough's South Bay so far away that to the fisherman they must have appeared as distant as the stars. In just a few hours the boats would return on the morning tide with their dawn catch and the pier would be bustling again with scraped-off fish scales, buckets of guts and seagulls hovering and diving for snatches of brine-fresh carrion, and if the catch was good the trawlermen would live like three-day millionaires until Monday morning came around once more, and the lure of the next tide beckoned.

'Wealthy aristocrats and military officers used to fish this coast for big-game tunny,' said Dinah, when she noted Bucky looking over to the pier. 'It was the top spot for it.'

'What's tunny?'

They walked.

'Bluefin tuna. There were world record hauls using rod and line recorded here. I'll take you to a chippy where you can see photographs hanging on the walls of fish measuring sixteen feet in length that had been hauled up from this very harbour.'

'They still catch them now?'

Dinah shook her head.

'My grandad was a trawlerman and he used to tell us about the old days, back before commercial fishing reduced the herring and mackerel stocks so much that the tunny had nothing to feed on and disappeared from the North Sea. Now it's mainly whiting, coalfish, plaice, sole. Some shrimp, lobster and crab too. Half of it doesn't even make it onto people's plates though.'

'Where then?'

'It ends up as fishmeal. They feed it to farm animals.'

Bucky was only half listening. He longed to be horizontal in a room by himself, with only his melancholy for company. The Foreshore Road was now thronged with Friday night people loose with drink. Dinah led the way among them with Bucky shuffling a step behind. They passed pubs festooned with Union Jack flags whose entrances were thick with vape smoke that gave them a mysterious and ethereal appearance; they passed stalls selling doughnuts scooped from bubbling vats of oil, and others selling nothing but polystyrene trays of fish and chips.

Behind them music and screams soundtracked a small funfair and the town's archaic castle watched on silently, a dramatic silhouette hunched over the headland.

The sounds, smells and artificial colouration of the night heightened the growing sense of disassociation that Bucky was experiencing, as if his mind and body were slowly separating into two entities, and the slow panic that had stalked him earlier was now crawling through him, from the ground up, a parasite. He paused for a moment outside an amusement arcade in which there was a maze of machines whose visual allure was garish and seductive. He saw shifting shelves of coins, mechanical grabbers hovering over treasure troves of unobtainable toys and the occasional £10 note, and one-armed bandits that periodically sprang into life with strange digitised jingles, adding to the polyphony of whirring and clattering.

Close by, at the corner of the arcade's open front, was a test-your-strength punching machine.

'Oh, man,' said Bucky. 'I've not seen one of those things in a long time.'

Dinah turned back towards him. She rooted in her pocket for some change.

'Fancy your chances, do you?'

Bucky smiled, but said nothing. Three young men, teenagers in tracksuits, boys really, each held fast in the conflicting grip of both pubescent machismo and deep insecurity, walked past them, and as they did one knocked against Dinah, causing her to drop some coins.

'Watch it, you,' she said, but the boy barely gave her a second glance as one of his friends pushed a pound into the slot and the punchbag levered down into place.

'Little scrotes,' she said, out of the side of her mouth. 'I bet I know their mothers.'

The boy who had paid shaped up to the machine and then lunged forward and punched the ball. A digital screen displayed ascending three digit numbers that crept up to a halt at 643.

He grunted indistinct words of dissatisfaction.

He tried again, but this time he swung too hard and only clipped the ball. Scuffed it. 399. His friends howled with derision. Before he could try a third attempt, the boy who had bumped into Dinah stumbled forward and punched at the ball blindly but without any real power. He scored 691 and whooped with pride. Out of embarrassment, the first boy jumped on his back and they tumbled to the floor. The third – the youngest-looking of them – was laughing and gurning so wildly it looked like he was trying to eat his own face.

'No technique,' Bucky said to Dinah, tutting. 'No technique at all.'

The boy who had paid for the machine straightened up.

'What's that?'

'Oh, nothing.'

'It sounded like you reckon you know better.'

Confused, Bucky shrugged. Dinah interjected.

'*He said* you have no technique.'

Now the boys were interested in the two of them.

'Don't see many of you lot in here,' said the third boy, who had not thrown a punch, and though he was facing both of them, he was looking directly at Bucky.

'You lot?' said Dinah.

'Americans.'

'Man couldn't punch a trifle without busting up his hand,' said his friend in patois that was at odds with his pale complexion and Yorkshire accent. 'Believe.'

Bucky held out his hand.

'Let me borrow one of those, sweet pea.'

Dinah pressed a grubby coin into his palm. He slowly took off his gilet and made a show of carefully – leisurely, fastidiously – folding it.

'Would you mind?'

He offered it to Dinah who draped it over her forearm while Bucky unbuttoned his cuffs and again, with a quiet sense of pageantry, slowly rolled up his sleeves. The boys spoke under their breaths and they tittered, but they were curious. Bucky tilted his head to touch his left ear to his left shoulder and then to the right. He stretched out his elbows behind him and rolled his shoulders.

'Thinks he's Tyson Fury,' said the boy who had thrown the first punch.

'Tyson? I saw the original,' Bucky replied. 'Iron Mike, Atlantic City in '85.'

'Who?'

By now they had been joined by two other boys and two girls who had wandered over to watch. Bucky cracked his knuckles and then pushed the pound into the slot. The metal lever dropped down and the ball hung there, slightly higher than his head. He stood facing it squarely and tested his range, then he adjusted his old Air Jordans so that he was now at a slight angle, sideways on. The ball hung suspended. All eyes were on him as he prolonged the moment.

Bucky punched the ball so hard and so fast, and returned to his original stance so neatly and quickly, that the gathered teenagers barely saw the movement. Instead they heard bells ringing and saw the numbers shoot up through the seven and eight hundreds at rapid speed and only begin to slow down in the high nine hundreds.

996 ... 997 ... 998 ... 999.

It was the highest score that the machine's three digital digits could register.

The fake sound of a roaring crowd came through speaker and a disembodied voice in a fake American accent announced: '*It's a KO!*'

Around him the kids tried to look unimpressed, but their faces failed them. Instead they conceded quiet mutterings, first of disbelief and then begrudging respect. The ball was released again.

'It all comes from the hips,' Bucky explained to them. 'You twist from the hips and you punch *through* the ball. Don't aim for the ball – aim for beyond it. Through it. Watch this.'

He threw the same punch again.

999.

Bells, whistles, the roar of the crowd. *'It's a KO!'*

'Man's a pure warrior,' declared one of the boys who had joined them. The others nodded in acquiescence. They had to. It was undeniable. It was irrefutable. Bucky knew that a pure, clean punch could not be argued with. It was one of the few remaining truths in an era of manipulation and denial. Violence was timeless.

'Here, come.'

Bucky stood aside and gestured to the boy who had thrown the first two blows. He stepped forward, but with a flush of embarrassment at being singled out this way.

'Now, look at the way my feet are planted and the angle at which I'm standing. Here, you try.'

The boy assumed the position.

'That's it. Left shoulder first if you're a southpaw, which I can see you are, and chin tucked to your chest to protect it. Now, first we shape up, then we check the range – you don't want to pop your shoulder out of its socket. I've seen it happen and that shit hurts almost as bad as popping it back in. Hurts like hell.'

One of the girls winced.

'Then, as you swivel your hips from this angle, the upper half of your body has more power behind it, more leverage. It's not just about your arms or your fists or your wrists, it's about your everything. And remember to punch through.'

The boy swung a right hand straight down the middle and the ball flew back and locked into place with impressive speed.

901. The teenagers cheered. The boy tried to play it cool, but a beaming smile broke through his mask.

'Now, *that's* what I'm talking about. Technique. You don't need to be tough or strong or big – or young – to throw a proper punch, you just need technique. Once you have it, you don't lose that shit. It never goes.'

Bucky asked Dinah for another pound and inserted it into the machine.

'Here, the next round's on me.'

As the boys jostled each other and peevishly squabbled over who would get the first go, Bucky and Dinah stepped back out into the street and headed along the road that led towards the Majestic, which was illuminated on the clifftop now like a great stone lantern. A low fret was creeping in from the sea and spooling around the bollards, lamp posts and sheltered seating areas that looked out across the black water.

'Wow, Bucky. That was quite something.'

'Oh, that wasn't much of anything.'

'You can really punch though, can't you?'

'I surprised myself.'

'You hit 999. No one does that.'

'Yeah? Turn that number upside down and what have you got?'

'666.'

'You know numerology right? Room 333 and all that. So what does 666 mean?'

'The number of the beast. The mark of the devil.'

'Well,' he smiled. 'It must be that I've got the devil in me.'

He suddenly felt more tired that he had in a long, long time. He was exhausted. Spent. His body was once again crying out in protest at being denied the painkillers that he had been taking so for long. He stopped. The Majestic seemed far away, as high as the moon.

'Is that crazy tram still running?'

'I'm afraid not.'

'Then I think I'm going to need to get a taxi back up there.'

'Really? It's not far.'

'Might as well be the moon, sweetie, the way this tiredness has got me.'

★

59

After she had helped Bucky into a taxi, Dinah walked up through the town centre and into the residential streets of the North Bay. She looked through the windows of the terraced houses as she passed by, seeing frozen moments of 'lives being led in quiet desperation'. This was a phrase she had heard somewhere, and thought of often. She couldn't remember who said it, or maybe she never knew, but she did immediately and implicitly understand that it had applied to her marital situation for some time now. Too long. And now the older she became and the less things changed, the more determined her resolve to avoid submitting to that same dissatisfaction entirely. She could not allow it in the way that she had seen others around her allow it; her own father, for example, who had a heart attack during an argument with her mother about the thermostat, and never recovered; and then her mother left alone, far too many decades into a marriage that made her unhappy to ever move on, her grief swiftly giving way to resentment and the unrelenting bitterness that alienated Dinah and made her barely recognisable.

And now here she was, stuck with Russell, weighed down by him, anchored to a shared past that was exactly that – the past.

There were outlets, escape routes from life. There had to be. Beautiful distractions. She knew that it was music, soul music, that took her out of herself – music and dancing and the occasional new experience, if there were any to be found in the town in which she had spent her entire life.

She turned the corner by the Rusty Jug, which was still festooned in weather-worn bunting from whatever the last international sporting event or royal occasion had been, and there were a couple of late stragglers slouched outside, eking out the last dregs of their pint glasses and blowing smoke into the quiet nothingness of the suburban street.

One of them called out to her.

'Now then, Di.'

She paused, struggling to see the face in the shadows of the Jug's short awning and wondering whether she should be worried. Russell and Lee had crossed enough people in the town for one or two to occasionally surface and share their grievances with her instead of them, so she was relieved to see that it was only Mick Fox.

'Hello, Mick. Good night?'

'A quiet one. Are you at the Weekender?'

'I wouldn't miss it. I'm helping run it.'

'Doing the door, are you?'

'No, love. I'm looking after Bucky.'

'Bucky Bronco?'

'That's it.'

'*The* Bucky Bronco.'

'Yep.'

'Didn't he disappear after "Until the Wheels Fall Off"?'

'Kind of.'

'Didn't he run off and join some religious cult?'

'I don't think so.'

'Or OD'd?'

'Definitely not.'

'I heard he OD'd. Or was killed in Vietnam.'

'We hear lots of things.'

'He's still alive then?'

'He was when I put him into a taxi twenty minutes ago.'

'I also heard he lost a leg during a bank robbery.'

Dinah laughed.

'Well, which is it, Mick — it can't be death, war, religion and amputation all at once, can it?'

Mick Fox shrugged.

'Which hotel is he in? I'd like to go and buy the lad a drink.'

'That would be telling, Mick. He's jet-lagged to buggery anyway.'

'Yeah, I expect he is. He must be getting on a bit. Bloody hell, Dinah, Earlon "Bucky" Bronco though. *Here.*'

'I know. It's mad.'

'Have you heard him sing yet?'

'Don't be daft.'

'What's daft about that — he's a singer, isn't he?'

'Do you fit boilers for free when you're down here on a Friday night?'

'Of course not.'

'Well then.'

'Still. What's he like?'

'Sorry, Mick, I have to get back. I've got to be up at the crack of dawn. You'll be able to see for yourself if you come down on Sunday.'

'I wouldn't miss it for the world. I'll be there with my dancing shoes on.'

He did a neat little spin, right where he stood.

'How's the sciatica?' Dinah asked.

Mick held out his hand and shook it, as if to suggest it was so-so.

'The worst pain is in my right arse cheek, so the doc's got me on the Tramadol again. I've been hallucinating geckos in my bedroom the past fortnight. Bloody geckos. What's that all about?'

'Are you meant to drink on it?'

Mick shrugged again, drained his glass, ignored her question and instead burst into the chorus of 'Until the Wheels Fall Off' at full volume. His off-key voice echoed down the terraced street and followed Dinah long after she had turned the corner to walk for the final two minutes home, until she finally heard a distant, but audibly angry, shout of protest, and Mick's singing come to an abrupt halt.

★

Lee was in the kitchen making toast from half a loaf of bread. His fringe hung down over one eye like a broken set of venetian blinds. Dinah lifted the lid on the slow cooker and saw that the stew sat untouched. The power had been turned off and a skin had already formed across the congealed contents. Several empty, crushed cans of Carling were discarded on the counter and one was in the sink along with the morning's dirty dishes. Her son had the hooded eyes of the severely stoned as he leaned a little too tentatively over the toaster with a knife in hand, carefully observing its contents.

'Where's your dad?'

Lee nodded towards the cans.

'The wrong side of them. Did you bring my chocolate milk?'

'This place reeks of weed. Couldn't you open a window?'

'It's freezing out there.'

'Have you even been out?'

The toaster popped up and Lee began to smear a thick layer of margarine onto the two slices that he added to an existing pile of four.

'Did you get my chocolate milk though?'

His voice was a childish whine that he had never grown out of, never grown beyond. Dinah knew her love for her son was diminishing; she felt it strongly, but she refused to succumb to guilt over this recent realisation, and in fact wondered if love and the capacity to give it had a limit. And if so, at which point, she wondered, did it finally run out? Was there a discernible moment when all the love for someone is gone? Would she recognise it when it happened? She certainly felt this was the case with Russell; it was glaringly obvious, but with children it was meant to be different. Again, she did not feel guilty about considering such thoughts. The maternal bond had been weakening since the boy had hit puberty and turned into a taciturn lump, and had only further weakened since he left school, underqualified and overly idle. But, she reasoned, you can't give up on your kids. Or maybe you can? The thought was liberating.

'No, I didn't.'

Lee scowled.

'I asked you do one thing—'

'And I asked you to do one thing too,' she snapped back.

He looked at his mother with parched, vacant eyes, two windows into a void, and she thought about how people talked about 'the miracle of childbirth' – but they never mentioned the miraculous way a child, specifically her child, could avoid doing something so simple as a few minor domestic chores of his own volition for weeks at a time. He literally did nothing but fester in his room, sleeping all day and disappearing down Internet wormholes all night.

'To, you know, tidy up a bit?' she said. 'I've been on my feet since dawn.'

'I have tidied up.'

'Changing your bong water isn't tidying up.'

'I flushed the toilet, which is more than Dad does.'

'Well, that's true, but the bar couldn't be set any lower. You could at least have a shower. You smell like a butcher's drain.'

'I'm going to,' Lee said. 'After my breakfast.'

'Breakfast? It's gone 11 p.m.'

'Not in the Philippines it's not. They're seven hours ahead. It's 6 a.m. there. Ning will be up soon. We've got a play date.'

Lee had never met his fiancée Ning in person, but he was nevertheless intending to marry her as soon as he made enough money from cryptocurrency and buying and selling vintage computer games on eBay (even though Dinah knew he spent what little money he laid his hands on solely on weed and overseas bank transfers). Ning's full name was Maningning, and Dinah couldn't even think badly of the young lady for taking advantage of her son in this way. If anything she admired her for tolerating Lee's company for several hours each day in order to play a long game which would almost certainly lead to nothing but disappointment for at least one of the two star-crossed, headset-wearing young lovers – and she doubted that it would be her son's Filipino Juliet. The girl was *smart*. And at least Lee was no longer enamoured by the insidious gym-ripped grifters who were turning online misogyny into a very successful hustle in the lucrative land of the virginal, the frustrated and the lost. All that business had threatened to take a much darker turn a year or two back. So, in a weird way, his infatuation with Ning was good for him.

'What do you even talk about on these "play dates"?' she asked. 'Aren't they what kids do?'

Lee folded some toast into his mouth and chewed noisily in a manner that she knew was one of his many micro-provocations that he had learned from his father, and which she had learnt to rise above, though it still silently irked her.

'You've asked me this before.'

'And you never really answered. I'm just interested, Lee.'

'It depends. Films, the weather, feelings. Her English isn't so great. Most of what she knows has been learned from Hollywood films. *Frozen*, in particular. So mainly we just game.'

'What, like tiddlywinks? The hours must fly by.'

'Ours is a relationship that exists beyond words.'

'A bit like mine and your father's then.'

'Her English will improve when she moves here.'

'You're still planning that then, are you?'

'Of course.'

'And where will her kids live? They can't all fit in your box room.'

'She doesn't have kids.'

'So who are those children I've seen running around in the background?'

He shrugged.

'Just kids in the crèche at the office she works in.'

'Oh yes. And what does she do there again? It's strange that she always calls you from a crèche in a business that doesn't have any furniture.'

'It's different out there. You've never been so you wouldn't know.'

'Strange that she's always at the office so early too.'

'It's because of the climate. It's the rainy season so people work earlier. Everything's different out there. What's with all the questions anyway? You don't even know anything about the Philippines.'

Lee picked up his towering plate of toast and a cup of tea.

'I can't believe you forgot my chocolate milk,' he said as he left the kitchen.

'And I can't believe a twenty-six-year-old man would get in a peeve over a drink for small children,' she shouted after him. A moment later she heard his bedroom door slam shut with just the correct amount of aggression to further irk her.

Dinah lifted the lid off the slow cooker again, looked inside and then replaced it. She shook her head and began to gather up the empty beer cans.

★

Bucky had the taxi stop outside of a corner shop that was still open. It being late, the owner, a tired-looking Turkish man with tramlines shaved into the side of his head, was about to bolt the door, but let him come in with a solemn nod of the head.

He bought a large bottle of Coca-Cola and a large bottle of whisky – one of the standard Scottish ones. A Glen something. Then, almost as an afterthought, he added some ibuprofen and aspirin, a packet of twenty cigarettes and a lighter. It came to a lot more money than he expected.

'How much are those cigarettes, my guy?' he asked.

'£12.60.'

Bucky whistled through his teeth. He'd not bought any in a long time. The shopkeeper bagged his items and then locked up as Bucky left,

The car dropped him right outside the Majestic. As he stood outside, he tore the cellophane off the cigarettes and lit one up, his first in many years. It tasted harsh and dirty and was far from the pleasurable experience that he had romanticised in his mind, but there was a comforting familiarity in the action of inhaling and exhaling, something almost meditative, so he continued anyway. Also, it had cost him; if nothing else, he'd smoke it down to the nub out of a stubborn sense of ingrained thriftiness, even if it did make him feel nauseous. Bucky felt the first rush of nicotine flooding his system.

From here he could see along the coastline, beyond the opulent streets of South Cliff to where there was little else but the jagged shape of the cliffs' silhouette and the ancient sea-blasted rocks below, the distant hiss and fizz of a tide in retreat.

The lobby was quiet as he crossed it. Bucky made sure to give a wide berth to a man who had slumped sideways in the seating area, a large near-empty plastic cider bottle lovingly cradled in one arm like a newborn child. He looked peaceful and contented.

The other lift worked. It arrived. He stepped in.

Between the first and second floors the old elevator jolted and Bucky dropped his Coke. It rolled across the floor and clattered to a halt, a foaming creamy-brown mess thankfully contained in

66

the bottle, which he slowly stooped to retrieve. He felt a little light-headed from the nicotine hit, a little dizzy.

Four doors down from his room, loud, repetitive music was thumping and there were screams and laughter from within as he passed it.

Bucky let himself in and went straight to the bathroom where he rinsed out a tumbler and poured a good double glug of whisky, two fingers deep. He drank it straight. It was rough. He swigged more straight from the bottle. The drab room felt smaller at night as if starved by sunlight, its dimensions had been reduced even further. There was very little space for manoeuvre around the bed. He sat on it and kicked his shoes off, swallowed some painkillers and, once the Coke had settled, mixed another drink. But the Coke was warm and there was no way he wanted to drink more whisky without ice; he knew he could, and possibly would, sink the whole bottle if it created a distraction from the incoming withdrawal symptoms. He slipped his shoes back on, took another neat swallow – firewater they used to call it – and then went in search of an ice machine.

Though he couldn't see anyone, his whole floor felt alive with Friday night activity. He heard more music from one room, a too-loud television from another, an argument abruptly ended by the sound of something substantial being smashed – furniture upended perhaps, or a broken lamp – from a third. Bucky turned a corner onto a landing just like the previous one. He heard unseen children, a woman sobbing. There was no ice machine so he continued, his feet feeling like dead weights as he shuffled across the carpet. He turned another corner where there was a winding stairwell that must lead up to one of the corner turret annexes. To his right, a service elevator marked STAFF ONLY. He took it. It stopped at a floor and the doors wheezed open. Shabana was standing there with a mop and bucket in hand.

'Oh, hi, Shabana. We meet again.'

'Hello, Mr Bucky.'

'Just Bucky is fine. They still got you working at his late hour, huh?'

The doors began to close, so Bucky stepped out of the lift and into a storage space full of cleaning products, laundry bags and bathroom accessories.

'Always,' she smiled.

In the low light Shabana's complexion appeared as smooth as marble. She was a classical sculpture, at odds with its tawdry modern surroundings, but unlike him, not weathered by the storms of time.

'Cleaning at this time of the night though?'

'The night-time is when people make the most mess, especially weekends. English people, they like to be sick in many places. They drink too much beer and wine and cocktails, then they fight each other, then they hug each other, then they vomit on the carpet or over the fruit machines in the entertainment area or in the plant pots, and now every Friday or Saturday night, my boss is calling for me and saying, "Shabana, please remove the vomit from behind the velvet curtains in the Palm Court Ballroom," or "Shabana, please fetch a mop for the blood that is running from the man's nose and dripping onto the carpet after he has been punched at the wedding reception," so I do. Always I do.'

'That's rough. I hope they're paying you well.'

'They pay just a little bit more than what you Americans might call Jackie-shit, pardon my language, but it all helps towards my studies.'

Bucky laughed.

'You're a scholar?'

'Of course, yes. Just because I carry a mop does not make me a cleaner for the rest of my life, any more than you having legs makes you a table.'

'That's well put. What are you studying?'

'I'm studying civil engineering so that one day soon I can return to Afghanistan and help rebuild this wonderful country that has been destroyed by male idiots.'

'I'm sorry about that. And I'm sorry for America's role in all that. Truly.'

'Are you a politician?'

'Me? Hell no.'

'A soldier?'

He shook his head.

'I'm a lover, not a fighter, sweetie – and I'm not much good at that these days. I'm a little out of practice. No, I've done all sorts of things. I guess I used to be a singer.'

'Then you have nothing to be sorry for. The artists are rarely to blame.' She narrowed her eyes. 'Are you a famous singer? Are you a celebrity?'

'I don't think so. My bank manager doesn't think so either. It is the reason I'm here in this freaky town though. To sing, I mean. Or that's the idea anyway.'

Shabana narrowed her eyes further still.

'You have come all the way from America to sing your songs here?'

'Yes, all two of them. Trust me, the notion is a crazy to me as it is to you.'

'What type of music do you make?'

'Right now, none. But back then? Soul music.'

'OK.'

'You're not a fan?'

'I like rap.'

'A hip-hop head, huh?'

Shabana nodded.

'Yes. You look surprised. I grew up listening to Kanye and Kendrick, but I also like many of the young rappers too. Do you like rap?'

Bucky weighed up the question.

'Well, it's not that I don't like it; it's just my radio is pretty much tuned to a local station back in Chicago that plays the deepest soul cuts, and that's about it. That's my world, as small as it is. Rap can be a bit frenetic for me. A bit ... repetitious.'

'It sounds like you're stuck in a rut. You just haven't heard the good stuff.'

Bucky smiled. He laughed again.

'You know, perhaps you're right. I guess I should broaden my cultural horizons. Maybe you can hook me up with something good?'

'Only if you play me some of the songs that you sing.'

'Have you got the Internet in this place?'

'Of course. This hotel may look an old shipwreck, but believe me, the Internet is everywhere.'

'Well, alright then. But right now all I'm after is a little bit of ice from an ice machine for my late-night drink, and then a big, big sleep.'

'You should definitely sleep. You look tired.'

'Like you wouldn't believe.'

'Unfortunately there are no ice machines here in this hotel. And as far as I know there are no ice machines in England. If you go to your room though, in five minutes' time I will leave a cup of nice cold ice outside your door.'

'Shabana, you're a true angel.'

'Then after that, I will pick up more people's sick.'

Bucky laughed.

'Like I said, an angel. Truly, heaven sent.'

★

It was late, very late, and Bucky had drained two more large whiskys when he decided he wanted one more cigarette, or needed more ice, or might even go to hear one of the songs that Shabana wanted to play him – something, anything, to take him out of the room, out of himself. Sleep was circling but his internal clock was ticking to a different time zone. His mind was in England and his body was in Chicago, yet his addiction was somewhere over the deep, dark Atlantic, high above the mysterious and desolate depths of it. The withdrawal was making its presence felt with a slowly building internal scream as broad and fearful as that same ocean. It was quiet for now, but not for long.

There was something about his room at this time of night that made him want to flee it. It felt like a space of infinite isolation haunted by all the fellow souls who had spent solitary nights there before him. A century and a half's worth of ghosts. Bucky was not a man prone to superstition, but he felt it; it was tangible. A sense of residual dissolution.

Now shoeless, his shirt wide open to the waist, he left the shrinking space of his room in search of reassurance, and instead hobbled along the hallways, which in some places felt sticky, the viscid remnants of generations of spilled drinks, beach sand, sweat and other trampled solutions ingrained in the carpet. Bucky's socks made no sound as he prowled the corridors. Twice he took an elevator, once up and then down, the lift jolting again so that he stumbled and banged his head. He had to stop to catch his breath somewhere near a short landing that led to another spiralling stairwell when two children shot past him. Were they the same two boys with the football and the scooter that he had seen earlier in the day? They moved so quickly and his sleep-starved whisky vision was so blurry and his tree-trunk legs unsteady, the landing so night-still and finally silent, that he found himself questioning whether they had even been there at all.

Then the hotel became a vast and confusing network, an endless Escher-like network of stairways and corridors, handrails and doors; of short landings and long landings soundtracked by snatched eruptions of laughter and screams and further unseen doors slamming; and the sudden, urgent thud of unseen footsteps above Bucky and behind him, though there was never anyone there when he stopped and turned around; and music too, music playing in different rooms, but always muted and muffled behind the endless rows of wooden doors that looked to him now like coffin lids stacked in sequence. But then between the noises sat long silences in which Bucky felt as if he were the hotel's only inhabitant. The entire place was a perplexing puzzle that he sensed he would never solve.

He was in a semi-somnambulist state that he briefly considered could conceivably be sustained all night, were it not for the pain in his hips overriding the booze and the very final traces of his last half tablet, which he was already regretting not having saved until the morning, when its effect would be much needed.

He belched, and a sickening backwash of whisky and Cola splashed at his throat.

With his drink still in his hand, Bucky pushed his way through more doors and stumbled into a large empty ballroom. It was dark but bright moonlight fell through the huge floor-to-ceiling windows that looked out over the sea below. The light had a strange solidity to it. It hung like long billowing drapes that bent when they met the ballroom floor, spreading flat across it. He walked towards the light. He tried to hold it. He grasped at nothingness.

Old parquet tiles creaked underfoot as he slowly padded across them in his socks. He felt peculiar – not so much drunk as disembodied, as if he were watching himself from the curved stalls that ran around the balcony above. Tables and chairs were haphazardly positioned around the edge of the dance floor, but there was no sign of human activity – no dirty glasses, stray coat or dropped earring awaiting reclamation, only clean tablecloths and unlit candles. The moonlight gave everything a spectral appearance; the cavernous room felt as if it existed in a time slip and had not been used in a hundred years, though for a moment he imagined the gay chatter of its refined guests and the gentle tea-dance music of a different age. Bucky looked around him. He was standing astride the centuries in this ghost room. Great white columns rose up on either side of the rotunda area that overlooked the sea and in the muted magnetic light, they towered over him, appearing sky high – 'Like a stairway to God,' Bucky was surprised to hear himself say aloud, in a voice that was slurred. His tongue sat thick and dry in his mouth, so he drained the remains of the whisky and warm Coke, its ice long melted.

Above him hung dormant chandeliers, ancient. Without the energy of electricity to give them life, they too were also reduced to nothing but ghostly relics from a bygone era, ornamental rather than functional, simply there. 'Just like me,' said Bucky raising his empty glass to the ornate and intricate glass-ware. 'Hell, *you* know.'

He walked to the windows. Their long blue curtains were tied back. He gripped one in his hand to help his balance and its thick velvet texture felt comforting. He pressed his brow to the windowpane. The glass was cool and the night felt fathomless, bottomless; the sea out there, its tidal patterns determined by a moon that belonged to a universe that held a thousand million other moons, most of it unknowable. A place man could never conquer and colonise, only guess at.

Hell.

And the sea itself was a shifting abyss, its charcoal water shot through with fins of silver light in a state of constant rearrangement and reconfiguration.

In that moment it felt like the loneliest place on earth, the sea, far lonelier than his hotel room, for it suggested an existential desolation that was expansive.

He held his head there, one hand gripping the long curtain. The cold glass felt nice and calming. It stemmed a growing headache. Glass was made from sand. Sand was made from rocks being broken down by the ocean, and time. Everything joined up, until it didn't. One day soon he would be in the soil with his Bell.

On the sea's horizon he saw the occasional flashing light, tiny signs of life, so small and so far away.

The lights were there, and then they weren't.

He did not feel at all well.

★

Noises came from Lee's bedroom next door – her son's inane chatter, mainly, punctuated by gunshots and explosions in the game that he was playing with his fraudulent fiancée who was 6,574 miles away. Dinah knew the exact figure because Lee had quoted it on several occasions, as if it legitimised their relationship and made him seem less single, less tragic; as if, somehow, their love transcended such trifling details as geographical distance, and the fact they had never met, and never would. Dinah knew a lesson in heartbreak would have to be learned in a time-honoured tradition: the hard way.

Russell was still out and could stay out for all she cared. It was Friday night and he had a circuit of idiot friends who considered her husband, in their words, a living legend for some of the antics he had pulled over the years, including streaking at a televised cricket match or, on another occasion, being arrested while comatose and incontinent on a bouncy castle. They would happily let him sleep off a session on sweat-shined sofas beneath the bare, dim bulbs of their depressing little post-divorce and/or custody-battle studio flats, up three flights of tightly winding stairs. It was a town of bedsits, of once grand town houses now carved up to accommodate these modern ways of living.

Dinah took off her eye mask and reached for a set of earplugs from her bedside drawer, carefully inserted them, replaced the mask and then lay back in bed. A moment later she leapt up and slid the bolt on the bedroom door. Though it had been an especially long day – she had been up at 5 a.m. to drive to the airport – Dinah felt energised by her time spent with Bucky Bronco, writer of 'Until the Wheels Fall Off', 'The Bees & the Birds' and, the holy grail of collectible soul singles, 'All the Way Through to the Morning'. Here he was, right here in her home town, ready to sing these very songs this weekend. Even though she was slightly surprised to find him an old and uncertain man who wasn't quite the portrait of indestructible power and youthful virility that he sounded on those sixties tracks, he was still the same person in possession of the same lungs, heart and soul, who had cut those singles in the first place. And not only that, she reasoned, but she sensed that *he* needed *her* in some small but significant way; and if it was not her approval he wanted, then he certainly required her local knowledge, her support, and something else, something deeper, that as yet remained unspoken. Bucky was a man depleted, a man in need, that much was clear.

She lay still in bed, scrutinising the darkness until it came alive in colours that danced behind her closed eyelids.

★

Grief sat inside him now like a solid thing. Over the recent months he had pictured it in turn as an anchor, an anvil, a millstone, or something else immovable that he was forever shackled to.

As he drifted off in a spinning-room haze of booze, jet-lag and withdrawal, Bucky now saw his grief: an ugly chrome-star shape, all sharpened gleaming angles and bladed edges. When it moved it stabbed at his insides. It was real; he felt it, tangible and cruel. Merciless. Minutes felt like hours and hours like seconds until time itself was under question, distorted beyond all reason and recognition.

He held his hands up to his face to check he was still real, but they seemed to be at a great distance from him and the sight of them offered little comfort. He drew his knees up to his chest and pulled the duvet over his head. Down beneath it everything appeared yellow and there were choirs of voices overlapping. *Baby, baby.* He felt burning, the ache of longing swirling in the hot whirlpool of grief. He felt the rough sheets on his skin. There was a chatter of voices now, chuntering in unison. *Baby, baby, you and me.* And the swash of the sea was out there, close by, all ship-slap and tidal tones, time curving around the corners, and voices singing, *You and me until the wheels come off,* so real it was as if they were in the room with Bucky, in the bed with Bucky, confusing, a swirl of sound, and the splash and hiss of seawater in the shallows down below was deafening, and then there was another voice, a different voice – his voice? – saying, *so low, so long, so lonely*, and more voices, gospel voices, soul voices. *Until the end of time, baby baby, you and me until the wheels come off,* and Bucky turned in his bed and he turned again – *the wheels, baby, until the wheels* – and he felt himself the subject of a haunting, a haunting by his own music, the old music, from a different life, and he heard himself cry out loud, *Maybellene, my darling*, and the ache, the pain, it was in all his joints and bones and his blood and his spirit, which felt as if it were rapidly calcifying right there in his veins, and *Oh,* he heard himself say – or was it someone else, or the chorus of voices or perhaps death himself – *You and me until the wheels come off, and the rivers run dry and the sun burns out,* and he could smell himself and it was as if this Mr Death was with him now; Mr Death was real, Mr Death was close by, he was rapping dry knuckles at the cold window and a hundred voices said together, *the wheels, the wheels, until the wheels come off,* and the voices overlapped until they were rendered senseless, inaudible, a rubber-tongued rabble of gibberish, and he heard a snippet of a melody, familiar but warped, all bent out of shape and Bucky tasted bile at the back of his throat again, hot and sour, and sweat stuck him to the sheets and his legs were anacondas trying to squeeze their way beneath the door and along the silent hallway, and he retched a string of bile onto the pillow, and he feared there was a face at the window, he was certain of this face, certain that if he parted the tired curtains there would be a ghoulish face there and so he cried out, *Maybellene*, once more and cried out, *My Maybellene*, a third time and from the murk there came a quiet sobbing sound so sorrowful it made his heart ache, and the exploded chrome-star was tearing him up inside, and then he realised that the sobbing was coming from him, the sobbing was him, his essence, the core of Bucky brought out into the open, dragged into the dim predawn minutes. The graveyard of the day.

He came round – he did not wake, for he was sure he had not been asleep – to the tapping sound close by. It was a sinister and insistent clicking at the window, something dry like the tip of a single sharpened fingernail tapping at the glass, and he didn't dare breathe for even though there was a shard of daylight pushing through the gap in the curtains, this time there were no chorus of voices, no childish babble, no Mr Death or *baby, baby* or *until the suns burn out*, no nightmarish chuntering or contorted soul song, only the sound of a visitation high up on the third floor of a strange old building clinging to a cliff in a strange old country.

And, finally, sleep – of a fashion.

PART TWO

Until the Wheels Fall Off

In the early hours, when the sky still held a smudge of moonlight, the seagulls started up as if they were all adhering to some unseen signal. Perhaps they were. Bucky was awake immediately. If he had slept at all, he was not aware of it, felt none of the benefits of unconsciousness. One day had simply bled into another and he was a casualty of a particularly febrile bout of insomnia.

He lay flat, feeling like a negative portrait of himself, bleached and blurring from view – bloodless, almost. His body lay heavy on the sunken mattress and the pulsing aches that racked it were emotional as well as physical. The possibility of achieving a vertical position seemed intangible, laughable.

The avian racket came from all directions – above, below, moving around in the space beyond the streaked glass of his sash window, but most notably directly from the ledge outside. They were so voluminous, and sounded so close; it was as if the gulls were in the walls of the hotel, or in his room, his bed, beneath the covers, harassing and haranguing. The sound was tormented and tormenting, like several warring concertos of seagulls screaming in conflict. It was horrific, infernal, torturous.

Sweat soaked the sheets that had been kicked loose from the mattress during Bucky's nocturnal contortions and they snaked around one throbbing leg. The duvet half hung off the bed. He felt cold against the morning; it was a bone-deep cold, a steely and sorrowful ache that throbbed right through him. It was in his marrow and no heat would relieve it. Hot tears pooled in his eyes, turning the room glassy.

This withdrawal sickness had happened several times before, but never so far from home, and always with Maybell close by, to press a damp cloth to his brow, fix him some spiced soup with sausage and rice or pick up his prescription – or maybe even finding a little something else to tide him over until the full terrors told hold, just as they had now. Full retribution for his sinful weaknesses was being wreaked upon him by a vengeful God. He could describe it in no other way.

Bucky rose from his sweaty pit in a delirious stupor, like a revenant. He first sat, then swung his legs to the floor, stood and followed the meek thread of wan light that stretched across the carpet to the crack between the curtains. He paused for a moment, and then with what strength he could muster, he flung them open.

A large gull sat there, staring back at Bucky as if it had been awaiting him; as if its screams had been an attempt to draw him in closer. It was also responsible, he now realised, for the heinous tapping at the window during the long hours of the restless night. This realisation did not make Bucky feel any better. If anything it angered him even more, as did the seagull's petulant silence now.

Close up, it was a huge, overfed white thing, all flesh and feathers and scavenger appetite. Its beak was like two blades of a folding knife locked away. Its grey wings were similarly neatly stowed. The two webbed feet were perhaps the vilest things Bucky had ever seen, the leathery stretches of skin that joined its toes and the neat black claws prehistoric-looking. They spoke of attack, death, merciless evisceration. Ancient times.

But it was the bird's eyes that really disturbed him. Like two hellish black holes into nothingness, the message they appeared to convey was pure unadulterated disdain for Bucky. No – it was stronger than that. They spoke of malevolence. There was no impartiality here; the gull wished him harm, of this much he felt certain. There was an arrogance, too, in the way in which it cocked its head very slightly and gently tapped at the glass once more with the tip of its beak, slow and mockingly.

Bucky felt sick. Bucky felt trapped. Cornered. Christ, he wondered, what other torments would this day hold? He told himself it was only a gull, only a stupid seagull with a brain the size of a soybean, but was grateful for the thick glass that sat between them nonetheless.

He slowly crouched down towards it, but as he did the gull screamed without warning, screamed hellishly, and for a cursory moment he saw right inside its mouth and down the pink wet passage of its flexing gullet. He saw beyond it – deep into it – and sensed a timeless terror that was also wordless, something from the pre-time, elemental and inexplicable. This was the entrance into a dire and devilish new dimension.

The shock of the sound and the glimpse of the gull's inner workings sent Bucky stumbling backwards, where he flailed for a moment and grabbed at nothing solid before falling over, which sent a jolt of pain across his lower back. He lay crumpled on the floor, wondering if he had damaged anything permanently. When no major pain beyond the existing ailments presented itself, he lifted his head up to see that the windowsill was empty, vacated. All that sat before him was another dawning day in a foreign country – and on the glass a rheumy smudge of green excrement with two light feathers stuck in it, deposited with a kind of pop-art violence.

It was difficult for Bucky not to read the fishy splatter as anything other than a message, an augury, a prognostication of even worse times to follow.

★

The day was overcast but Bucky was glad of the cold, biting air on his face as he stiffly shuffled towards a park bench on a patch of grass below the museum.

His hand trembled as he gripped a cup of hot black coffee, so he rested it on the seat beside him while it cooled. His eyes fell upon a thistle that glistened with dewdrops. He knew he should eat something but all thoughts of sustenance were secondary to the dilemma of how he could locate some opioids. Or if not opioids, then anything narcotic that might at least blunt the edges of the sharp pains of longing that were scratching and clawing away, more aggressively than ever.

Hell. He was in it.

A living hell on a pitiless planet.

From the bench, Bucky had a clear view down to the beach, where several people were in the sea once again. Every time he looked folk seemed to be getting in and out of the briny water, even though to him it looked hostile and uninviting. These Yorkshire folk were either daredevil-tough or outhouse-rat-foolish, he thought. Or both.

There were dog walkers down there too, hurling sticks across the wet spumescent sand and occasionally stooping to scoop up their beloved hounds' deposits into plastic bags that hung from their wrists like fashion accessories. Dogs, he noticed, seemed to be everywhere in England, and appeared to be treated as if they were equals. Gods, even. Well, why not? he thought. Dogs had given a good account of themselves, historically speaking. Cats too. Unlike humans, neither seemed intent on destroying everything, except perhaps the occasional sofa and morning newspaper. Plus they had ingratiated and integrated themselves in ways that suggested they were far smarter than given credit for.

A figure walked up the steep park path towards him. Only when it got close did he realise that it was Dinah, her sea-wet hair hanging lank and stringy as she gently gasped for breath.

'Bucky Bronco, as I live and attempt to breathe.'

'Hell, Dinah, you weren't kidding about this sea-swimming madness, were you?'

'You should try it – I told you, it's good for you. It clears the head, numbs a few aches and pains and strengthens the immune system too. Prevents colds.'

'Being cold prevents colds? Now that's some twisted-up logic if ever there was.'

Dinah joined him on the bench.

'You'd be surprised, Bucky. And I'm surprised to see you up and about so early too. How did you sleep?'

'To call it sleep would be generous.'

'Have you eaten?' Dinah asked. 'Have you had breakfast?'

Bucky shook his head.

'Do you want some?'

Again he shook his head.

'Not right now. Usually I'm something of a trencherman but right now my appetite's gone west.'

'You should. At some point you should eat some breakfast.'

'Maybe I'll get me another knickerbocker-thingy.'

Dinah laughed. She took out a flask and poured a cup of coffee, then offered it to Bucky. He raised his own cup in response. They drank together.

'I'm afraid I can't stop for long. I've got to head over to the Spring Gardens, but first I need to go home and get changed.'

'Right. Who's at home?'

'Russell and Lee.'

'Your kids?'

'Yeah. But unfortunately I'm married to one of them.'

'Oh.'

'Yes, Russell. You might have the great misfortune of meeting him at some point, though I'll do my level best to prevent that. In many ways – intellectually, shall we say, and in terms of prospects too – my husband and son are sort of interchangeable.'

'I'm guessing you don't mean that to be a good thing.'

Dinah shook her head and then laughed, though the weight of her sarcasm made it sound more like a snorted-up hiccup. A long moment's silence passed until Bucky broke it.

'Don't worry, you don't have to tell me a damn thing, sweetie. Your life is your life; we only get one each. I'm just passing the time.'

'No, it's fine,' said Dinah, but didn't continue.

They sat drinking their coffee and watching the sea spread itself across the sands. When it retreated it left a sheen that appeared almost oily in the dull morning light.

'Sometimes,' said Bucky, before pausing. 'Sometimes we let the mistakes we make define us. We ruminate. We dwell. We dwell *deep*. Hell, I know I do. And now I sound like one of those cheap motivational slogans you see on some shoddy printout on the doctor's office wall.'

Dinah smiled. She appreciated Bucky not pushing the issue. He wasn't probing. And that compelled her to open up to him in a way that surprised even herself. 'We married young,' she said. 'Too young. Teenagers. And Russell has elected to stay the same age. Some people think that staying true to yourself is admirable but Russell is *literally* the same person doing all the same stupid shit as when he was seventeen, which is fine when you're seventeen or twenty, or maybe even twenty-five, but when your brain hasn't progressed at all, and you're still on the bones of your arse in your mid-fifties—'

She broke off mid-sentence and shook her head again. She sipped at her coffee. Bucky did the same. Each mouthful made him slightly more awake, marginally more present.

'What does he do?' asked Bucky.

'Now, that's the question, isn't it? And the answer is: these days, a whole lot of not much. I suppose you could say he's a committed semi-professional beer, wine and vodka-taster, and sometime shoplifter. Like I said, there's a certain charm to all that when you're seventeen, a sort of roguish rebel-without-a-cause appeal, but not when you're facing old age with zero prospects and even less motivation. Turns out everyone needs a cause, otherwise you're stationary.'

'What's your cause?'

'Surviving, I'd say. Putting food on the table and keeping them out of trouble.'

'I hear that.'

They drank in silence.

'Your old man's never had a job?' Bucky asked.

'Oh yes. He's had plenty of jobs. He was a driver for years. For a good while he worked for the Jacobuccis.'

'What's that?'

'The Jacobuccis. They're a big family round here. They own a lot of the arcades, the cafés and the ice-cream routes. Italian. He did deliveries for them, mainly for the factory. They supplied a lot of fast-food restaurants and chain pubs so he would take van-loads of ice cream all over the place, right across the North. But then the factory shut a few years ago, so he went to work for Amazon instead.'

Bucky considered what Dinah was telling him.

'Yep. Sometimes it seems like the working life is out to break a man rather than make a man. Or a woman. It's hard out here. They say poor is a state of mind and broke is a state of wallet; I have known both intimately. We all do what we've got to do to come on through. How did the new gig turn out for him?'

'Badly. He couldn't hack the pace, couldn't handle the regimentation. To be fair, it's backbreaking work, an impossible task running against the clock like that all day long, and Russell is his own man — meaning, he's a lazy bastard. He kept popping into some of his old haunts for a pint or two. Then he'd get behind schedule, so he got warnings, which stressed him out even more, or he "misplaced" parcels — some he chucked out the van window down a country lane and they were found by a farmer — and so the drinking increased. Then he lost his licence. And then it was over. Actually, it wasn't quite over — they put him in the warehouse, but his people skills were lacking, and he got into bother, and then it really was over. Sacked from a job they're training robots to do. Imagine.'

'That's rough.'

'It's rough for everyone, but that's still no excuse for being a total and utter penis.'

Bucky laughed. '*A total and utter penis.* Yeah, I like that.'

'You wouldn't if you were married to one.'

'And your son?'

'Lee. A budding total and utter penis.'

Bucky laughed again. Smiling, Dinah looked at him sideways, then did the same. She found herself surprised to be sharing such intimate details and opinions that she otherwise usually suppressed. What was it about Bucky's demeanour that was opening her up in this way? She wasn't sure; she only knew that she felt comfortable in his presence.

'I know, I know,' she said. 'I shouldn't say that about my own flesh and blood, but it's true. He's definitely his father's son. He stays in his room all day getting stoned, playing games and chatting to a woman online who he has never met, and never will meet, because she's slowly rinsing him for whatever spare cash he has. He's in love with nothing but an idea, a flat-screen female from a far-flung land.'

'We're living in crazy times, Dinah. No one ever told us the future would be this strange. It seems to me like the Internet is taking the human brain in directions that evolution hasn't accounted for.'

'You're not wrong there, Bucky.'

'They said it was meant to enlighten us but I'm not so sure. Personally, an old man like me, I don't bother with it. It feels like it's too late to start now. But I see the way people's behaviour is changing. Not being big on computers gives me a rare viewpoint on those who spend their days and nights in the digital world. I see the changes.'

Dinah sighed.

'You're right, he's a child of the Internet, a product of that generation, you know? The thing is, like his dad, he has no drive or ambition, which is OK, not everyone wants to rule the world, but he's stagnating. He's a young man marinating in his own juices and it's not pretty. He's got no assets, no interests, nothing about him at all. It's like he's entirely devoid of a personality, which I find odd, because even if it's a rotten one, a personality is not something his father could be accused of lacking. Russell is what some people call "a character", and all that that entails. But Lee – he'd be lost without Wi-Fi. He would literally be adrift in the world. He doesn't know how to function otherwise. I suppose, deep down, we secretly hope that our kids will look after us one day when we're old and incapable, but we just can't assume that those roles will be reversed. Lee can't do anything, and his father is too selfish to do anything for anyone even if he could. His development is, as you Americans like to say, arrested, and I might as well be single.'

'Sound like you're holding it all together for everyone?'

'Just about.'

They fell silent again for a moment, before Dinah suddenly thought of something.

'I'm sorry Bucky, I've been jabbering away about myself.'

'It's OK, Dinah. You don't need to apologise. It was me who asked.'

'It's weird, I don't normally discuss this stuff. Maybe it's because I feel like I already know you through your music. So let me turn the tables on you instead: any children back home?'

He looked down and shook his head.

'None that I'm aware of.'

'Oh.'

Bucky squinted out to sea.

'You know, one day you look up from your own navel and your parents are old. The next day you look up, look in the mirror and are surprised to find that suddenly you're old too. Time's a bitch.'

'That it is.'

When Bucky didn't look like he was going to say anything about being childless, or anything else at all, Dinah took it as a sign to leave.

'So shall I swing by in a bit – say, an hour or two?'

'Sure, sweet pea. I'm not fixing to go anywhere.'

'Will you be alright?'

'I have been for seven decades, just about.'

'And you'll get something to eat? You'll get some breakfast?'

'I'm sure I won't starve.'

'Because you've got to keep your strength up for the big comeback.'

Bucky forced a smile and nodded.

'Thanks, Dinah. I will.'

★

True to her word, an hour and a half later, Dinah was back in Bucky's room at the Majestic, taking in the sea view. She had showered and changed and enjoyed a few moments of silence as neither Russell nor Lee was around. She was glad to see that her husband had not returned home last night – such non-appearances stopped being a concern years ago – while her son would almost certainly be asleep for most of the daylight hours. That three different people were following three differing time-tables ensured the continued existence of her family under one roof. The simple fact that they were barely around together at the same time had prevented Dinah from kicking both husband and son out – or more likely, she herself would have to leave and set up a new life elsewhere as they were far too lazy and inept to do anything beyond their separate, selfish daily routines.

Bucky meanwhile had managed to walk the 200 plus yards back to the hotel and drink a small glass of warm, leftover Cola and nibble a few nuts and a dry biscuit to put something in his stomach. Now he was stretched out on his bed and attempting to disguise his hangover as jet-lag, his jet-lag as withdrawal, his withdrawal as non-existent. It wasn't working.

'Bucky, I probably should have asked you this before, but how would you feel about doing a quick interview?'

He rubbed his eyes and yawned, then sat up on one elbow. The bed creaked noisily.

'An interview? What kind of interview?'

'Just a chat for a magazine.'

'About what?'

'About you, Bucky.'

'About me?'

'Of course. Have you ever heard of *Souled Out*?'

He shook his head. 'Nope.'

'It's a very reputable magazine and website, and there's a journalist who writes for them who would love to have a short sit-down with you. Apparently she freelances for *Mojo* and some others too, so she reckons she might be able to place a piece with one them as well. Have *Mojo* ever interviewed you before?'

Bucky shook his head again.

'Honey, the only people who ever want to interview old Bucky are doctors and welfare folk. Lord knows, I could do with a little mojo in me today though. Hell.'

'That'll be the tiredness from the journey, I bet. Your body will still be in a different time zone. I thought perhaps you could have a little sleep later on, but first we'll just pop along to the Spring Gardens so you can see the layout for the Weekender. Size up the stage and soak up the vibe, so to speak. And then we can have a drink with Hattie.'

From his bed, Bucky looked at Dinah blankly.

'Hattie's the journalist,' she explained.

'Oh, OK. Well, if you think it's worth doing, sure, I mean, I'll do my best.'

'It can't do any harm.'

Probably it can, Bucky thought, but kept the notion to himself. He also couldn't help wondering if this journalist could score a little something for him. Was that still how it worked? He had been so long out of the game that he no longer knew the etiquette or even the terminology. Back in the day, the music biz used to be a hotbed of narcotic transactions and favours, but it had been such a long time that all he knew now were prescriptions and the old neighbourhood connections. Quite a few of the kids round his way still respected him, knew he wasn't a narc. He'd helped some out with a few dollars here and there.

'Great, let's go,' said Dinah, rubbing her hands together.

'What, now?'

'No time like the present,' said Dinah. 'Also, the venue will still be quiet, so we'll have no one bothering you.'

'Why would anyone bother me? I've done nothing wrong.'

Bucky felt his mood souring, but decided to fight it as best he could. Dinah was only looking out for him, he saw that. She was doing her best, this sweet decent woman. Also, leaving the room at least increased his chances of sourcing a little something – a little *anything* – to put some pep in his step and keep the incoming horrors at bay.

'You know, at first I thought you were just being modest, but you really do have no idea, do you?'

'About what, honey?' asked Bucky, as he slowly raised himself up off the mattress and into a standing position. His hips howled and he turned away from Dinah, wincing.

'About your popularity, you daft doughnut.'

'I mean, I just keep thinking that this is just some elaborate set-up, a conspiracy to get me here under false pretences, and that at any minute now a camera crew is going to pull up or leap out of that wardrobe there or some shit.'

Dinah laughed.

'Bucky, we wouldn't do that to you. And *I* certainly wouldn't do that to you. I thought we had established that having you here is a massive buzz for everyone involved. So let's at least accept that you're here because we want you here, and on your own merit, and then move on from that. OK?'

He nodded.

'No sweat. Sure. And I'm sorry – I guess the lack of sleep is making it a little harder for me to get acclimatised to being here. You've just got to bear with me. Old Bucky's bones are aching. I've led a rum life, but none of it has ever included going abroad.'

'You've never left America before?'

'Nope. Not to Mexico, not to Canada, not to anywhere. You could say I'm not best prepared for any of—' Here he gestured around the room, and the town that lay beyond it, to the sea, the sky and the high circling gulls whose shrieks soundtracked the cool, clear morning—'*this*. But I'll see if I can't string a sentence or two together in a manner that befits your king's English. Hell, I don't know. I'll do my best.'

'Deal,' she said.

Dinah raised a palm. Bucky hesitated, and then high-fived her.

'Right on.'

★

The main room in the Spring Gardens had a lingering morning-after-the-night-before scent of stale sweat, spilled sticky drinks and residual energy. The absence of people only highlighted that a substantial crowd had been very present twelve hours earlier, when a full house had danced shoulder to shoulder to a DJ set of soul classics from promoter Graham Carmichael, who had

90

been playing the same small box of seven-inch singles in similar rooms across the North and Midlands for well over four decades.

'As with Graham's hair but not his waistline, the crowds have been slowly and steadily thinning out over the years,' Dinah explained, as she and Bucky entered the building after a mercifully short walk down from the Majestic. 'But he'll always have his loyal – and local – faithful, and last night was packed by all accounts.'

'And this Graham owns this place, does he?'

'Not owns, oh, God, no. He barely owns more than a pair of shoes, the clothes he stands up in and a blind cat called Frankie Valli. No, he just puts the odd Weekender on. And thanks to a forthcoming appearance by the near-mythical Earlon "Bucky" Bronco, plus full DJ supporting cast, Graham might actually just about break even for once, through advance ticket sales alone.'

'No pressure then,' said Bucky, a worried look flashing across his face.

'Oh, don't worry about that. Any losses he incurs are always offset against the pleasure he derives from the Weekenders – and, of course, a chance to step into the spotlight and take to the wheels of steel. Look – there's the silly old sod now.'

'I can't believe you're here,' said Graham, striding across the dance floor and clasping Bucky's hand in both of his. 'Graham. Welcome.'

Graham, he noticed, had a very large, very round feminine-looking ass for a man.

'Neither can I,' Bucky replied. 'Thank you.'

'Always the first to arrive and last to leave,' said Dinah, sniffing the air. 'Blimey though, Graham, I think you need to get some fresh air in here. It smells like a locker room.'

Bucky looked around the hall and took in the tiled floor, the high stage, the lighting rig and the extensive sound system. As he did he experienced a hot, stifling swash of dread so acute and sudden that he felt his bowels turn unexpectedly loose. Graham was explaining the venue's sprung dance floor to him, but Bucky returned from his dissociative state to cut him off mid-sentence and excuse himself to the bathroom, where he noisily and violently did the business that had evaded him upon waking.

Bucky's body clock, which felt like a busted mess of springs and random numerical digits, was purging itself. His body was now calling out for drugs in a voice that was deafening only to him, while at the same time embarking upon a process of continued detoxification in reaction to – or perhaps revolt against – the sudden denial of its usual steady supply. His body had become a battleground over which he had very little control. He expelled again, a hot splashing jet that felt, for a moment at least, almost transcendentally beautiful.

At the washbasin he swallowed several Tylenol down with some handfuls of water, and then chased them with a nip of the remains of last night's whisky, which he had decanted into a water bottle tucked into the inside pocket of his gilet.

In the bar area he was introduced to the journalist Hattie, who seemed impossibly young for someone who made a living writing about what he considered old man's music. They took a table and she placed a notepad and phone between them. Dinah brought them drinks – sparkling water for Hattie, more black coffee for Bucky – and sat at the next table. He wanted another cigarette; already one addiction was stepping in for another, though the howling need for the golden numbness of the pills was only getting louder. The kicker was, he had known that this day was coming for years – it always did. What he hadn't expected was that it would be here, wedged between a dreary sea and a low-ceiling sky in a foreign land.

Hattie was petite, and her hair was tied up and hidden beneath a beret. She had a smattering of freckles and slightly crooked teeth that he found fascinating.

'So,' she said, pressing record on her phone. 'This is such an honour, Mr Bronco.'

Her accent was unexpected.

'The honour's all mine. And "Bucky" is just fine. Where are you from, sweetie?'

'Germany.'

'Oh, cool. Anywhere I might have heard of?'

'I doubt it. I'm from a tiny place out in the sticks, in an area called Samerberg.'

'OK. I've got to admit, my German geography is pretty whack. Is it that near Berlin?'

Hattie shook her head. 'No.'

'How about Hamburg?'

Hattie laughed.

'No, it's even further away from Hamburg than from Berlin.'

Bucky fell silent as he racked his brain. He stared at his drink, at the table, at his fingers as they curled crablike around the handle of his coffee cup, and he tried to think of another town or city in Germany that he had heard of.

'Frankfurt,' he finally declared. 'Are you from near Frankfurt? Or Friedberg? I've only heard of that because that's where Elvis was stationed.'

'No,' smiled Hattie, 'although Friedberg is not far from Frankfurt and I like this guessing game. The effort is appreciated. So, actually, Samerberg is in Bavaria, down near the border of Austria. It's just a smattering of hamlets and little villages, really. Farming and hillwalking country. A lot of mountains.'

'Now, I know that Bavaria is famous for beer, right? And…'

Both Hattie and Dinah hung on Bucky's words again as once more he racked his brain for a cultural connection point.

'Sausages? Or is it offensive to say that?'

Hattie laughed again.

'No, I mean maybe it's *a bit* of a German stereotype, but I think in this case it's fair to say we Bavarians like our sausages, particularly the white sausage. My village isn't known for much else, except a pretty famous footballer from the eighties grew up there, and also a great German poet called Romy Landau.'

'Oh, that's cool,' said Bucky. 'So what brought you to England?'

'You did.'

'Me? How so?'

'I came here to interview you.'

'You came here to do this? Just for this conversation, I mean?'

Sipping her drink, Dinah smiled and shook her head, but kept quiet.

'Yes. Of course.'

'You mean, you just got on a plane and came here?'

'Yes. Just like that. Up in the air and across the sea. I wasn't going to miss this opportunity to hear you sing; no, I wouldn't miss that for the world. Also my editor said that seeing as I was coming to watch you perform anyway, we should take a chance and see if I could interview you too. And here we are.'

'Have you even heard my music?'

'Are you crazy? Of course I have.'

'I told you, Bucky, you're too modest,' Dinah said from her table, and then to Hattie: 'I thought he was just being humble, but it turns out he doesn't have a clue, right, Buck?'

He raised his palms, only able to offer an exaggerated look of bewilderment in response.

'People have been trying to track you down for years to do an interview,' said Hattie.

'Well, heck, no one ever knocked on my door. I've not been hiding.'

'You weren't easy to reach though. No manager, no record company, no website, no email address. Nor are you registered for publishing royalties. No social media presence.'

'Thank God.'

'And you're not even in the phone book, not that anybody uses phone books now. But we're here now and that's all that's important.'

'Tell me,' said Bucky. 'A young lady like you, all the way up a mountain in Germany or whatever. How come you know my music? Because back home, no one spins a single of mine.'

'I heard "Until the Wheels Fall Off" on reruns of an old TV show called *Beat-Club* when I growing up. I must have only been about six or seven, but I fell in love with it straight away. They mainly played rock 'n' roll bands so when I heard such a pure example of soul music, it really stood out. Your voice, it grabbed me. I remember I recorded it directly from the TV and used to listen to it that way, on my headphones. This was before YouTube.'

'But I was never on a TV show called *Beat-Club*. I've never even been to Germany.'

'*You* weren't on it, but your song was. They had dancers instead.'

'Dancers?'

'Yes. Doing a routine. It was pretty – what's the word? Corny? But the music was great.'

Bucky looked from Hattie to Dinah, and then back again. He shook his head, further stunned by the revelation.

'Well, anyway,' said Hattie. 'Perhaps we should address the elephant in the room: Bucky Bronco is back.'

'Well, yes, I guess he is.'

'Not that you're an elephant, of course.'

'No, but I reckon I feel like I'm an endangered species.'

Hattie smiled.

'The obvious question is: why here? Why now?'

'You mean the singing game?'

'Of course,' she laughed. 'The singing game. Unless you're planning on doing a tap-dancing routine instead?'

Bucky didn't notice the ice-breaking attempt at humour. He was too busy frowning into his coffee, baffled to hear that after all these years in obscurity, his meagre output had reached an audience in Germany too. And though this discovery should have been making him feel real good, he was once again wondering at what point he might conceivably ask this woman if she could get him any drugs. But she looked so young, so innocent, and, besides, if he asked her, maybe she would write about it in her article, and how would that look? *Bucky Bronco returns from the wilderness, depleted and desperate.* It was all so confusing and hopeless. *Bucky Bronco: a broken man.* Time was, he could be dropped in any city in the US of A and he'd have been able to find a bed, a meal and a little something – something illegal. *Earlon Bronco: back from the dead … but can we be sure?* With a sinking heart he realised he was now officially too old and too ignorant of the new ways to get into any real old-fashioned trouble. What made it worse was that all these new folk – these *fans* – all seemed so damned nice, so encouraging. They were on his side, and that was an outlandish concept to consider so late in life.

Hell.

'Hmm,' he said. 'Because I was asked, I guess.'

Noticing the journalist's slight discomfort at the bluntness of his curt response, he elaborated.

'What I mean is, I must be reachable somehow because right out of the blue I got a call inviting me to come and sing a couple of the oldies to the fine folk here in Scarborough, England, and I guess I must be prone to flattery or something, because the next thing I know I'm holding a return plane ticket in my hand and trying to work out where in the hell this place called Scarborough even is. Then I've touched down and I'm standing in the rain, scratching my head, with Dinah here assuring me that the invitation is genuine, so here I am, as dazed as a stray dog in the noonday heat, talking about sausages and some such.'

'Many people thought this day would never come.'

'Me included, honey,' said Bucky, lifting his coffee and taking a sip. 'Me included.'

'Some people thought you were dead.'

'Me included,' he smiled. 'Hold the front page though: Bucky Bronco rides again.'

'It's the soul comeback of the century.'

'That's nice of you to say, but there's a hell of a lot of century left to go yet.'

'The decade, then. It's just that I mean, you cut those two singles, one of which was never even released, then disappear for decades. So do you mind me asking what happened?'

Bucky put down his cup, but missed the saucer and slopped some coffee onto the table. It pooled there in wobbling droplets, like black mercury. Beneath the table he grasped one wrist to stop the trembling.

'No, I don't mind. But it's not an easy question to answer – we're talking a period of fifty years here, so there's no simple answer that I can give you in a sentence or two for your article. How do you boil a life down to the barest bones?'

Hattie nodded.

'I understand—'

Bucky interjected.

'Let's just say I got into a few scrapes here and there, for sure. I got married. I worked, I didn't work. I drank too much, I didn't drink enough. I got by, just like most people got by.'

'But you didn't record again?'

'No, ma'am.'

'Or tour?'

'Nuh-uh. Never did tour.'

'Or perform?'

Unused to having to pick over his life in such detail, Bucky glanced sideways to Dinah, as if for reassurance. He shook his head. Gripped his trembling arm tighter.

'So you recorded "All the Way Though to the Morning" – which still sounds *amazing* now, by the way,' Hattie said. 'But you never released it. So what happened in, say, the year after that? 1968. The year you dropped off the map.'

Bucky drank more coffee and fingered the packet of cigarettes in his pocket. Both arms felt as if they were well full of writhing snakes and the sharply angled chrome-star was cutting up his insides. Dinah was looking at him intently. All his muscles ached. He was cold, but sweating. His thoughts were rapidly fragmenting, smoke in the wind. He tried to pull them back in.

'You really want to know?'

Hattie leaned in, Bucky could smell her perfume and for brief moment he was reminded of a woman he had a little thing with, back in the late eighties. Images came flickering back from a blurred past: a walk-up apartment in Chicago in the summer. A bare mattress. The stifling heat. Limbs entangled. The taste of salt, of sweat. Hattie nodded.

Bucky sighed. The weight of history was pressing him deeper down into the pit of withdrawal. All those memories that he had put into holes and buried. They hadn't disappeared though, merely corroded.

'Well, alright then. Just give me one minute, honey.'

★

Bucky had to go to the bathroom again. It was the coffee and it was the things his drug-starved body was doing. It was staging a mutiny against the moment. He felt hot and cold from one second to the next.

He sat on the toilet, doubled over. Worms were turning in his mind, and uncovering those memories that he was dangerously close to being forced to fully excavate and examine. Afterwards he took a long time sipping at some water from the tap, washing his face and then patting it dry with some stiff paper towels. When he returned to the table, Dinah and Hattie were deep in conversation but stopped as soon as they saw him, both smiling. He knew they were talking about him. He was fading and they could not hide their concern.

'Are you aware of Mr James Brown?' he said, slowly lowering himself back into his seat, and digging the nails of one hand into his thigh in an attempt to jolt himself back into full consciousness.

'Of course. The Godfather of Soul.'

'A title he gave himself.'

'Along with The Hardest-Working Man in Show Business,' said Hattie.

'Another name he gave himself, but I guess he earned it. It's certainly not something I could be accused of. Anyways, April 15, 1968 and JB was playing in Detroit, Michigan, so me and my brother Cecil – everyone called him Sess – decided we would go and see the main man in action for the first time. Now, if memory serves, Detroit's only a four or five hour drive east of Chi-town, so off we went in Sess's beat-up, hunk of junk '57 Chevy. We were just kids, excited teenagers, you know? I was seventeen, one single recorded and another in the bag, and Sess was turning twenty, already two years into college. See, Sess was smart, much smarter than me. Book-smart. He had a whole career plan to become a lawyer – not just any lawyer though, but someone who would help the community, *our* community, help the people, *our* people, in fighting injustices and righting wrongs. All of that. His route was the right route: to play the game, to work at things from the inside. First, you become part of the system; then, you master it. Change from within. So Sess was going to do it the hard way, the right way: through education and qualifications, and by that second year of schooling, he was, by all accounts, thriving. Anyway, Mr Brown, that night, he was cool, a real showman. Not the greatest singer but as a performer? *Hoo-ee.* Forget about it. Untouchable. He was as sharp as a pin, screeching and sweating – and me and my big brother Sess were screeching and sweating right along with him, and also looking pretty damn sharp in our black leather coats, fat collared shirts and black sunglasses, even though I say so myself. We were as high as kites on the energy of it, but nothing else. Maybe a little reefer, I don't recall. No hard stuff though. That wasn't our bag back then. Like I say, we were just teenagers, practically kids.'

Hattie and Dinah were both listening intently to Bucky, who had the distant look of someone with only one foot in the present moment, and the other ankle-deep in the morass of memory. His energy was waning but he knew he had to see the story through. It had been so long since he had verbalised it. There was no turning back.

'But what are you going to do after a JB concert? Crawl into your bed with a nice glass of warm milk and some cookies? Hell, no. We were two hot, hip cats in Detroit for one night only, with a few dollars roll in our pockets. Detroit in 1968, man – the motor city. Berry Gordy had the soul scene sewn up, the best of the best. His Motown palace had them all. Tammi Terrell and Marvin. Miss Ross and her Supremes, Little Stevie Wonder who was much the same age as me but already on album number eight by the time he was old enough to vote, and – oh, man – the Temptations, those boys were bad but, by God, they could sing. David Ruffin, what a voice. A true and pure tenor, no one better. No one better.'

Bucky paused, fully lost for a moment in recollections of music past. Dinah cleared her throat.

'Would you guys like some more drinks? I'll fetch us the same again.'

'Thanks,' said Hattie.

'Sorry, sweetie,' said Bucky. 'I tend to go off on tangents. I've not spoken on this subject for quite some time. Pretty much buried it, you know?'

'No, please. This is perfect. It must feel good to relive such a night.'

He shook his head and shrunk into himself. A long silent moment passed before Bucky was jolted back into being.

'I've lost my thread.'

'You were talking about Detroit, April 1968. After the show.'

Bucky drained his coffee, now cold. He swallowed it down anyway. Another icy shiver ran the length of his spine.

The symptoms of the withdrawal were now on him like a bad bout of flu. He had gone from taking six pills a day to one, to nothing, and the crash-landing from that high was a punishing one. It was hitting full force now. There was no smooth descent here, only a plunging heart-in-mouth free fall.

The pills were all he could think about. Those pure little pills that contained a taste of heaven.

Dinah returned with more coffee, more water.

'So, yeah, anyway,' Bucky sighed and turned the cup around on its saucer. 'We went in search of a hot spot. Somewhere to carry on dancing and, hell, maybe we'd meet a nice Michigan chick or two, you know.'

'It sounds like a blast,' says Hattie. 'I wish I could have been there. I wish I'd been alive there then.'

Something about Bucky's face told the journalist she had said the wrong thing. Something about his grimace suggested the story was about to go somewhere unexpected, if he could even finish it at all. He shook his head again. Beneath the table his hands were snatching at his trousers. They were gripping them to ease the shakes.

'Well, you know, Detroit is a tough town and I guess we took a wrong turn because five beers later, we found ourselves in a neighbourhood where some folk didn't much like the look of two handsome-as-all-hell outsiders. Long story short: we got jumped by some greasy knuckleheads. I mean, without saying barely a word, these guys were on us, like white on rice, as they say, pounding on me and Sess, but me in particular. Kicking, stomping, the whole nine yards. Brutal. And all for what? I'll tell you what: all for nothing. Shit. They wouldn't have stopped either, I have no doubt about that. And these weren't kids I'm talking about – these were men. *Men.* Working men, fathers, whatever. But, see, Sess was down on the ground and backed up against a wall, but because there was only one or two on him at this point, he was able to get up on his feet. That's when a knife was pulled. Later everyone but Sess said it belonged to him. It didn't, I know for sure it didn't – my brother wasn't like that, my brother was a scholar and a gentleman, a budding lawyer no less – but it *did* end up in his hand while he waved it at them to get them to back the hell up.'

Bucky paused, blew on his coffee, then took a sip. Dinah and Hattie were hanging on his every word.

'And I guess that's when he caught one of them. It was just a nick, a little flick, like I say, to get them to back the hell up, so's Sess could get me and him the hell out of there before these men killed us stone dead, but this guy, this one guy, well, he held his hands up, or he was too close, or too slow, or whatever the hell, and the blade must have caught him on his wrist. No big thing. Just a nick, a little flick. Then it seemed like there was sirens, and the homeboys all fled. All except for this one fella, who collapsed. Just folded over there, right where he stood. Seems he was bleeding out from one of the main veins, lickety-split. He turned grey, grey as a ghost right there at our feet. I don't mind admitting I'd have been on my toes too, but for Sess. I said, Brother, we need to go. But he said, No. No way, man. Sess stayed, and I stayed with him too. Of course I did. You see, Sess himself called for the medics before Five-O even got there – you won't remember *Hawaii Five-O* but it was the big show that summer. Anyway, my brother stayed because he still believed in justice then; he thought because we hadn't done anything wrong, and it was them who pulled the blade, that the whole sorry situation could be straightened out and maybe those homeboys would do the right thing and say it was just a brawl that got out of hand, no harm done and all that bull. I mean, *they* attacked *us*. But how naïve we were.'

Bucky drank some more coffee. He didn't want to talk any more; he wanted to swallow several painkillers and drift away on a gentle golden tide towards a setting sun. But now the recollection was reaching its dire conclusion, that one point that he'd hoped never to revisit in conversation.

'So what happened?' asked Hattie, urging him on.

Bucky sniffed.

'Short story even shorter: the Man gave Sess twenty-five-to-life.'

'What?' spluttered the journalist.

'You're kidding,' said Dinah.

'Murder. First degree. That shit's mandatory. *Man-da-tory.*'

'Oh, Bucky,' said Dinah. 'I had no idea. And what about you?'

'Me? I did eighteen months on remand in juvie before they came back with a not-guilty. I mean, they had to. *Had* to. Because all the evidence showed that I was guilty of nothing but getting my jaw broke and my spleen ruptured and being a young man from the wrong neighbourhood in America in 1968. But my brother, hell...'

Bucky paused and shook his head. He drew a deep and sorrowful breath.

'They threw the whole goddamn book at him. I reckon they must have seen a strong, smart proud man standing defiant before them; someone who had confounded expectations by not fleeing the scene and instead trying to help the guy. He made a statement, co-operated all the way. And still the jury saw fit to find this articulate beautiful man with a big brain and an even bigger heart guilty. They didn't want a guy like that on the street. Dumb-ass gangsters were a dime a dozen to them, but in Sess they saw a threat of a different kind. They buried him. Shipped him to Stateville Correctional, put him in the F-House where there's no place to hide. It was especially designed that way, you know – there were no hidden corners, so that inmates could be watched constantly, and they had this tower in the middle, with armed guards pointing a gun at them all times of the day. And that was the last I saw of my big brother Cecil Bronco. Hell.'

Bucky stared into his coffee. Stared hard at the rainbow film of grease swirling on its surface. He felt his eyes dampen again, his vision become glassy.

'He didn't get out?' Hattie asked, though she suspected she already knew the answer.

Bucky didn't take his eyes off his coffee cup, swimming behind a veil of tears. He fought them back. Refused to let go entirely. He never had, and vowed he never would. Bucky took another deep breath, then exhaled slowly.

'Sess was killed in a riot in '73 – or so they said. Because who really knows? My big brother was twenty-five. They sent him off into the shadow realm.'

'Christ,' said Dinah. 'That's awful.'

'No one was ever named as being responsible for his death. And now isn't that a surprise?'

They all fell silent for a moment.

'And what about you?' asked Hattie. 'What happened when you got out?'

Bucky raised his cup, blew on it and took a sip, but the coffee was cold. He suddenly had a tension headache which appeared from nowhere. Perhaps, he thought, all those decades of holding the tears in had caused it.

'Well, the rest of the sixties, my sixties, were over for starters. Goodbye to all that. My second single went down the pan, along with my career before it had even begun. It was never released and already I was yesterday's news. In fact, I wasn't even news at all, until a few weeks ago when these guys got in touch.'

'So you didn't sing after that?' said Hattie.

'I couldn't,' said Bucky. 'When Sess was murdered, a part of me was murdered with him. And it *was* murder, whichever way you cut it. By then there were other pressing concerns to think about, serious things, like staying alive myself and keeping out of prison. All faith leaves you in those moments. Life becomes all about survival. And I never did get to make that album.'

As he sipped more cold coffee, both Dinah and Hattie, silenced by Bucky's story, sensed that to say anything now would be a mere platitude. Pointless.

'You know, some folk reckon on soul music being an expression of sorrow and pain but for me, until then, it was always about joy. The joy of being alive. Just the privilege of it all. But when that joy dies, so does the need to articulate it. Pain is a lot harder to live with, to carry around with you. Your heart can't hold it. And sometimes music just isn't big enough either. So there was no joy left in me, not for a good while, or at least, nothing lasting. Maybe a few moments here and there – a good sunset or a good lay. A nice meal and nowhere to be but at home in your favourite reclining chair, and being happy with that. Hell, all that joy was beaten out of me in that Detroit street, just as it was beaten out of Sess on that landing or that exercise yard. The difference is, I made it through to the other side and my only brother didn't. But the joy didn't die entirely; there were still a few sparks, a few embers, but they had to be slowly stoked back to life over many, many years. The love of a good woman helped.'

'So what did you do then?' Hattie asked. 'How did you get on?'

'A little bit of prizefighting and a lot of drugs. All sorts of other stuff. Whatever it took to survive in that America where the deck is always cut against you. A long-odds life. Those are stories for another day. I'll tell you one other thing though, I never could listen to James B again. But, hell, ladies, I sure could use a bit of fresh air as I've not spoken on this stuff for a long, long time.'

Hattie reached for her phone and stopped recording.

'I appreciate this,' she said. 'I really do.'

'Bucky, I had no idea,' said Dinah.

'You know the worst thing?' he said, standing up on rigid legs and taking out his cigarettes and lighter. 'A story like this is really no rarity among me and mine.'

★

Bucky wandered over to the concrete sea wall that curved its way along the coast, a short-term measure against a long-term problem of irreversible erosion.

He leaned against it and lit a cigarette. There was a plaque explaining the purpose of the sea defence, but Bucky knew that one day the plaque would be gone and the wall would be gone too, just as everything that stands against the sea is scrubbed away eventually.

It's the same with the life you're born into, he thought. Things get stolen from you, chipped away in increments so subtly that sometimes you don't even notice until whatever it is they're taking from you is gone. Or maybe at other times it happens in one or two big events. Tragic occasions, seismic shifts. A crack appears, and it's beyond repair. Either way, it's all a slow downward slide made only slightly smoother by the occasional golden hour here and there to cling to. Damn though, he missed Maybell. Missed her like summer sun on a wet winter's day. And he missed Sess too, whose face he was ashamed to acknowledge he had just about forgotten; save for a press cutting of his mugshot, he had no photograph of his brother. Sess was just a memory now, a presence trapped in a past that was out of focus, a folded yellow clipping. What, Bucky wondered, would Sess have been like as a man? The tragedy was, he would never know. Things changed, he thought, and things stayed the same. The sea goes out and the sea comes in again. Back home there were youngsters enduring the same or similar tribulations he'd gone through, every single day. Worse, even. At least his family life had been good. Parents who were present. There was always food, a roof, community, laughter and music.

He smoked. A feather floated down onto the water.

It was cold and there had been condensation on the inside of his hotel room window that morning, and now he didn't know where the smoke ended and his breath began. An English autumn.

Behind him people were arriving at the venue whose doors had opened at midday. There were single men, couples, a small cluster of young women. Some stayed outside, catching up with old friends, drinking coffees, smoking through their hangovers and savouring the slow start to a weekend of music and dancing. From inside the Spring Gardens there was a loud and sudden blast of music that Bucky recognised as 'You Didn't Say a Word' by Yvonne Baker – those horns were unmistakable – before it was cut dead, the volume of the strangulated burst heightened by the reverberating sense of silence that followed in its aftermath. Then, a moment later, a crude snippet of a garage rock song that he knew was by the Kingsmen, possibly 'Little Latin Lupe Lu', a cut he hadn't heard in decades. Even from out here, it was way too loud, and when Bucky looked over his shoulder towards the source of the music, he could see that inside the building a dizzying swirl of lights were being tested: there were flashing reds, greens and blues, the shimmer of a disco ball scattering shards of white diamonds everywhere, and a strobe light that resembled a migraine made manifest. He turned back to the sea and to the sky, both of them dull and vast, each mirroring the other, their washed-out tones offering respite from the sensory racket behind him.

He knew he couldn't go back in there, not today. There was too much stimulation. His shredded nerves would not be able to cope. Bucky felt like the empty shell that a crab has crawled out from and abandoned. He felt like a fragile glass which, if touched, would shatter with a thousand hairline fractures; or a sand sculpture that would crumble if the breeze changed direction. Everything was coming apart.

He knew that the right pills or powders would fix this feeling, or at least dull the sharp edges of that bladed monstrosity that was cutting him up from inside with an even greater sense of malevolence and violence than before. He would swallow anything if it stilled the moths that were fluttering around the cave of his heart, trapped and seeking a soothing moon. He would take anything offered to him if it calmed and cooled the hot, bubbling tar-pit of his bowels.

But all he had was the whisky and useless painkillers, so he washed another two tablets with a large gulp of it now. The whisky tasted of burnt oranges and wet ash, lonely nights and bitter mornings. Voices of doubt grew like stalactites in the dark, dripping caves of his mind – a chorus of echoing voices that belonged to real people who Bucky knew from back in the neighbourhood.

Did you hear about ol' Bucky? He went and got hisself into a hell of a mess over in England?

Bucky in England? You sure?

Yup. Bucky is jonesing bad over there.

More people were arriving at the venue. A few were gathered in a huddle and clutching records, rare singles that they were showing off or trading, or hoped to have played by the disc jockeys. They were all dressed in outlandish and archaic styles that were unfamiliar to Bucky: wide jeans turned up at the bottom, long flowing skirts, tight patterned sweaters, sleeveless shirts that seemed inappropriate for a chilly October, suspenders, leather loafers and lots of sew-on patches – patches everywhere. Even though the day was grey, one kid was sporting a broad black pair of wrap-around sunglasses just like he and Sess used to wear. Collectively they appeared as if they wandered in from an alternative 1970s that he had never experienced. So *this* was the scene he had been unwittingly soundtracking – while back at home he was janitoring or labouring or hustling or criss-crossing the line of the law, and always avoiding winding up back in the can or dead.

A couple of the kids, a boy and a girl, teenagers probably, had adopted a casual air of aloofness as they tried and failed not to look over in Bucky's direction while he drew on the last of his cigarette. He had always prided himself on being able to read a room, gauge a mood or recognise a subtle shift in the ambience of a place. Prison taught you that, and the streets taught you that too. It was a survival technique known by any fool back where he came from. You feel the eyes on you, hear the footsteps at your back. You interpret the intentions to be found in the different sounds of knuckles rapping at your door. You use your senses. All of them.

He ground out his cigarette on the sea wall and watched the breeze steal the briefly burning embers and sweep them out to sea. Bucky felt terrible in both mind and body. No, it was worse than that – he felt *excremental*.

★

It was time to leave, but his old hunting gilet was hanging on the back of a chair at the table in the bar and he knew he couldn't go without it, so with great reluctance he turned and hobbled back inside, towards the lights and the noise. Heads turned towards him, and he heard his name being spoken in whispers, which only heightened the existential sense of dislocation, loathing and paranoia that he was experiencing on top of the targeted physical torments. The two kids who had been eyeballing him now headed him off before he could get through the venue's main doors.

'Excuse me,' said the boy. 'Are you Mr Bucky Bronco?'

'Sorry,' said the girl, for no reason that Bucky could discern. 'Sorry.'

Bucky stopped, not just out of politeness, but also to catch his breath. 'I am. And you don't need to apologise, sweetie.'

'We can't wait to see you play tomorrow,' said the boy. 'We've got tickets for the whole weekend.'

He held up an arm and showed his wristband.

'We're huge fans of "Until the Wheels Fall Off",' the girl gushed. 'I've been literally dying to meet you.'

These English people, he thought. So polite and tentative sometimes, but blunt too. And then there was the morbid gallows humour and the straight-faced sarcasm he had detected, not least in Dinah. They were a breed apart.

'That's cool,' said Bucky. 'Thanks. Thanks a lot. But try not to die.'

He felt weak as a kitten and all he wanted to do was be back in his hotel room with the curtains closed and a duvet over his head or, better still, at home in his tiny house, pushing a pill from a fresh sheet, popping it with a cool glass of water or, *even* better still, pouring himself a tall cold glass of Pabst Blue Ribbon, and then tilting back in his recliner with the afternoon air blowing in through the window, the radio dial tuned to Classic Chicago, or maybe no music and just the sound of birdsong. And the smell of Maybellene still close by, clinging to the clothes of hers that he kept in the wardrobe. He knew he'd have to face them at some point, but not now, not yet. Better still of course would be Maybell herself, leaning in the kitchen doorway, talking about something or other she had seen or heard that day, anything, it didn't matter what, just to have her there in front of him, to hear her voice once again. Hell, his broken heart was tearing itself open further still. It was hatching a new level of sorrow.

'How have you found Scarborough?' the girl asked.

By turning right at Greenland, he wanted to answer, like the Beatles when they'd been asked about the other direction across the Atlantic.

'Very steep,' he said. 'But hospitable. The folk seem nice and the food's a trip.'

The boy pulled a flyer for the Weekender out from his pocket. He had a sharpie pen too.

'Could I possibly get your autograph please, Mr Bronco?'

Autograph? Bucky wanted to get away, far away. Even here in the entrance, on the front steps, the music was too loud and his anxiety was rising like flood waters. He wondered if these kids had a local connection, a hook-up. Something to get him through the next two days was all he required, but they didn't look the type. Too healthy, too well-bred. Innocents, really. You just couldn't tell with the English – their pale complexions and their neglected teeth suggested they could all be junkies, every man jack of them. The drug laws, too, he was unfamiliar with. Were they stricter in Europe than the US? Weed, for example, was fully legal in some places back home, but was it here? Did they differ in the UK to Europe – was the UK even in Europe anymore and what was all that Brexit thing about? He'd paid no mind to it. And were the rules in the UK the same as in England anyway? Hell. He had no idea.

'You kids really know my music, huh?'

They both nodded.

'You're in my top five most-played tracks on Spotify,' said the girl. 'Twice.'

'That's crazy.' He took the paper and carefully wrote his name and then handed it back. 'You kids be sure to enjoy yourselves this weekend, OK?'

'We will,' said the girl. 'Can I ask, you know when you go on stage—'

'Oh, definitely,' Bucky said, and turned away from the two teenagers and into the venue, feeling weaker than ever.

★

The bar was beginning to fill up but the main hall was largely devoid of people, and so the music was booming around the empty cavernous space. Everything felt uncertain beneath him, as if ancient tectonic plates were shifting deep down in the substratum, and a yawning chasm might suddenly appear to swallow him up and deposit him into the infernal fiery centre of the planet, burnt to a crisp, reduced to ash, in a half second. Utterly immolated. The thought was enough to accelerate Bucky's heart rate and squeeze droplets of sweat out onto his brow and temples. He wiped them away as more eyes followed him. He retrieved his gilet and was about to leave when Graham Carmichael intercepted.

'Bucky, I hope you don't mind, but can I introduce you to a couple of people who want to say a quick hi?' he asked, but before Bucky could find the words to utter an excuse, Dinah was at his elbow.

'Are you alright, Bucky?' she said quietly.

He silently shook his head and she noticed that he couldn't – or wouldn't – meet her eyes. She saw too, the sweat patches, the trembling hands.

'Can you give us a minute, Graham?'

'Of course, Di. I've got to split anyway,' he said, turning away. 'Like now.'

'What's going on? You look a little peaky.'

'Peaky?'

'Off colour. Maybe it's the jet-lag still?'

'Yeah. It's not really that though. The thing is, Dinah—'

Suddenly they were interrupted by a man striding across the bar towards them.

'Jesus Christ,' Dinah muttered. 'Not now.'

'Is this him then?' The man addressed the question to Dinah but was looking at Bucky. He was sizing him up. 'Is this him?'

Bucky saw a short man who didn't seem able to stand still. Faded tattoos decorated his forearms and in one hand he held a can of Carling. It was Russell, her husband.

'What are you doing here?' she said. 'You never said you were coming.'

'You must be him then,' said Russell, ignoring his wife as he stepped forward and slapped Bucky too hard on one shoulder. The feeling reverberated through his aching body. He felt like a rung bell.

'You're a big unit, aren't you? I mean, you're not hard to miss. Russell Lake.' He tipped his head towards Dinah. 'I expect she's told you all about me.'

'My husband,' she said, unable to disguise a contemptuous sigh.

'Of course,' replied Bucky, offering his hand. 'Russell, hi. Dinah has indeed spoken highly of you.'

Russell scowled doubtfully.

'Well, I know that's a lie but I appreciate you Americans have mastered the art of talking shite, and in a way I respect that. Takes one to know one *et cetera*. What are you drinking, Buckaroo? Di will get them in, won't you, love? She's got a tab.'

'Bucky was just leaving.'

'Leaving? Already?'

'He's not on until tomorrow and I said I'd take him out to try our local delicacy.'

'Ketamine?'

'Very funny.'

'But you've been waiting for him to come here all year.'

'Here…'

Dinah reached into her pocket and pulled a small stack of raffle tickets and gave them to her husband. Bucky recognised a song being played over the PA. It was '6 By 6' by Earl Von Dyke.

'Drinks tokens. Fill your boots.'

'Don't mind if I do. What are you having, Mr New York? These are on me.'

'Bucky's from Chicago—'

'Same thing.'

'—and we'll see you later on.'

'Great to meet you, Rusty,' said Bucky as he left.

'It's Russell,' her husband called after them, but when neither Bucky nor Dinah turned back to acknowledge him, he looked around the room and, seeing that no one had noticed this minor humiliation, headed straight to the bar, his eyes already scanning the glass optics that were glimmering in the flash of the mirror-ball's sweep.

★

Bucky's parents were both born believers. Perhaps it was this, he had often reasoned, that prevented him from straying from the righteous path entirely, as so many of his friends and contemporaries had. That he was still alive and still free over seven decades into this creaky old roller coaster of a ride called life put him in the minority amongst those he had shared street games, schooling and long hot summers with; death, drugs and incarceration had stolen so many vital spirits away. Poverty played its part too. Poverty, bad parenting – there were all sorts of reasons.

But the Broncos weren't poor. They didn't have much, but they had enough, and their family unit was tight. His parents had faith, and something else that was priceless: the ability to afford their son's bounteous love. Love was the glue that kept it that way. Which is why several times a week he and Cecil were taken to church services and to talks, to fundraisers, to socials and to church picnics, always in pressed shirts and diamond-shiny shoes – 'Sunday best on a Monday through Saturday' was one of his mother's mantras.

Their pastor was a family friend blessed with the name of Presley; being called Presley in the late 1950s, back when Bucky and Sess were still in grade school, had its benefits, and Pastor Presley used to joke that he was the uncle-once-removed of the boy from Tupelo who all the kids were going nutty over. It was here in Pastor Presley's congregation that Bucky first found his voice, proudly singing along to all the old organ spirituals like

'I Don't Know How to Get Along Without the Lord' and 'The Lord Will Make a Way Somehow' and newer renditions such as 'There Is a Fountain Filled With Blood', recently recorded by Miss Aretha Franklin herself, and 'Touch the Hem of His Garment', a hit a few years previously for Mr Sam Cooke. Bucky didn't quite appreciate how at that time Pastor Presley was something of a hip cat himself – maybe not as young and wild as his namesake, but unafraid to embrace the new and the popular as a means to give praise, so long as each song had an uplifting message to bring singers and congregation alike that one step closer to Him.

By fourteen Bucky was leading the entire church in praise-giving, spreading the good gospel with 'This Little Light Of Mine' and 'How Can You Refuse Him Now?', while others sang along with tears of gratitude and adoration streaming down their cheeks, and one arm raised in appreciation. At fifteen he was spotted by Pastor Presley's brother, Walter Presley, co-proprietor of Sweet Chariot Records, and by sixteen he was singing backup in the label's in-house studio session crew. At seventeen he cut his first single. It had all seemed so natural that once he found his true voice, Bucky thought he would be singing forever. It was as if God had flowed right through him, and he just went with it. He took that pure path of righteousness all the way.

★

'Look, it's bloody Bucky bloody Bronco,' a tall lean man with the face and build of an unwound grandfather clock called out in a barely comprehensible accent.

'It's never,' said the woman beside him, who, in stark contrast, appeared almost as wide as she was tall, which wasn't tall at all, and had big meaty forearms, on one of which he was surprised to see a tattoo of what appeared to be a spinning wheel of fire encircled with the words *Until the Wheels Fall Off*.

'It bloody is.'

The couple, along with several others who had spotted him too, now with determination made a beeline for Bucky and

Dinah as they crossed the lobby and stepped back out into the street, but before the couple could reach them, a car promptly pulled up at the kerb right outside the Spring Gardens.

'Hop in,' said Dinah, opening the back passenger door for Bucky. 'Quick, before we're flattened in the world's slowest and most adoring stampede.'

Bucky climbed in. It was cramped in the back seat and it smelled strongly of the same synthetic alpine scents that always made him feel queasy, but he was grateful to be in there, with a closed door between him and the fans who he never even knew existed. Dinah joined him, and instructed the driver.

'The Whaler please, love.'

The car pulled away and Bucky turned to Dinah.

'How did you know?'

'That you needed to make what some call a "French exit", but which I prefer to term "a shrewd move"?'

'Hell, yes. That was like some presidential shit, right there.'

'It was when you said you needed some fresh air, but went out and smoked a cigarette, even though you told me yesterday that you had quit smoking a long time ago. I watched you, and could see that you didn't look right. It was that and – no offence – the sweating. You looked like you'd been in the sea for a dip so I ordered an Uber for us in ten minutes' time, *et voila*, fast forward ten minutes and you're in it.'

'Thank you. That was pretty thoughtful.'

They sat in silence for a moment.

'I don't smell though, do I?' asked Bucky. 'From the sweating, I mean?'

'Not at all. And sorry about Russell before.'

'It's OK. He seems a character. A live wire.'

'Oh, he's a flaming handpump. A right doyle. Another thirty seconds in his company and you'd have seen that soon enough. Never has a man been less aware, or in fact less concerned about, the negative affect he has on others. Reader, I married him.'

They were back along the Foreshore Road, passing the amusement arcades again. Bucky's head felt like an overinflated balloon, his skin stretched thin. The alpine air-freshener was acrid, sickening. A couple of swimmers were in the sea on paddle boards, and several dogs were chasing balls and sticks across the wet sand. Paw prints trailed them for a few moments, before disappearing like invisible ink. High up above a kite hovered, flapping in the breeze. To Bucky it looked like a large leathery pterodactyl that was about to attack. On the ground below a small staggering child was attached to it by a string and handle, and appeared moments away from being lifted up and spirited away over the water.

'Was it the interview?' Dinah asked. 'Was it too much for you?'

His hands were spread flat on his knees to prevent them from trembling. He saw another *Never Feed the Gulls* sign.

'The interview was fine. Sorry to drag you away. You didn't have to leave. I know how much this thing means to you. The music, I mean.'

Bucky licked his lips. He tasted salty residue. The sea's effect was everywhere. It had scratched at the flashing plastic frontage of the amusement arcades. It had chipped the paintwork of the window frames and the sea-view benches, and almost appeared to have scoured the faces of those who occupied them now as they passed by. He could see the aged residents of the town sitting in shelters on the promenade, facing the receding wall of grey water and waiting for – what? he wondered. Waiting for what we all wait for, he supposed: a sign of life, or a harbinger of the great inevitable. Or maybe they were waiting for nothing, and instead were perfectly content in the stillness of the moment, their minds entirely devoid of concern, as he wished his was. Perhaps they came and merely sat and then they went again, back to their first-floor flats with their electric blankets, cat hair and memories. He had seen them from his window in the Majestic. Some trailed lap dogs behind them, others little tartan-coloured shopping trolleys. He had watched as elderly couples clung sweetly to each other as the wind lifted and the sea exerted its strange magnetic power over the town, and the breeze echoed in the sonorous caverns of his sadness, and he once more tried not to think of Maybellene.

'So what is it, Bucky?' Dinah asked. 'What's wrong? Wait – don't answer that. You, sir, need to eat, and I know I bloody do, and we're nearly there. So hold that thought for a moment.'

★

The old black and white photos of big game tuna that Dinah had mentioned hung from the restaurant's walls. She ordered for them both: haddock, chips and mushy peas, the small pot of which Bucky eyed with confusion.

'This guacamole?'

'Mushy peas.'

He picked it up and sniffed it.

'I've heard of them. But what are they – peas turned to mush?'

'Pretty much.'

He tentatively tasted a forkful.

'And this is a delicacy?'

'That might not quite be the right word for it.'

'But people eat this on the side?'

'Yes, but only ever with fish and chips. Or pies. Think of it as Yorkshire salad.'

'Is there a war still going on that I don't know about?'

Dinah laughed, and speared a chip. Bucky did the same and lifted up his tiny wooden fork that was so small it was close to useless. It looked miniscule in his large hand. He held it in front of his face.

'I feel like Gulliver in Lilliput over here.'

She laughed again.

'I'm glad your humour is still intact,' Dinah said, through a mouthful of food that was too hot to swallow straight away. 'So, are you ready to tell me what's going on with you – I mean, only if you want to, of course? Are you ill?'

'No,' said Bucky. 'Well, yes. Maybe a little.'

'You do still look a bit rough, if you don't mind me saying. Perhaps it's something you ate last night? I hope it wasn't all that ice cream.'

'It's not that.'

Dinah folded up a slice of buttered bread.

'So what is it, Bucky?'

'You really want to know?'

'Of course. I can't help if I don't.'

'You don't have to help.'

'If there's a problem, I'd like to, if I can. A problem shared is a problem halved and all that.'

Bucky pushed the tail end of his battered fish around his polystyrene tray.

'OK, then. What happened back then was *life*, and what's happening now is sudden withdrawal from opioids after many years of reliance or, well, I guess if I'm being honest, addiction. Yeah, that's it: addiction. Basically, I left my stash of pills on the plane and now I'm *jonesing* hard. So, yeah, I guess I'm an addict and an idiot.'

'Oh, Bucky. You should have said.'

'It's embarrassing.'

'Embarrassing? It's not embarrassing at all.'

'Sure it is, it's downright shameful. I'm meant to be Earlon "Bucky" Bronco, the great lost hope of American soul. If my wife…'

Bucky busied himself tasting the fish. The oily crisp batter was surprisingly tasty.

'And also you guys are paying me good money to be here.'

'So what? You're a human being with human problems. Didn't you yourself say that's where the best soul music comes from – a place of joy and pain? Money and greatness has nothing to do with it anyway; everyone has problems. Rich or poor, famous or failure, soul singer or tone-deaf drunk howling at the winter moon, we all suffer one way or another.'

'This addiction though—'

'Hey, we're all addicted to something, Bucky. Russell to booze, my son Lee to skunk weed, gaming and porn. You see Graham Carmichael, the fella you just met? He can't walk past a betting shop without giving them every single penny in his pocket, and then when he gets home, he does the same thing online. These northern soul Weekenders wouldn't happen if he didn't manage to get sponsorship from local businesses behind him, because if it was up to him not a single artist or invoice would get paid. He doesn't have a pot to piss in, does old Graham. Everyone has their problems. You've not met Brian Waller yet, but he's one of the top DJs on the scene, people love him. He's on tonight. Well, Brian, he did a four-stretch inside for armed robbery, and has got kids all over the place. More than he can count, and he never sees any of them. But he keeps that all quiet, of course he does. And look at Stevie Simms.'

'Where?'

Bucky turned around but saw no one.

'He joined the army at eighteen and was in Afghanistan by twenty. Helmand Province, the heart of the heat. He was out digging up IEDs, a bloody war hero, but now he wanders around town looking like Rasputin, shouting at lamp posts about Bitcoin. He still loves his soul music though. Never misses a Weekender. Says the music is the only medicine he needs, a claim that I would personally dispute. My point is, everyone's a screw-up so don't be worrying what people think of you, and don't be feeling bad about yourself either. I can't say I know what it's like to live in America as you do, but it seems to me that you've done nothing wrong except be born into an era where life is a challenge, as it is for everyone one way or another. Besides – the stuff you've been through – the trauma, the loss, being locked up for something you didn't do, not to mention the way the music industry chewed you up and spat you out? No one could blame you for self-medicating. To be honest I'm surprised you're in such a healthy state, love. Lots of people would have given in long ago. But the one thing we do need to talk about is getting you right and doing whatever it takes to make you feel better.'

Bucky looked glum.

'Hey, come on. It's not the end of the world.'

'It feels like it is right now, trust me.'

'But it can be remedied, I'm sure,' said Dinah. 'Now tell me all about these opiates. Or is it opioids? I never know the difference. Either way, I bet they're bloody lovely, otherwise you'd not be wanting to take them all the time, am I right? That's the stuff they never tell you about in the articles and documentaries, isn't it: how good drugs can be.'

A smile crept across his face.

'I mean, yes, you're right. When they're good, they're golden. And when they're not, well – anyway, what's your addiction?'

Dinah ran a chip around the inside of her tray and scooped up some peas.

'God, I don't know really. Cold water, soul music and the wrong men, I suppose.'

★

Full of starch or what Dinah called 'stodge', they drifted back along the seafront. The winter-to-come was blowing in off the water and lifting litter from overflowing bins and wrapping greasy sheets around the feet of lamp posts. More strollers were out on the beach, throwing sticks and tennis balls for dogs that sprinted across the sand with the joyful abandonment of the newly emancipated. Bucky envied that sense of wonder, that ability to exist purely in the moment, instead of dwelling on days gone by or potential pitfalls to come. Some people said dogs were stupid but he had never encountered one who went to a therapist or had to pay taxes.

Hell.

Outside one of the arcades was a booth in which there sat the upper half of a life-sized fortune teller called Zoltar. He was wearing a bejewelled turban and clutching a crystal ball.

'Come on then,' said Dinah, plucking a 50 pence coin from her pocket. 'Let's see what the future holds for old Bucky, shall we?'

'Oh, no, I'm good.'

'Come on, you never know. He might give you next week's lottery numbers.'

'What is it with you and numbers?'

'Or maybe he'll tell you that there's something good just waiting around the corner for you.'

Bucky looked uncertain.

'You're not superstitious, are you?' she asked.

He weighed up the question.

'I guess I just never messed with voodoo.'

'Voodoo?' Dinah laughed. '*Voodoo*, Bucky?'

'I mean, I always thought it best not to mess with things you don't understand.'

'It's just a machine designed to fleece the tourists, nothing more.'

'OK then, sure, why not.'

Dinah inserted the coin and the booth creaked into life. Portentous music played as Zoltar's eyes flashed with red lights and he mechanically bowed his head to the crystal ball. He began to speak: 'Pay attention now, Zoltar has a word of wisdom for you: he who laughs last thinks slowest—'

'What does that even mean?' asked Bucky. The automaton continued.

'Stay alert, my friend, and laugh heartily – and quickly. For a small fee Zoltar will tell you more of his secrets. *His wisdom is priceless.*'

He closed his glowing eyes and returned to a position of stasis.

'Well,' said Bucky, turning away. 'There you go. I guess you're right. Wise is the man who makes fifty pence every twenty seconds.'

'Wait,' said Dinah. 'There's more.'

From a slot in the front of the booth, there stuttered out a small yellow paper ticket. Dinah tore if off and passed it to Bucky.

'Don't forget your fortune card.'

On one side of it was an illustration of Zoltar surrounded by the twelve signs of the zodiac, and on the reverse was a printed message.

'Go on,' she urged. 'What does it say?'

Bucky raised his eyebrows. He drew the card away from him until the words came into focus; for years he has been struggling with small type, but was, in the words of Maybell, far too vain to wear glasses. He slowly read it out loud:

You are the lucky one, you were born lucky and luck continues to follow you. True love is close by and you know where, so don't hide your feelings and instead let love rule. Anger is better directed at problems, not at people. Do not dwell on the past or your own weaknesses, and sooner than you think all of your dreams will be realised. Positive change is close by – simply open your eyes and embrace it. Believe in yourself, for you are braver and more talented than you know and more capable than you imagine. You are LUCKY.

'Lucky Bucky,' chimed Dinah. 'He's only one letter out.'

'Maybe that could have been my stage name: Lucky Bucky Bronco.'

'There's still time.'

He offered a wry half-smile.

'You think?'

'Of course. Zoltar is never wrong.'

'Well, you know, if both you and he say so.'

'We do. I've been coming to see old Zoltar for as long as I can remember and he's never let me down yet. If he says luck and love are right around the corner for you, then you better be ready for them.'

'Well, hell,' Bucky replied. 'I reckon I am just about ready to receive some good fortune. Been waiting for a bit of that my whole life.'

'And some love … again?'

Bucky felt himself blushing, his face turning hot against the chill of the damp autumn air. He turned away.

'Oh, hell, honey,' he stammered. 'One thing about life is, it never fails to surprise.'

★

The studio – the first and only recording studio that he had ever been in – had no windows. Back then, back before it was bought out and doubled in size to accommodate all those big major label bands who came through in the 1970s, it was a dingy basement space, nothing fancy. The soundproofed walls and lack of natural daylight accentuated its subterranean sense of detachment. Outside, day and night could pass unnoticed as Sweet Chariot Records' changing cast of session musicians cut track after track. In the summer three huge fans were wheeled in and turned on between takes, but with the tape rolling most of the time, this was rare, and the air became heavy and reeked of the sweat and cigarette smoke that encircled the players. Grass too. This is what Bucky remembered most – the stink of that airless bunker. Only a walled-in back lot offered a breathing space, and there was a bar three doors down that served a good strong chilli washed down with some nice ice-cold beers when anyone needed sustenance.

The first time down there, Bucky sang backup vocals on 'Midnight Is Just a Passing Moment' by Rufus Redwood, then 'I Love Love' by Seven Emeralds, and then he was back the next day to sit in on 'You Shut the Door on Love (Didn't You)' by Pee-Wee Prentice and 'When' by Margot and Connie – the Coney Sisters – and all of this while still at high school. With the money he made he bought a mohair suit, a pair of Italian leather shoes and put down the first payment on a new colour TV set for his parents. He bought some books that Sess needed for college and a silver chain and put money onto Pastor Presley's plate most Sundays.

Sweet Chariot ran a tight production line set-up. Bucky saw that right from the off. It was straight out of the Motown mould, but without the big budgets and creative vision of a Mr Gordy: work the artists hard, and when they were close to breaking, push them further still. And it paid off – for the those at the top of the tree, at least. For 'the talent' who actually recorded the music pseudonymously, and for standard hourly rates, it was a different story.

After nigh-on a year of this, Pastor Presley's brother Walter Presley, Jr, who some whispered was more than a little friendly with some of the biggest names to be avoided in Chicago's criminal underworld, turned up at the Bronco household one Thursday evening that was so cold folk were snapping dogs off fire hydrants, offering a contract to record two singles and an album. Bucky, who was a Capricorn – stubborn, the lone goat on the hillside – and turning seventeen in the new year, signed it without hesitation. It didn't occurred to him to have it looked over by his parents, much less a lawyer, or Sess, who was studying law himself and already had a good head for translating legalese into plain English, because it was also just words on paper, which had nothing to do with that feeling he got when he sang soul music, nothing to do with it at all, and, besides, at seventeen years old, forever is an incomprehensible concept. To try and put a contract on feelings was like trying to shovel crude oil with a pitchfork, so he paid those fifty-five pages never no mind, and signed. Fifty-five years later the mistake still haunted him.

When the first shoots of spring were pushing through the sidewalk cracks, Bucky was back in the airless basement space of Sweet Chariot Records's studio room number two, singing once again. But this time he was lead vocalist with his own backup boys and a tough, stone-faced band of seasoned session players behind him, guys who could cut five singles plus B-sides in a week, and stay high the entire time. Guys who entertained bad habits and bad women, yet still clocked in each morning, in an ironed shirt and a tie. It was one more quirky rule imposed upon an empire that Walter Presley was expanding in the tail-wind of labels like Stax, Atlantic, Motown and FAME. Over two long days Bucky recorded 'Until the Wheels Fall Off', 'All the Way Through to the Morning', 'The Bees & the Birds' and 'Too Much Love (Is Still Not Enough)'; hoarse and late to do his homework, Bucky didn't stick around to hear them being mixed, and was back in the classroom by Monday morning, fried but exhilarated at the prospect of leading two lives. By that Friday two tracks were already at the recently opened Midwest Music pressing plant near Pinckneyville, Illinois, and 'Until the Wheels' on the way to record stores and radio stations across the country soon after that.

But what felt like a beginning was actually an ending.

★

They passed a pub that was bubbling with daytime drinkers. Bucky stopped to catch his breath. Dribbles of dried seagull scat had hardened into discernible lines drawn down the face of the building.

'Can I buy you a drink?' he asked. 'A quick thank you – or maybe you have to run? I don't want you to miss out on the big weekend.'

'No, no, I've got time,' said Dinah. 'Things don't pick up until later anyway. Thanks, that would be nice.'

Bucky ambled up the steps and into a large room divided into panelled snugs and glass-portioned alcoves. He felt both hot and cold, tired and wired, and a sub-psychedelic carpet appeared to swirl beneath his swollen feet. The bar brought to mind the old time saloons from the Western movies of his childhood, but with a clutch of vape smokers in the doorways and a variety of pies gathering flies in a plastic case on the long counter.

Some of the drinkers inside were visitors, curious day-trippers down from the industrial towns of Teesside for a Saturday's jolly, but the majority were locals supping away their end-of-week pay. A select few were the hardcore mainstays for whom the pub was more than a room in which to while away a few stray hours, but rather a place of worship, where morning blessings, afternoon baptism, evening communion and last orders confessionals could be ritually undertaken. The leathery cushions of their chairs bore the imprint of routine, regularity, repetition. Same seats, same drinks, same jokes. A Union Jack flag sagged above the bar, its sun-bleached reds and faded blues speaking of past days of hope and possibility.

Bucky ordered beer for them both and then as an afterthought asked for a whisky each too, then gripped the four drinks in hands as gnarled as burls growing on an old English oak. As he walked several heads turned his way and sized him up without discretion. Though he still felt an uneasy sense of disassociation – as if he were seeing everything from behind a wall of glass – the fried food had fortified him somewhat, and helped to quell the tremors and the trembles. If only, thought Bucky, he could lay his hands on something other than booze to blunt the edges of that lingering, liminal in-between time, before the defiant October cocktail hour relinquished control and finally submitted to a long night of darkness. Something to dust the day with resplendent magic. Something to deflate the stinging sensation of withdrawal that was swelling ever more inside of him.

Close by on the wall there hung another flag, this one blue and featuring a white flower. A rose perhaps.

'What's that?' Bucky asked.

'A flag.'

'No, Sherlock, shit.' Even as he said them he heard the words coming out back to front. 'Sorry, I got that backasswards. What, I mean to say is—'

'I know,' laughed Dinah. 'I'm just joshing you. It's the Yorkshire flag.'

'Yorkshire has its own flag?'

'I guess it does.'

'Why?'

She shrugged.

'Some historical reason, no doubt. I think the different counties of Yorkshire have their own separate flags too. It's deep-rooted and complicated. No doubt a senseless scrap in a field was involved at some point.'

'England really is a strange old place, isn't it?'

'Sure is. I'll drink to that.'

They clinked glasses as a puce-faced pensioner with an emphysemic cough and a scowl of the perennially disappointed walked by their table.

'Dinah,' he said, touching a finger to his flat cap and hacking something solid into a grey handkerchief. She smiled and nodded – 'Reg' – as he passed by, then seeing Bucky's quizzical look, she added: 'My stockbroker. The best in the west.'

He laughed. 'O-K. So do you know everyone in this town?'

'More or less. I'm a lifer.'

'You've never left?'

She shook her head, sipped her beer. 'Nope. And there's little hope of parole either.'

'The desire to leave for somewhere else never grabbed you?'

'Oh, it grabbed me alright. I just never acted upon it.'

'How come?'

She took a bigger swig of her drink.

'The usual. Work. Husband. A kid. Fear.'

'Fear?'

Dinah shrugged.

'Fear of the unfamiliar, I suppose. I admire people like you, who are able to just hop on a plane and go somewhere so different to where they come from.'

Bucky smiled at the irony of this but stayed silent and instead drained his whisky and winced at the cloying aftertaste that lodged in his throat and coated it with a cauterising afterburn. He scanned the room, only semi-casually looking for someone who might be able to sell him what he needed. You never lose the radar, he reasoned. That ability to spot the dealers, the hustlers. That was street life. You never entirely grew beyond it. Hell. In any other circumstances this town – this pub – could feel like a place of mischief, mystery and possibility, but in amongst the low laughter, loose voices of chattering conversations and bar stool ruminations, Bucky detected the reek of underachievement – of plans gone awry, and ambitions unrealised. Not amongst everyone; he'd hate to been seen as casting judgement over the lives of those who he didn't know, especially given his own short-comings. But it was ingrained. He could smell the combined acceptance of life's many challenges amongst its slowly sozzled patrons. He recognised it. It was more than familiar. Only a couple of the wilder faces appeared to emit the glow of the utterly, joyously free, and who even knew how they would be come midnight, for that blissful state of the heavy drinker rarely maintained an equilibrium. Dinah interrupted his reverie.

'I bet you've been about a bit, Buck. Seen America, I mean.'

He shook his head and drained the dregs of his pint.

'Nah. A tiny percentage of a fraction, I reckon. You and me, Dinah, I guess we're more alike than we realise.'

★

The day had drifted, the morning yawning into afternoon, the afternoon tightening into a cool autumnal evening. Evening glancing towards night.

After Dinah left Bucky slowly drank a second pint of beer and waited for the opportunity to score to present itself, and when it didn't he had another, and a whisky. Twice. Finally, after he slowly circled the room in search of a face – the shifty glance of an invitation, even – of someone who was not only holding but selling, and instead saw only heavy-lidded yellow eyes, fidgeting fingers and gold chains, he stepped out into the street to smoke while reviewing his options. Though he had told Dinah that he would try and put in an appearance at the Spring Gardens later, he knew he wouldn't. In fact he sensed that whatever happened, the night was unlikely to end well, which would then leave him with tomorrow to face. The thought of the crowd, the music, the clamour of unfamiliar faces looming at him was enough to make him down his final whisky, grind out his cigarette and lurch down into the town. He was trying not to think about drugs, and Maybell, and Sess, and he was failing.

Soon the earth-line was tilting; Bucky had lost his centre. The street elongated and then shortened and he felt like a faded version of himself, a negative portrait, bleached and blurring from view. Bloodless, almost. What remained of his energy, his essence, was draining away like bucket brine sloshed down a fishmonger's drain. His equilibrium was shot.

The air felt viscous, his limbs heavy as reality pooled around him – street sounds, passing faces, fading daylight. How is it possible, he wondered, to feel high and low simultaneously, but yet not meet in the middle? 'And how long,' he heard himself say out loud in a voice that was surprisingly calm, 'before some semblance of stability can be achieved?'

A seagull swooped shrieking overhead, a hellion of the sky, then another and Bucky flinched, shrinking in his thin skin, all sense of reason rapidly capsizing. His hands fumbled for his cigarettes, his lighter. The inhalation and the exhalation of the smoke had already became a crutch, a meditation to slow the galloping horses of his carousel mind; how quickly he was hooked on the nicotine sticks once again. He turned down a side street and lurked for a moment, enjoying the lack of movement around him, before flicking the half-smoked cigarette into the gutter. He watched it burn there for a moment, drunkenly entranced.

His face flashed across a door's dusted glass, a blank mask whose faint twist of a grimace only hinted at the cold turkey torment that was tying internal knots. He walked into his face, into the shop. Bucky briefly wondered if this was where Dinah worked, and found himself hoping that it was – hoping for something or someone familiar to cling to in a moment of crisis – but instead saw that behind the counter there perched a frayed-looking man with wild grey hair and the burst tomato nose of the committed drinker. The man looked up from a book and offered half a smile that revealed teeth like the worn-down nubs of a schoolteacher's chalk. Behind him hung a blue flag with yellow stars. Bucky couldn't remember if that was a Jewish thing or a Scottish thing or a Europe thing, or what the hell. Again his ignorance towards all things international – all that occurred beyond his home country's borders – shamed him.

He was in a junk shop. Its every inch of wall and shelving space was stacked, strung and hung with silk scarves, stuffed animals, militaria, old tin signs advertising oil and toothpaste and choc-olate, top hats and peacoats, watercolour paintings of farmyard scenes and storm-wracked shipwrecks, cigarette card collections, peacock feathers, pipes, children's toys such as jigsaws and spin-ning tops, nautical equipment – sextants, binoculars, maps and telescopes – rope and fur coats, mildew-mottled books, maracas, medicine bottles, ashtrays, cuckoo clocks, decorative knives, foot spas, horse brasses, cassettes, buoys, lobster creels and even an ancient copper diving helmet whose glass screen was cracked and brass fittings were patterned with patches of green from decades – centuries, perhaps – of salt water and sea-air erosion.

The shop's scent was the universal junk-shop smell of damp, dust and decades past. Bucky breathed it in and drew comfort from the musty familiarity. He distractedly fingered his way through a box of tatty old seven-inch singles – Black Lace, Black Uhuru, Black Sabbath – and then ran his hand across the shelf until it settled upon something cold and solid: a stone. A rock. One side was roughly hewn and scarred with the marks of excavation but the other was cleanly sliced across and keenly polished, for there within it sat the fossilised remains of something so alien and primeval as to be completely incongruous in its modern-world surroundings. The trapped creature was oval-shaped, with a skeletal-looking carapace across its back; it resembled an oversized woodlouse the size of a large dinner plate. Its head, body and tail were all intact, as if it had crawled to a halt just moments ago.

'That's a trilobite,' said the shopkeeper, looking over his glasses; then, as if reading Bucky's mind, added: 'About 450 million years old, give or take a fortnight or two. I could do you a good price on it.'

Bucky laid his hand over the fossil. He pressed his palm to it and splayed his fingers, felt the coldness of the polished stone. Four hundred and fifty million years. The awesome enormity of the number sent an electric jolt right through him. Jesus died two thousand-and-change years ago, he thought. Jesus died yesterday compared to this strange fellow. An inconceivable and ancient world sat beneath his hand, and who knew what life it lived, but live it once did, and no doubt with the same sense of desire, danger, struggle and survival that defined all living creatures. For a moment time crumbled and Bucky imagined fertile plains and impenetrable forests, and skies that screamed with animals twenty times the size of Scarborough's seagulls, with leathery wings, talons and evil intent. For a moment he felt a connection to past existences. This thing, this little louse that crawled the earth 4,500,000 centuries ago, had had a heart. It still did now, calcified in stone and pressed between the pages of a story called time. It was held fast there, close by. His pressed his hand closer, tighter to the trilobite. They were both born of the same planet, walked the same spherical surface of an earth made from water, rock, fire and gas. Bucky breathed in. Bucky breathed out. He closed his eyes. Felt alive.

★

When they pulled up to her little house, Dinah had the taxi driver wait while she ran inside. Lee was in the kitchen, heating noodles in the microwave. She had two minutes. She took the stairs two at the time, peeled off her top and skirt, sprayed deodorant and then stepped into a clean dress. She put some make-up essentials in her handbag while she swilled some mouthwash.

Dinah went into Lee's bedroom and straight to his stash box. She snapped off a sizeable bud of weed from the small branch that her son had, and put it into her tampon holder, which she also placed in her bag. In the bathroom she spat out the mouthwash just as the timer on the microwave bleeped its completion. She ran down stairs and stuck her head round the door.

'Alright, love?'

Lee looked at her, a forkful of noodles raised halfway to his mouth.

'Off out with your new *friend*, are you?'

She ignored the sarcasm.

'Seen your dad?'

He shrugged.

'Well, have you?'

'I told you, no.'

'Well, you didn't though, did you?'

He ignored her and stared at his phone. Music was playing from it. Inane music, featuring a pitched-up cartoon voice.

'Doing much tonight?' she asked.

'It's date night,' he said, through a watery mouthful of food. 'I'm seeing Ning.'

Dinah rolled her eyes.

'Send her my love, will you?'

This got Lee's attention. He turned towards her, but his mother had already left, the front door gently closed behind her.

★

He hit another hill. There were so many strenuous hills. He felt them in his hips and in the balls of his feet, taxing the last of his energy. He felt them in his knees, his lower back. Hills were fine to look at, Bucky thought, but why did they have to go and put buildings at the top of them? Chicago, they at least had the good sense to build on a flat plain that was once, so they said, a prehistoric lake in the time of his trilobite friends. That made sense. But Scarborough? Hell, the English must be sadists for the pain, sure enough. Or maybe all the flat parts got colonised already and this was all that was left.

A shadow fell across his path as something slowly passed by in his peripheral vision. It was that same truck he had seen twice already, the one with the ornate advertising hoarding decorated with sinister clowns, rearing horses, high-wire performers and the slogan: *The Circus Is Coming to Town!*

He got a better look at it this time, but still he couldn't see who was driving. The damn thing was following him. At least that's what it felt like. Maybe he was paranoid. But still, what was the phrase: *Just because you're paranoid, it doesn't mean they aren't all up on your ass anyways?* Something like that.

Bucky shuffled along in an aching fugue state, his head down and broad shoulders hunched. It was still Saturday and it felt as if it had been Saturday forever, and would always be Saturday; it would never end and he would always be here, haunted, heart-heavy and fearful of everything for an infinite amount of Saturdays. Like the fossilised creature that once crawled this same planet, he felt trapped by time, with only the ebb and flow of the nearby tide to tell him that he wasn't suspended like an ancient Egyptian mummy or one of those four-thousand-year-old bodies brought up from a bog, near perfectly preserved for all those centuries, blinded by the sunlight and already beginning to decay at the first exposure to the modern age.

He found himself in a park. It was landscaped, conceived by Victorian imaginations, with several sloping pathways and privet hedges and hidden corners containing ponds and small statues and flower beds that would surely be in bloom come spring or summer but which now sat fallow and colourless. He slumped down on a bench in one such discreet alcove that was set back from the path. The claws of anxiety mauled at him from inside and exhaustion hung from his eyelids like chandeliers made of stone. A light, downy feather sat on the bench beside him.

His mind wandered back to a place of comfort and safety, back to hot Chicago summers, the smell of the city. Each neighbourhood had its own tone, its own energy. Back then he and Bell had no need for vacations. Nobody did. Holidays were at home. There was no sense in fixing to go somewhere else when everything they needed – food, family, friends, music – was right there on the doorstep. Familiarity, hell, it was underrated. He'd never been big on exploration but every day was an adventure if you viewed it right. You made your own fun and it rarely needed to cost more than the price of a bottle or two. No abundance, but always enough. That's how he used to feel anyway, for a while at least, when he was younger. But, Christ, he cursed that mean old bastard called death. Bucky wished he had been taken first, he really did. Maybell was just better equipped to deal with the day-to-day act of living than he was – and it *was* an act, because pretending was a part of it, always had been. Pretending you were thriving rather just surviving; pretending you were strong when you felt weak; pretending you didn't give a damn when really you were scared of every shadow; pretending you were happy, you were cool, you were chilling. You were pretending you were golden.

It was exhausting, the whole charade of it.

The park was busy with squirrels. As Bucky walked by several of them slinked along branches and scurried from beneath bushes, and when he sat they slowly moved in towards him from all angles. One well-fed squirrel appeared particularly plucky as it advanced, only pausing to look up at him just an inch or two from his right shoe. He remembered the small packet of airplane cashews that he had pocketed. Bucky stood but before he had even torn them open, the squirrel scaled his lower leg, its sharp claws gripping his trousers and scratching at the flesh beneath. It was unexpected but not entirely unpleasant.

'Whoah there, little fella,' said Bucky, as he held one cashew out at waist height. Fearless, the squirrel ascended higher and curled one miniscule four-fingered paw over the top of his old leather belt and with its other quickly grabbed the nut, sunk its teeth into it – and then quite casually turned and descended his leg. He couldn't help but respect the brazen creature's tenacity.

★

For a time, after he was out and the second single had been pulled from the Sweet Chariot Records schedule before it had even been pressed up ('I'm afraid that train has already left the station, son,' shrugged Walter Presley, Jr), and no one would give a break to an unqualified singer whose most significant moment to date was criminal, Bucky was forced to fight, literally, for money. He had triumphed in many street scraps over the years and though he hated confrontation – he never knowingly started a single fight in his life – he found he was scarily good at violence. He could duck and dip and swing and slip, feint and roll; he could take a punch and give two back. His chin was strong and he never went down. Such skills had been further honed in the can, where he had passed his time with books and boxing, so when he was offered $100 – *$100!* – to go toe-to-toe with a big lump, an ageing doorman called Daryl or Devonte or some such, on an unlicensed undercard in a warehouse somewhere on the outskirts of the city, he took the fight – and the prize money when he snapped the jaw of his opponent, and left with barely a mark on himself. Once the initial fear had subsided, footwork and clear tactical thinking had made victory so much easier. The series of fights that followed across the state of Illinois were not so simple but Bucky needed the money – he was getting married the following summer to a sweet young thing called Maybellene, who had stolen his heart and persuaded him to give up the crooked knuckle game because the endless black eyes and bust lips were not a good look. A promise of the straight life once they wed was one that he was all too glad to keep.

★

Bucky sat back down again and a moment later a sulky cat emerged from the undergrowth and skulked past with the haughty gait of a tired pole dancer.

'Well, hello there, Miss Kitten,' Bucky heard himself saying.

It stopped mid-step to blankly size him up for a moment, then carried on its way. Bucky lit a cigarette and smoked in silence. A blue-grey miasma hung in front of him for a moment before the breeze dispersed it.

England, old England, sat before him. Bucky's feet were planted on ancient land, though of course, he drunkenly reasoned, all lands are ancient. He had made sure never to fall for the class-room myth that America was founded a few centuries back. Ridiculous. In God we do not trust. But still. This here England, this rugged, ragged Yorkshire, was something else. It had a richer, deeper flavour to it. You could feel it beneath you and you could see it in the faces of the people too. Maybe it was because it was an island, a little rock that could be conquered at any time, from any direction, that made it a land of noble savages or maybe savage nobles. A rum place, for sure.

The people spoke the same language, but were a different breed to those back home. There was a raw fatalism to them, a molasses-black humour, and maybe it was arrogance – or maybe it was a cavalier attitude to life that enabled the population to drink their own body weight in whatever liquor was to hand at any given moment. A nation of pickled people.

Bucky stared out to sea where a vast bank of cloud that looked like a spaceship, a huge malevolent sky-wide colony, was moving at speed towards the land, the town, towards him. The metal bench was cold beneath his bones.

From a manicured hedge nearby a small rabbit took two tentative leaps out onto the path, but almost immediately it turned and retreated when a teen noisily tore around the corner on a skateboard, its wheels roaring on the pitted tarmac. He shot past Bucky, knees slightly bent, his arms hanging low as he did a board slide on the next bench along, and then slid to a sideways halt at the bench beyond that. He deftly popped his deck up into one hand, sat, pulled a joint from behind his ear and lit it with the flick of a Zippo lighter that disappeared deep down into a trouser pocket. Bucky couldn't help but be impressed at the fluidity of the young man's movements and the ease with which he appeared to be gliding through the space around him. Such unselfconscious physicality came only from the confidence of youth. He just about remembered when he had felt the same: fearless and unencumbered by the collective toll of negative experience – those marked cards dealt from the stacked deck of life.

A sweet, strong cloud of mossy-smelling smoke billowed towards him, as did the looming mass of incoming rain. Damn, thought Bucky. That smells *good*. Without allowing himself time to hesitate, he lifted himself up and walked towards the skater. He saw the rabbit watching with wide wet eyes from its trimmed hedge hideaway.

As he approached, Bucky nodded and having not noticed him before, the skater seemed surprised.

'Easy brother,' said Bucky. 'Are you good?'

The skater considered him for a moment.

'Yeah,' he said with a slight hesitation in his voice, though he made no attempt to hide the large joint he was holding in one cupped hand. 'Safe.'

'Sorry to cut in like this, but I wondered if you were holding.'

'Holding?'

'Don't worry, son, I'm not a cop.'

The skater pulled on the joint and then spoke through an exhalation, his voice thin and scorched by the smoke.

'I didn't think you were, to be fair.'

'Well, hell, that's good to know.'

'Are you American?'

'Certainly am.'

'Where from?'

'Chicago.'

The skater nodded.

'Sweet.'

An awkward moment passed before the young man spoke again.

'Do you like it?'

'What's that?'

'Chicago. Do you like it?'

Bucky considered his answer: *did* he like it? He wasn't sure. It was like asking if you liked the moon or breathing. It was pretty much all he had ever known. It was simply there and he was a part of it. Somewhere in the distance, up on the residential streets of South Cliff, he heard the prolonged angry honk of a car horn, seagulls. A dog barking.

'I guess so. I don't know much else.'

'Same. Are you proud of where you come from? Americans always seem to be flying their flags and shouting "USA! USA!" for no real reason.'

'Nah. My parents were from there, so I'm from there. The whole flag thing is not for me. Besides, I could just as easily come from Namibia or Greenland or Egypt or Tonga.'

'Tonga? Where's that?'

'No idea.'

'So how come you're here in this hole?'

'Hoo-ee,' said Bucky. 'It's a bit of a long story. But let's just say I'm only passing through – I think.'

'Wise move, man. Stay too long and the town will get its claws into you and never let you go.'

The skater hesitated and then held the joint out to Bucky. He took it. Had a hit.

On top of the alcohol, the effect of the weed was instantaneous. It folded over him and then coursed through him, a calming green wave that washed away the bobbing flotsam of his cluttered mind. He felt a pleasurable slump, a sense of relaxation from head to toe. A letting go. It had been too long.

'Mind if I sit, brother?'

The skater shrugged. 'Sure.'

Bucky took another hit and then passed it back.

'So what are you after?'

'After?'

'You asked if I was holding,' said the young man.

'Oh, yeah. I guess I was just wondering if you had any drugs I could buy?'

The skater looked at him sideways and then laughed. His chuckle was surprisingly high-pitched.

'*Any* drugs?'

'Yeah.'

'Like, any in particular?'

Bucky thought of that Brando line in *The Wild One* when he was asked what he was rebelling against. *What have you got?*

'I know what you're thinking,' he said. 'An old cat like me. But, brother, I'm a long way from home and just need a little something to get me through the weekend. Something to cool a troubled mind.'

The skater nodded and then pulled out his wallet. He opened it and slipped out a strip of tablets.

'I've got these.'

'What are they?'

'I'm not sure.'

'Well, will they take me up or bring me down?'

The skater looked at the pills in his hand and smiled.

'Yeah, I don't really know that either. But you're welcome to take some.'

'I mean, at this point, I reckon I'm game for anything.'

Bucky took the strip of tablets – 'May I?' – and popped one out into his palm. It was small, circular, white. It gave nothing away.

'This could be anything.'

'That's half the fun,' said the skater. 'It's like a lucky dip. Or an unlucky dip.'

Bucky turned it over.

'I mean, I've got the constitution of a bull, and one pill of anything wouldn't do much to me anyway, so do you mind if I relieve you of two? Also, how much do you want for them?'

The smoker relit his joint and spoke through the smoke again.

'Nothing, man.'

'You sure?'

'Consider them a gift. Your country gave us skating, hip-hop and cheeseburgers, so now I'm giving you … whatever these things are.'

Bucky smiled.

'Well, that seems like a fair international trade. God bless America and God save the King. This must be the special relationship I heard about. Right on.' He swallowed the pills dry, sat back and took the joint that the skater passed to him once again.

'Yes, it's mighty generous of you. If ever you find yourself in Chicago and in need, just look me up. Bucky Bronco is the name. I think the young of today are unfairly maligned if you ask me. Demonised, even.'

'It's no problem. They were free anyway. I nicked them off my dad.'

Out at sea, chimneys of rain were falling; the pregnant cloud had not been able to hold its load until it reached land.

'What does he do – is he a dealer or something?'

Bucky passed the joint back.

'No,' said the skater. 'He's a vet.'

★

She came to him then. Maybellene.

Feeling sedated but serene, Bucky lifted his chin from where it sat heavily on his chest and there was his wife, not as he last saw her, not as he left her – depleted, emaciated, reduced – but how she lived most of her life: in laughter and radiating love. She was wearing her usual house clothes and her busted-up slippers, and her arms were extended, open, her palms facing upwards in supplication. She was walking towards him now, right there in the park, and she was radiating that same sense of love, happiness and tranquillity. He could feel it as a physical thing, an incandescent heat. Supreme warmth.

'My Maybell,' he heard himself saying. 'Is it really you?'

She did not reply, only nodded and smiled. Bucky felt a sob rise up from his chest like a bubble and then he heard it escape from his mouth. It became something audible. He couldn't quell it.

'God, I miss you. I don't think I can…'

'You can. You can, and you must, and you will.'

138

Warmth washed over him. The feeling was total, all-encompassing and beautiful. He rose to greet her, his arms also outstretched. He felt light, weightless and unburdened. Bucky felt joyous. He felt free.

★

The sprung dance floor of the Spring Gardens's main ball-room was already thick with bodies, sweat-drenched Rorschach patterns spreading on the dancers' shirts and the occasional squeak of rubber or creak of leather on polished wood heard in those split-second moments of temporary silence as the musicians and singers of fifty or sixty or more years ago hung on a note, drew breath or paused for dramatic effect, and the dancers of today spun or swayed or knee-dropped the pains of ageing away, the decades shed like dead skin around them.

Dinah circled the dance floor. DJ Kath Bullard announced: 'And next up for you lovely people we've got a classic cut that will get every last one of you moving, it's "Blowing Up My Mind" by the Exciters, and this one goes out to your friend and mine, Dinah Lake.' She was surprised to hear her name, and surprised to see heads turning her way. She looked over to the stage where Kathy was rifling through a box of sevens perched next to the deck on a trestle table. They gave each other the thumbs up.

The snare beat led the dancers in unison and Dinah was pleased to see a handful of younger people – teenagers, some of them – energetically bopping in amongst the usual faces of those who she had watched grow old over the decades, on other such dance floors across the North and Midlands. Many of them she had seen in Stoke and Whitby, Blackpool and Burnley, Darlington and Driffield and Halifax and Rotherham, and here too in Scarborough once or twice a year, always autumn or winter – and, yes, some she remembered from back in those final glory days of Wigan too. Most were young then and old now; they had aged, but the music was timeless. New blood was needed but so long as there were a few fresh folk each time, then the Northern wouldn't or shouldn't die out completely. Nostalgia played its part, she knew that. She welcomed it, almost. There was no reason nostalgia had to be a bad thing, not when a jubilant sense of energy filled the room on a dreary October evening. The ecstatic glow of temporary, yet total, emancipation was visible on the faces of those who had seen their old jobs replaced by new technologies, or had children they were estranged from, or had debt collectors at their door, or housebound loved ones they had to care for, or cars they could no longer afford to put petrol in, or who had lost sons and daughters and siblings to debt, addiction, disease, depression or war. Nostalgia was not a crime, not when up against an endless flow of news that reported on economic decline, food shortages, rising cost of living, domestic murders, knife crime, gun crime, Internet crime, climate crisis, financial crisis, National Health Service crisis, famine, mass displacement, people smuggling, child abuse rings, babies drowning in cold Channel waters, oil wars, culture wars, wars that had been going on so long you couldn't remember the reason why they started in the first place. If anything, Dinah was glad of the indulgence of nostalgia, glad of the memories that music unlocked. Glad, still, to be alive, when the world was a spinning, raging, burning orb of floods and fires and mayhem. The music was an anchor. It was a reliable constant.

Kath Bullard dropped the needle on 'Get It Off My Conscience' by Lovelites and she felt the magnetic pull of the music. It was drawing her in from her very centre. She joined the moving bodies and inhaled the sweet smell of muscles in communal movement once again.

★

He awoke to a blood-curdling shriek. It was so close and so loud it felt as it came from inside his skull.

When he opened his eyes, Bucky was lying lengthways on the cold metal bench and a huge seagull was looming over him. He knew with great certainty that it was the same gull that had been at his window. The skater was nowhere to be seen.

The seagull was huge, the size of a small dog.

The seagull dipped its head towards him and shrieked again.

Once more he found himself faced with the levered beak and torrid flesh-pink marbling of the vile creature's tremulous throat. It screamed in anger, in warning, in pain. It shrieked from somewhere remote and primeval, somewhere from deep prehistory – a noise as bottomless and incalculable as England itself.

Fear flushed through Bucky, followed by an adrenaline surge so strong it was as if his blood was bubbling. Poised, the seagull arched its back and slowly spread its wings wide. Its span was even broader when seen close-up from below, its slowly unfolding boughs of bone and feather stretching to block the last of the day's watery sunlight, before curving slightly inwards as if to enshroud him as he lay prostrate and befuddled on the bench. The bird's beaded black eyes were rimmed red and glass-like, its cold penetrating gaze full of contempt. It was these, more than anything, that galvanised Bucky up from his prone position to become a flailing, animated bundle of action as he leapt forward and attempted to grab the gull. Too late. With a flap of its wings the bird rose up, hovered for one heavy moment – Bucky briefly, subconsciously, marvelled at the creature's ability to achieve flight at all – and then casually landed at the other end of the bench.

This only angered Bucky even more. He had not moved so quickly in years. He would throttle this meddling, taunting bastard with his bare hands, hands that he now knew were still capable of damage. He would grab its neck and crush its craw, use his belt or shoelace as a ligature if he had to. String that bitch up. He would tear out its feathers and grab it by its contemptible little legs and slam the gull's plucked carcass on the bench again and again and again; he would stamp it on the ground, stamp it flat and crunch it into the soil, then boot it into the bushes for the foxes and coyotes or whatever damn critters roamed this damn town at night to gnaw on in the predawn hours as the sea crashed onto the shore down below. Yes, he would show this no-good bird that though he might be old and ailing, Bucky

Bronco, who had done some hard time and defended himself against bigger men, and beaten them, who had survived injustice, grief, addiction and hunger, who had come of age an underdog in America during the second half of a century, and was not to be messed with.

Yes, he'd kill that seagull and roast it on a spit over a fire made from the burning corpses of every music business shark who had ripped him off or told him he would amount to nothing.

He lunged again, arms extended, hands grasping and grabbing at nothing but evening air. The seagull squawked and flew higher this time, its wings pulled back and its head dipped once more as it hung suspended above him like a toddler's mobile dangling above a nursery room crib. Bucky scrambled up onto the bench now and though his joints jolted with shocks of pain, he barely felt them, and instead, acting purely on attack-mode instinct, he leapt from the bench to swat or stun or grab the stupid bird, but it casually moved a foot to one side as if controlled by pulleys and levers. For one elongated second Bucky was airborne, he was travelling through the void of empty space in a park by the sea on a far-flung foreign island, and in that instant he felt unencumbered by doubt, fear, loneliness, anxiety, bereavement and physical decline, and, in fact, felt entirely weightless and free.

But then gravity came roaring back into his reality and he hit the ground with a dense thump that sucked all the air from his body. He was a punctured airbed. A beached jellyfish.

The seagull retreated with a cruel croak of laughter, a cold-blooded cackle, before sweeping away, and Bucky found himself miraculously back on his feet and charging down the park's sloping path after the goddamned thing at a speed and velocity that he would never have thought possible. Then he tripped and fell again, but this time he did not – could not – get back up.

The pills he had swallowed were very strong. Very strong indeed.

★

The wedding was a small affair. Maybell wore white, Bucky was in his mohair. He was trim and taut then. Lean. Maybell proudly told him that he wore the suit well. Pastor Presley presided, even though Bucky had stopped going to the church after the Sweet Chariot business, after prison.

Later, when the commitments had been made and the rings exchanged, they ate ribs and cornbread, coleslaw and cake in the function room that adjoined the church. There was much music and dancing. Both of his parents were in attendance, as well as Maybellene's mother – her father had passed when she was an infant, killed in the Korean war. She never knew him. There were only photos and her mother's stories and a medal to remember him by.

The absence of Bucky's brother Cecil Bronco was keenly felt on his side of the family. Sess was still alive then, but buried deep in the penitentiary system. In just a few short months they would receive the news of his death in a curt two-sentence telegram sent by the state.

After that Bucky went AWOL for a while, drinking and drugging his way through the murk of grief. Only Maybellene bought him back round, with love, understanding and tenderness. Patience too. Patience for the destruction he reaped upon himself. She had never met Cecil, but she knew he was highly thought of by everyone in the community. His was accepted as a story of great injustice and which, for a while at least, was the subject of localised campaigning and a hope that the truth would come out. But truth doesn't work like that when up against a vast system. Truth stood no chance when up against the might of America and its many mythologies.

A funeral was held. Pastor Presley presided once again, even though it was only symbolic, for Cecil Bronco's body was never seen by those who survived him. Another truth supressed. His battered corpse would have told the real story of his demise, and that could not be allowed.

There was no music this time. No dancing.

★

As Bucky slowly shambled back to the Majestic, the waves were up again and several surfers were out on the water. The day was soon to dissipate into darkness but still a dozen or so men and women were making the last of the light. They paddled out, each clad in black wetsuits that clung like second skins. The water appeared oily. The surfers patiently awaited waves big enough to ride on in, each wobbling shorewards, some slick and others flopping from their boards at the first attempt, but all seemed to Bucky to be so agile, so free and entirely devoid of concern for anything other than the next rising, curling, breaking wave.

Once again the elevator jolted on the way up, and Bucky jolted with it, slamming into its flimsy wall. The tight little box rocked and he envisioned the entire thing coming loose from its ancient cables and dropping down the shaft, plunging him briefly into nothingness, and then into the floor which he imagined was made from the original wooden boards which would surely smash and splinter on impact, and then send him further down, back into the dank netherworld below the hotel. He thought, briefly, of the falling bodies from the Twin Towers, the slow silhouettes of them in the air that September morning. Then he thought of America, the noise and smell of it. He thought of the guns and the strip malls, the school shooters and the cops and the angry talk-show hosts. It was a miracle he'd survived it really. Many like him hadn't. By comparison, maybe England wasn't so insane after all. It was eccentric, sure, a fever dream, a dusty old island that needed a lick of paint, but it didn't feel dangerous. No cops would want to stand on his neck. Or would they? Hell. Maybe America had been lying to him all along – the idea that anyone could make it if they tried, but hadn't he always known that anyway?

He thought of his little house with the sagging couch and the old mattress and the refrigerator that leaked yellow water, and he thought about how Maybellene was not there and never would be, and with her gone he realised that, actually, he felt nothing for the place. It was just walls and memories now.

Back in his room, and still feeling both sore and a little stoned and challenged by the room's apparently shrinking dimensions, Bucky rifled through his suitcase, pulled out a wad of paper, unfolded it and then smoothed it out on his wide thighs. He could barely remember those songs he had written over a half century ago. Representing the bad times that followed in their immediate wake, they had been almost entirely erased from his mind.

He knew he needed to refresh himself, and now seemed like a good time to focus on something other than seagulls, nausea, the grazes on his knees and the gravel in his throbbing hand – and himself.

He had never bothered with the Internet and email and YouTube and all of that bunkum, so the songs had never been given the opportunity to rise up from the primordial murk of memory to remind him of what could have been. Regret was already something he could do perfectly well himself, thank you very much.

Two weeks ago he had gone to the neighbourhood library to look up the lyrics online to 'Until the Wheels Fall Off', 'The Bees & the Birds' and 'All the Way Through to the Morning'. Without them he knew that he would be stuck.

Bucky had been surprised how, once he had read the first line as a prompt, the rest had easily followed. They hadn't been entirely forgotten after all, but instead had laid dormant for all those intervening decades.

The folk at the Weekender had told him there was no need for a band or backing tapes: they had everything ready. All he had to do was rock up and sing along to the instrumental versions that they were providing. That *all* was crucial. It suggested that to Bucky, hitting the stage and tapping into the teenage version of himself – that young, green Bucky who had the world at his feet and fame for the taking – was as easy as slipping down into a deep, warm bath. It wasn't. Only last week had he finally built up the courage to play the songs, which a neighbour's kid had downloaded onto a CD for him; it was the first time the boy had cause to buy a CD, and to him it might as well have been a gramophone cylinder he was passing over. Bucky had slipped him a double sawbuck for his troubles.

Singing them out loud, even just to himself, was a trip. When those first notes of 'Wheels' kicked in, the years fell away and he was straight back in the past at the click of his fingers. Memories engulfed him: flashing recollections of peals of hysterical laughter, the taste of the red Ripple wine they all drank, sticky dance floors, the creak of leather shoes and coats, Clove cigarette smoke, hungover breakfasts at that corner diner after being up all night, his parents cutting some rug at Christmas, the names of girls he had forgotten – Lula, Sadie, Patty – Sess's big silent smile that day he got the grades he needed, Bucky as a kid on an upturned bucket singing his lungs out on the street corner for chump change, the sharp saddle of that first bike he had, losing a tooth in a fist fight, his first teacher, church.

The lyrics came easy then, but they hurt. Singing those words to that music meant more than revisiting an old song – it was a ritual that in that moment, alone in his living room, had raised the ghosts of the dead: those of his parents, long gone but never forgotten, and dear Sess too, murdered by a system, and Maybell most recently. And all those others, friends who had passed as well – from cancer, from poverty, from life. One or two by their own hand, which always made it worse. Singing was painful because these were not just songs, they were elegies for the dead. Elegies you could dance to, but elegies all the same. Hell, he had to admit it: they were laments for so many missed opportunities too.

★

Steam rose from the dancers who had stepped outside to smoke and take in the air.

Dinah drew on her roll-up. Out on the horizon the lights of dormant trawlers twinkled and the sea exhaled another throaty breath onto the shore. Inside, the music was still playing, but she could tell by the selection of tracks that the dance was close to reaching its conclusion. She had looked for Bucky everywhere: in the back corridors and closed-off lounges, in the turret room up a tightly winding stairwell, by the bar, the bins and even at

146

the bottom of the steep grass verge that climbed up the lower slopes of the slowly sliding cliff behind the Spring Gardens, but he was nowhere to be found. Bucky had not so much left the building as never entered it in the first place.

She was concerned, unable to give herself over to the night. Not when Graham Carmichael had asked her to sit in on the door, or find a medic when some daft lad had turned an ankle trying to execute an overly ambitious spin, and not when Bucky Bronco had failed to show his troubled face – a face, she thought, that failed to hide its own twisted, soul-sick history.

This time tomorrow the last great living voice of Northern would be closing the weekend with his one-and-half hits and everyone would be able to boast that they had seen Earlon Bronco in the flesh. Or would they?

Out at sea a fomenting storm was gathering strength. The first winds of it lifted more litter from rubbish bins that overflowed like molten candles. It blew past Dinah, off into the treacle-thick darkness of what lay beyond the soft glow of the town's last lamp post.

★

He wanted to find more whisky. Needed to. Bucky left his room but before he could get to the elevator, he saw Shabana coming along the corridor. She wasn't wearing her work clothes this time but was instead more casually dressed and wearing some subtly applied make-up.

'Hello, Shabana,' he said.

'Hi, Bucky, are you feeling any better tonight?'

'Better?'

'You were looking pretty rough last night when I helped you back.'

Bucky looked confused. His mind scrambled to remember.

'Helped me … back? I'm afraid I'm drawing a blank here, sweetie.'

Shabana laughed.

'I think perhaps you were a little jet-lagged.'

Now it was Bucky's turn to laugh.

'Jet-lagged. That's a very diplomatic way of putting it, I guess. But, seriously, I really don't remember much – did I make a fool of myself?'

'No, no more than lots of the guests here do. Probably less, in fact. And you were singing?'

'Singing? Oh, Christ.'

'But you were good, Bucky. I guess you weren't kidding after all.'

Bucky raised an eyebrow.

'You doubted me, Shabana?'

She shrugged, non-committal. He beamed back.

'Also you were wearing precisely only one sock.'

He groaned and shook his head, then drew his sore palm down across his brow and face.

'Oh, man.'

'You were just a little bit lost when I found you wandering the corridors quite late, that's all. You'd be surprised how often that happens. Even now, me myself, I can take the wrong stairway and find myself confused. And that's without going down to the secret floors underground.'

'You mean there's more to this madhouse?'

Shabana nodded.

'Oh yes. There are several floors that are hidden, where no guests are ever allowed to go. But I have seen down there and it's like stepping back into history. There are many secret corridors and halls that are dark and dusty like big caves and rusty old Victorian pipes that leak seawater that they used to pump up from the sea, and there are abandoned kitchens that have not been used for many decades, and there are passageways and dark corners and an empty shopping – what is the word, arcade? – and another room that was used by the RAF in the Second World War, and the diagrams and maps and plans are still up on the wall in there, and there are bricked-up doorways and a room that was once used for brewing beer, and another that was a bakery. There is even space where cows were once kept. I'm telling you, this place is crazy; it is a time warp, which is funny because this entire hotel is shaped by time. It is defined by the calendar.'

'What do you mean "defined by the calendar", Shabana?'

'Oh, it's very interesting. When this place was built in, I believe, the 1860s, it was the largest brick-built structure in Europe, a place fit for royalty, and it seems the architect was obsessed with time as a structure. So if you studied it carefully, you would see that there are four corner towers, which represent the seasons: spring, summer and so on. The twelve floors represent the twelve months, while up on the roof, there are fifty-two chimneys.'

'Like the fifty-two weeks in the year. Sorry, I interrupted.'

'That's alright. And what else? Oh yes — also there are three hundred and sixty-five rooms, one for each day of the year, though I've never actually counted them.'

'That's insane — the fact the architect must have specifically designed three hundred and sixty-five rooms, not because that was what was required, but because he was following a numerical impulse. That's true obsession. I have a friend here in town who is interested in all this type of thing. She goes nuts for numbers.'

'Well, here is one more thing that is nuts then,' said Shabana. 'Apparently Hitler intended to use the Majestic as his base once he had conquered Britain, and told the Luftwaffe that if anyone so much as put a scratch on the hotel during their bombing campaigns, they would have the Führer himself to answer to.'

'Wow.'

'Yes, wow. But now…' Shabana hesitated and then leaned in towards Bucky and in a lowered voice, said, 'Now it is not entirely such a special place. The building — yes. But some of the guests? Not always so. No offence to you.'

'Oh, none taken, sweetie. I wanted to see a bit of England, and I guess that's exactly what I am doing. And, you know, I think I'm sort of beginning to quite like the place. Hey, you know what else is funny? I hope you don't mind me remarking that you speak better English than me.'

'That's because you're American. Americans speak American. There's a big difference.'

'You think so?'

'I know so. You say 'erbs instead of herbs. And you call aubergines eggplants. Eggs don't grow on plants, man.'

Bucky laughed.

'That's true. And I guess we do. But thanks for helping me out last night, I really can't remember much of it at all.'

'You're welcome. And you are a pretty good singer. I even recognised some of the words.'

Here Shabana started singing a melody that was familiar to Bucky. It was the main melodic hook for his unreleased second single 'All the Way Through to the Morning', but it followed a slightly different cadence. And instead of going from the bridge into the chorus, she started doing what sounded like a freestyle rap, delivered with impressive diction and dexterity.

'Wait a minute,' said Bucky, taking a step back. 'Hold up *just a minute*. First of all, how in the hell do you know that song? No one apart from a few soul fans know of it. Also, it's fifty-some years old and was never even released anyway. And secondly, you're *a rapper*? I mean, hell, what's happening here?'

'Well, firstly, only about a million kids know that line: *You and me, we're gonna be alright, because tonight we're going to dance all the way through to the morning*. And secondly, hell yes, I'm a rapper.'

Bucky shook his head. He raised his hands, palms out. Shabana saw the scrapes there on his skin.

'Alright, alright, alright. Let's rewind for a moment.'

'You're hurt, Bucky?'

'What?' he said, turning his hands to look at them. 'Oh, that? It's nothing. What do you mean by "only about a million kids know that line"?'

'You don't know about the rap song?'

'What rap song?'

'The hit, Bucky. The hit.'

She started singing again. As she did she swayed and clicked her fingers, gesticulating enthusiastically with one hand. The line followed the exact same melody that he himself had laid down in that studio back on that warm Chicago spring day in 1967, but just at a slightly shifted tempo.

'*You and me, we're gonna be alright, because tonight we're going to dance all the way through to the morning...*'

'No, sweetie, I really don't know what's happening right now.'

'Oh, my God,' said Shabana, a look of surprise registering on her face. 'No one has told you.'

'Told me what?'

'You really don't know?'

'I think perhaps you need to tell me what it is you think I don't know before I can tell you whether I do or don't know it. But, before that I could really use a drink. I'm a little bit tight right now and I don't intend on sobering up any time soon. Maybe I could buy you one?'

'You know, in Afghanistan, under Muslim law, drinking alcohol is forbidden. It is considered *Haram*.'

'Yes, sure. Sorry. I forgot.'

Shabana covertly reached into her pocket and flashed a small pipe and a sizeable Ziploc bag of weed. Bucky registered his surprise, but then smiled and nodded.

'OK, OK. So what does Islam say about that type of 'erb?'

'I don't know. But if you come with me, I'll show the best place in the whole of the town.'

★

Jobs that Bucky held between the ages of twenty and seventy years old: grocery bagger, overnight bakery/deli clerk, laundry room attendant, dishwasher at the Chicago Symphony Orchestra, concessions-stand worker at Wrigley Field baseball stadium, gas station attendant, produce inspector, rebar welder, delivery driver for a brewery, delivery driver for a frozen food company, telephone salesman (advertising space in corporate catalogues), meat and seafood clerk, janitor at a high school, video-store sales assistant, telephone salesman (time share condos in Florida), maintenance technician, janitor at a college, security guard at a hospital, valet at a golf course, limousine driver, postal worker (seasonal), forklift truck driver in a factory, deputy junior warehouse supervisor, security guard at a residential rehabilitation clinic, assistant boxing coach, community youth group leader, assistant property manager, grocery bagger. It wasn't that Bucky was unreliable or unemployable – in fact, his diverse employment record suggested he was, in fact, quite the opposite – but rather that working life in America for someone with a criminal record that included prison time (despite all charges being dropped), and without any real formal educational qualifications beyond the high school diploma, was one of short-term contracts, minimum wages, exploitative companies, sadistic and/ or morally dubious bosses and minimal chances of such benefits as healthcare and a pension. He simply had to keep moving on in order to maintain a regular income to cover the cost of the rent on his and Maybell's first home together, a two-room cold-water walk-up that they occasionally found themselves sharing with rats, mice and other such vermin.

And so it went.

★

Bucky followed Shabana up a narrow stairwell that felt secretive and barely used. The steps were steep and tightly winding. They stole the last of his energy.

Shabana produced a key from her pocket and unlocked a door, then they stepped out onto the roof of the Majestic and for the first time Bucky appreciated the hotel's name. The two of them were at the top of the building, surrounded by the four turreted towers and below them swept the full display of the town's South Bay, twinkling with the neon lights and gaudy signage of its amusement arcades. In the distance he could just discern the silhouette of the castle perched on the headland like a protector against past invading foes.

'Wow,' he said.

The wind was whistling around the sharp stone corners of the hotel and the chilly breeze roused Bucky. Whatever he had swallowed earlier was still in his system, along with the booze and the few hits of weed the skater had shared with him, but it had all settled down into a manageable buzz. He breathed in the clean sea air, filling his lungs. Then he exhaled long and deep until the dregs of the panic he had felt rising throughout the day dissipated. He expelled it like an imaginary black billow of toxic smoke. The aching longing for opioids was still there, and waves of sickness kept coming and going, but up on the roof above everything gave him a strange sense of hope that perhaps all was not yet lost.

'Wow,' he said again.

'I had my own key cut,' said Shabana, as she carefully packed her small pipe with weed. 'If they are going to pay me so badly, then I'm going to need to find ways to get me through the day. And whatever the weather it's always nice up here. The hotel is so big, the management never find out.'

She held up the pipe.

'Oh, totally,' said Bucky. 'You've always got to hold something back for yourself, otherwise they'll steal your soul as well as the best years of your life if you let them. Nearly a half century of working low-end jobs has taught me that much. You never give them your all. Never.'

Shabana offered him the pipe and the lighter but Bucky signalled for her to fire it up. She did.

'But I thought you were a singer?'

'Was. Barely.'

She passed him the pipe and he felt the heavy weed smoke fill his chest once again. A warmth washed over him and he was instantly high, but favourably so. A reciprocal spirit of generosity suddenly gripped him.

'Say, would you like to come and see me sing?'

'You're inviting me?'

'Of course.'

'Where and when is this singing taking place?'

'Tomorrow, just over there.' Bucky waved vaguely in the direction of the venue. 'It's at the Spring Gardens. They say I'll be on around 9 p.m.'

'Oh—' she said. 'I mean—'

'There's no obligation at all.'

'It's just I have a shift.'

'Sure, I completely understand. Money comes first. But if you can swing it, I can get you in on the list.'

'List?'

'Yes, the guest list. I'm sure it won't be a problem. But I totally understand if you can't or it's not your thing, and, to be honest, between you and me, I can't even promise that I'll make it onto the stage, or if I do whether I'll even be any good.'

'Of course you will, Bucky. Of course you will. You'll be great. You've just got to have some faith in yourself. And, of course, so long as I can switch my shifts, I will do my best to be there. But about that song we listened to last night.'

'Right, right,' said Bucky. 'I really have no recollection of last night. But it's crazy that you know it.'

'But I don't know it.'

'You were just singing it though?'

Shabana took the pipe from him and went through the ritual of relighting it and smoking some more. Then she shook her head.

'No. I was singing "Honey Trap" by Lil Widowmaker.'

'Little what?'

'Lil Widowmaker. The rapper.'

'I've not had the pleasure.'

'Well, you should, he's great.'

'I'll have to take your word for it on that one, sweet pea.'

'Well, that's the thing, Bucky. That's what I've been trying to say. You don't just have to take my word for it.'

Shabana took out her phone and cued up the song. It started to play. Bucky moved in closer to hear it above the sound of the cold night's breeze and the purl and whisper of the sea breaking onto the shore below. He heard the voice of a wasted-sounding kid, rapping at a slow and monotonous pace over a minimal beat that was dragging its feet. There was a blank disaffection to his delivery, a sort of anaesthetised deadness to it; it was the barely coherent drawl of young America, thought Bucky. Deliberately detached and lethargic, tired already at such a young age. But then just as Bucky was beginning to wonder if the song was going to wallow entirely in its own misery for the duration, he heard the kid drop the main hook from 'All the Way Through to the Morning' and the song stepped up a gear. Shabana joined in with the chorus, her phone in one hand and her pipe and lighter in the other, as she effected a shuffling little dance up there on the roof.

'That's my song,' exclaimed Bucky. 'This Lil Windowcleaner kid *stole my song*.'

Still dancing, Shabana laughed and shook her head.

'Not stolen, man, sampled. There's a difference.'

'You sure about that?'

'Of course.'

'Really? Sounds like the only decent thing about it is my vocal melody.'

'Thieves steal, but artists sample. And samples pay.'

Bucky frowned deeply, doubtful.

'Is this kid big?'

'Huge.'

'How huge?'

'How do you not know this? The track just blew up on the Internet four months and is just about the biggest thing in the world right now. I can't believe no one has mentioned this to you.'

'Honey, I've barely left the house in four months. I've had other things on my mind this past while. But just out of interest, how many plays has this song had anyway?'

Shabana turned the phone towards him and pointed at the number.

'Holy moly, I must be high because to me that looks like seven hundred and sixty-one thousand plays.'

She laughed again.

'No, Bucky. Take a second look. That says seven hundred and sixty-one million. *Million*.'

★

They never had children. Either Bucky or Maybell – or both, though this was unlikely – was unable to, and they accepted this fact without the need to investigate further. That way, the apportioning of blame and the attendant guilt associated with the notions of either *being barren* or *firing blanks* – two phrases whose connotations of failure and inadequacy they deemed demeaning – could be neatly sidestepped. It strengthened their bond, drew them closer. They simply accepted that, between them, they could not create a child and after a while, once they had grieved the death of a certain possibility, they felt duly liberated. Their life was exactly that: theirs to enjoy together, and that was something to be nurtured and celebrated. Those reserves of love that would otherwise have been apportioned to a child or children were instead spent on one another.

Over the years Bucky had heard it expressed on several occasions that couples who did not choose to rear children were somehow selfish, and though the decision was made for them by Mother Nature, wasn't the world busy enough? Some might even argue that to put more people onto a planet when half of its population was struggling to feed itself was much more of a selfish act, but he, or they – that is Bucky and his devoted wife – didn't particularly subscribe to this notion either. All he knew was that they couldn't and wouldn't and didn't have children, and that was that. He never truly missed something that he never had.

The only matter that really concerned him on that front, something that nagged at the back of his mind, was that with neither he nor Cecil having bred, and every other living Bronco now dead, he was the last in the family line, the closing page of the final chapter of a story that stretched back centuries. The buck stopped with Bucky. Let death do what death does. Nothing much mattered any more anyway. He'd be gone soon enough.

'Hell,' he said, kicking the flimsy frame of his hunk-of-junk bed.

'Hell,' he said, throwing an empty glass at the wall.

'Hell,' he said, punching the mirror and crumpling concertina-like onto the bathroom floor.

★

The sea that night was riotous, a primal roar of tidal power. It moiled and boomed and bared its teeth. Bucky could hear it laying siege upon the lessening land. It was eating up the coastline imperceptibly, one crumbling clod of clay or crushed lump of sandstone at a time. It was chewing chunks from England. What strange secrets, he thought, the water kept, what deep and lonely subterranean caverns it harboured down below where no sunlight ever reached.

He turned on his bed, tangled once again, cold now, but sweating still. Bucky had never slept so close to water before, if you could call it sleep. The sea's constant snarling unnerved his half-waking state. His legs would not lie still and his skin itched and the waves grew ever taller, ever bolder, before collapsing into weeping heaps that disturbed 100 million tiny pebbles and flung them at the barren beach with spite. It was erosion and resculpturing at a granular level. Here in the gloom of his room, the proximity of the splenetic sea heightened his fear and amplified the totality of his aloneness, and somewhere in amongst the frothing white noise of the frothing white water, Bucky heard himself talking in a low babble, a gibbering chunter in tongues.

He startled himself with the snatches and snippets that he shouted out – 'my soul has a hole as deep as history', 'love is contagious', 'save me!' – before he realised they were all fragments of his own songs, lyrics he had not uttered, never mind sung, since the last century. Hell. At one point he felt the mattress move with the shifting weight of another, his wife Maybell turning and sighing beside him, but when he reached out a hand to touch her as he had done so many thousands of nights before, the absence was almost too much to bear. It was always worse at night, this loneliness, this sense of loss, but tonight it was a curling tidal wave. He was drowning, alone and hopeless with the storm slamming against the façade of the hotel, rattling his window and whistling an ice-cold melody of tremendous misery.

Close by, a seagull screamed above the storm.

Sleep was elusive. Grief total.

PART THREE

All the Way Through to the Morning

She awoke to the sound of retching. She awoke to the sound of gagging.

In the bathroom Russell was vomiting up the excesses of a Saturday night that ended long after the last blistered and beaming stragglers had left the Spring Gardens and its lights had been extinguished one by one.

Dinah knew that his descent would have ended up in one of several grim houses or flats scattered about the town, probably doing dabs of white powder with half a dozen people the same age as his son, or younger, possibly while deafening music pounded and hardcore porn flickered on a flat-screen TV that was too big for a room, in which a neglected dog or cat scratched at the door to be let out to do its business, only to be ignored by the desperate little gathering's inhabitants. She knew this because her husband had been living these nights for decades. Once she may have joined him, but not anymore. That stopped decades ago. On the slow walk home, with cheap amphetamines coursing through his blood, the dawn birdsong will surely have sounded metallic to Russell, and the sky's slow, mechanical grinding will have been like a machine starting up for the day.

Dinah turned away from her husband when he left an unflushed toilet in the bathroom to flop back down beside her, a thin string of gruel clinging to his unshaven chin. The morning light made it sparkle and the stench of the night was cloying. A bitter taste akin to battery acid coated his mouth. He carried the fusty residue of shame upon him. She could smell it. Was used to it. But never accepted it. He reeked. And in that moment, something shifted. Something snapped inside of her. 'Russell,' she said to the wall, 'I want a divorce.'

Russell was snoring.

★

Bucky Bronco also lay in his bed surrounded by the sad scraps of a Saturday. Pieced together they might conceivably make sense, but it was too early for rationality, and instead he was lost in a sorrowful fog of inertia. He remembered the park, pills, wandering the corridors of the Majestic once more, but little else. And, wait – was he up on the roof?

Mainly overriding his feelings of regret and embarrassment was that of the loss of his wife exactly one year ago to the day. This fact was unsurmountable, inescapable. How was it that a woman so humble and beautiful and so full of life could be allowed to fade from view? How was it fair that her spirit disappeared in such a way? Bucky had watched it happen, distraught and powerless, smarting with the injustice of a godless world, though he of course knew that justice had nothing to do with it. Death was not prejudiced; its choices were not arbitrary, and therefore were not even choices at all. Death had no conscience, no motivation, and to think otherwise was silly. It just happened.

But the fact that death just happened was the root of religion and all manner of other philosophies; it was simply too tragic a thing to merely accept without explanation or justification.

Meanwhile, as Maybell had rapidly faded, it took everything he could do not to fall apart himself. Only the stitching of duty and guilt held him together.

He had hated that cancer – something that the doctor had called bad blood. *Bad blood.* Bucky cursed it every waking minute. He wished he could have pulled that cancer out of her and into a sentient shape, and then pounded the hell out of it, just as he used to punish the punching bag when he was young, strong and fearless. Just to be able to tear it apart for a couple or three rounds, to humiliate it a while, before destroying it entirely. At least then he would have felt like he was doing something. Fighters don't lose that instinct, it never goes, but not everything is so simple, so base as brute violence. This enemy was invisible, invincible. Absolute. He wished he could have transferred his blood to her but by then there was nothing he could do about any of it, and that was the part that crushed him.

Maybellene was a big lady – she had loved her food and her candy and was a wonderful cook, everyone said so – but by the end she had shrunk down right there in the chair. Bucky had been forced to bear witness. She was reduced by this most vicious of opponents, right in front of him. All her sparkle gone as it dimmed down to darkness.

That was a year ago and now here he was, a world away, weighed down by the trauma of loss, the theft of something irreplaceable.

Bucky forced himself upright, and pulled apart the curtains to see rain falling with timeless Northern fury. It was Yorkshiring down with vertical vengeance. Even the gulls were in retreat.

He watched it fall behind stream-patterned glass, and was surprised to find that he welcomed the rain. Somehow the Sunday downpour matched his Sunday mood, and made him feel less alone in his sorry state. Rain was indifferent. Rain ruled the world. It amplified his insignificance; it reminded him that just when you think you're at the bottom, there's always further to plummet. Bucky smiled to himself at such a sorry thought. He thought about what Bell would say: 'Hell, you just let your smile be your umbrella, honey.'

The wind was blowing hard. The flags that flew on the hotel's four corners were snapping sharply and far below Bucky's window, beyond the terrace once used for taking afternoon tea, but which latterly was a spot for smoking and swilling low-priced lager, the sea was becoming a rising maelstrom of foaming white. Great rolling ropes of woven waves tumbled over one another in a rabid race to the shore. The sky rumbled as the clotted cream spume crashed onto hard, wet sand that hissed and gurgled back at the onslaught, and knotted fronds of bladderwrack were drawn in and out of the boiling shallows by the pull of its muscular undertow.

Bucky saw that the beach was empty save for two diminishing shapes in the distance: one that of a tiny dog darting away from the curdled peaks of dirty foam and the other, its owner, stoically sunken deep into their coat. Bucky never knew the sea could be so sinister, so temperamental. Only in films had he seen it this tempestuous, but living inland he had never before been confronted by its shifting kinetic energy.

He squinted out to the horizon and his bones ached with longing and a hunger that was almost carnal. But they ached with life too. His heart was still beating, and that was at least something. For too long he had been numbing himself from the reality of his aliveness.

He thought about Bell again, heard her voice again, as clear as a glass of gin: 'Best get yourself some garters, Bucky Bronco, because there's no one else going to pull up your socks for you. You're on your own now, sweet pea.'

★

It was a rare moment when all three family members were in the same room at the same time, a Sunday morning summit of boiling kettles, sore heads and spilled cereal.

Dinah was showered and dressed, determined to start the day early, with only one thing on her mind: to deliver Earlon 'Bucky' Bronco to that stage. To have a helping hand in one of the greatest comebacks the Northern scene would ever bear witness to. If she was to be midwife to Bucky's rebirth, then so be it. There could be no greater calling. Certainly any more minutes spent in this house, clearing up after these wastemen she called her family, was a tragic misuse of her time. The clock of her life was ticking ever more urgently, and she was growing sick of a life seemingly spent in their service. No more would she indulge her husband, her son; they were on their own. Serious consideration was also being given to the thankless retail job that she had been doing too long now. There had to be other ways to get by.

As if to confirm these overdue decisions, she silently watched her son honking goofily at his phone screen while an unattended pan of bacon spat greasy spots of fat onto a hob top that she had scrubbed clean Monday gone. Russell sat across from her at the table with his sleep-starved head in his hands and his yellowing fingers clumped tightly in his thinning mop of curls. The excesses of Saturday had rendered him uncharacteristically silent, and Dinah hoped his hangover or comedown, or whatever self-induced punishment he was suffering, was prolonged, crushing and torturous. She prayed it kept him fragile and feeble for the next day or two at the very least.

Without looking at it, Lee flipped his bacon and carried on scrolling. There was more stupid music, more donkey-like honking.

She stood to wash up her bowl, her mug.

'Christ, Russell. Put it away.'

He slowly lifted his head and looked at her with red-rimmed eyes. A weak protest.

'What?'

'Your thing. It's hanging out. Put it away.'

It was sitting shrivelled on his thigh like a stillborn shrew, like a Walnut Whip. Dinah realised with absolute clarity and finality that never again would she touch it. Of this she was certain, as sure as the tide turns twice a day. Not ever.

'Oh, leave us alone,' he said, though he tucked it back into his shorts nonetheless.

'Gladly.'

★

Three feathers fell from the ledge above the entrance to the Majestic. Dinah reached out and grabbed one, her hand snapping shut. When she opened it a barbed ball of down was pressed flat in her palm. She smoothed it out and slotted it into the button hole of her bold red shirt with the gold trim – the same shirt she had been wearing to Weekenders for years, decades even. And though it was a little tighter across the chest, and the cuffs a little shorter at the wrist, she prided herself on still being able to fit into it. The shirt symbolised so much, and held within its fibres many memories connected to music, her music, soul music.

She pounded several times on the door before Bucky answered, sheepishly avoiding her eyes as he stood aside to let her in. The room was a mess of strewn clothes, upended bottles, a toppled chair. There was a new stain on the carpet, a smattering of crumbs and the smell of smoke in the stale air that took her back to past times, to her childhood when it seemed as if everything – buses, cinemas, the damp woollen coats of grandparents – carried the scent of cigarettes. She saw that there was something unidentifiable in the bin. Liquid matter.

Dinah parted the curtains and tried to open the window, but found it held fast, by paint and nails and time. The gull's nest below it was empty. While Bucky tried – and failed – to explain yesterday's no show at the Spring Gardens, and failed also at remembering the course that his Saturday night had taken, Dinah made him a strong black instant coffee and gave him two tablets, which he took from her without question. She stopped him just as he was about to swallow them.

'Wait – don't you want to know what they are?'

His hand hovered halfway to his mouth.

'I mean, I guess.'

'It's diazepam.'

'OK. What's that?'

'A type of Valium, I think. It'll take the edge off things. I sometimes pop them to help me drift through an eight-hour shift. Only have one now, and save one for later – but only if you need it.'

'Sweetie, at this point in my life I reckon I need to take double what any other man – or woman, excuse me – can swallow. I've just got one of those cast-iron constitutions from a lifetime's commitment to an intoxicant of one type or another. It's one of the benefits of being what you might call bulky.'

'You could use a glass of water.'

'Water? Water's for washing with. No one drinks water.'

'What is this, medieval times? We've not got cholera, you know.'

'I don't know,' said Bucky, 'Perhaps a brandy would help,' though his mouth was dry and the word slurred beneath the weight of his intoxication.

'No, not brandy.'

Dinah went into the bathroom, emptied Bucky's toothbrush from a tumbler, rinsed it out and then refilled it.

'Here, drink this, you berk. And when did you last eat?'

Bucky shrugged and shook his head. He sat down on the unmade bed. Swallowed the pills. He sipped his coffee, sipped his water and thought of a year ago today.

'Alright then. So first we need to get you properly fed.'

'Again?' he pleaded.

'Again.'

He saw Maybellene in the chair there, so deflated, so small. Retreating in her skin before his very eyes. That bright day in October. The sun so at odds with the situation. Her voice gone, talking only with her eyes now. And outside, birdsong.

'It's the anniversary, isn't it?' said Dinah.

'What?' Bucky was pulled back into the moment.

'Your wife. A year ago today.'

He nodded slowly.

'Hell, Dinah, it's like you can read my mind.'

'Well, you don't get this kind of messy for the sheer hell of it. There are always reasons, right?'

Bucky rubbed one dry eye with his fist and yawned.

'Right.'

'I can't even begin to imagine how you're feeling.'

Bucky rubbed his other eye.

'Like a dog that's been kicked into a ditch.'

'Did you two have a song?'

He swigged more coffee. Looked up.

'How do you mean?'

'You and Maybellene. I just wondered if perhaps you had a special song that you made your own. *Your* song. Something shared between you down the years.'

He ran his hand over his face and scrubbed himself back into being.

'Well, actually we did. Do you know that Don Thomas cut "Come On Train"?'

'Only every single word. Of course I do. Released, I believe, on the short-lived NUVJ Records, 1972. No – wait. It was 1973.'

'Sounds about right. Well, anyway, that never failed to get us cutting some rug together. We must have spun it ten thousand times, maybe more.'

'What does it remind you of?'

'So much. The early years of our marriage, a lot of late nights. A lot of laughs. An entire era. It reminds me that I got to experience something special, something eternal.'

As Bucky talked Dinah pulled the song up on her phone and the familiar piano chords of its intro rang out.

'I didn't know her, but I reckon your wife would be fine with hearing it one more time – if you don't mind?'

'Honey, I don't mind.'

As the vocal kicked in Dinah started doing some soft shoe moves, drawing one foot to the other and then back again, sliding and gliding easily while moving from heel to toe. She bowed slightly at the waist and clicked her fingers. There was an impressive lightness to her dancing, as if she were unburdened. Bucky smiled. He wished that he could move so freely. Bucky laughed. He had not played the song in a long while, and definitely not the past year. Suddenly Dinah spun and then dropped to the floor in a half-split, one leg straight out, and then immediately bounced back up again, kicking the same leg out in front of her to head height.

'Whoa,' said Bucky, just as Don Thomas hit the sustained long note that he held in the middle of the song, a heartfelt tremulous vibrato to his voice that got Bucky in the sweet spot every time – and despite the hangover and the overbearing weight of grief, Bucky suddenly joined in, pitch perfect.

Dinah clutched his wrists and urged him to join her as the song built to a climax of drum fills, plucked notes and Thomas roaring and howling away. Though her moves seemed far beyond his capabilities, Bucky couldn't help but sing along at the top of his voice, and for a moment, just one brief moment, he too felt light, he too felt temporarily unburdened.

★

When he was in his mid forties – forty-six he reckoned, or maybe forty-seven or so – Bucky went through a bad patch on the employment front, in that there wasn't any. Recently he had been learning just how much tougher things became as you got older and your body wasn't quite the finely tuned muscle machine it was at the age of twenty-one. He had been overlooked for a string of the more manual jobs, and that filled him with fear, so he did what he always did in these circumstances: kick back and ride it out.

Back then he had a friend, Ernest, Ernie – now long dead – and Ernie kept homing pigeons up on the roof of his apartment building. He bred them and flew them, and every day for close to a year, Bucky left each morning with a kiss and a brown-bag lunch from Bell, and he walked over to Ernie's. Beside the pigeon coops there was a little old shed up there too where Ernie kept seed, rolls of chicken wire and so forth, and Bucky would stretch out on those stuffed sacks, and the dry, stiff graininess of them would gently massage his back, and he would read the newspaper and doze the afternoon away with his boots on. Then, when the day was done, and his sandwiches eaten – maybe Ernie would have joined him in a couple or three beers – he would saunter back home to Maybellene's cooking and the neighbourhood news. He saw four different seasons in all their glory up there. He had never been as broke or happy, before or since.

★

Hattie was across the pub at the bar when Bucky and Dinah took a table close to the carvery. Half-butchered torsos of pork, ham hock and beef joints sat on hot plates at head height. Dinah caught her attention and waved her over.

169

'You don't mind do you, Bucky?' she said, but before he could answer the German journalist had joined them and the two women were catching up on the night before – people they had seen, songs that were played, who had embarrassed themselves on the dance floor, and who had emerged victorious. Bucky felt the warm internal flex of the Valium, and though it didn't quell the aches and pains, it did slightly dampen his desire for opioids. Nor did it offer the soft focus lucidity of his favoured golden hour, though he did feel a certain gilt edge to the day, the usual sense of dread dissipating into a low hum of disquiet.

Dinah ordered three Sunday dinners for them and when they came Bucky found himself quite able to eat what was on offer, even if it was his first time tasting both Yorkshire pudding and some anaemic-looking sprouts, a vegetable that he had always avoided. The gravy was good and thick, and he found himself pouring an extra portion that pooled in a puddle that was the size of his large fist.

'This fellow properly tied one on last night,' Dinah said, gesturing to him with a forkful of folded roast beef.

'Tied one on?' said Hattie. 'To what?'

Dinah shot Bucky a glance, a wry smile. 'Overdid it.'

'Oh, drunk, you mean?'

'Drunk, stoned and then some,' said Bucky.

'You didn't say where you ended up.'

'Up is right. Up on the roof.'

'What roof, where?' asked Dinah.

'The roof of that nuthouse you've got me in.'

'You climbed up on the hotel roof?'

'Not so much climbed as led there, really.'

'By who?'

'A pal of mine.'

'Christ, you're a fast mover, Bucky Bronco. You've not been in the town two minutes.'

'Sweetie, I'm flattered, no one's called me a fast mover in a good long while.'

He shoved a roast potato into his mouth, and the way the crispiness of its exterior contrasted with the soft fluffiness of its

'Hundreds of thousands of dollars, you turnip,' Dinah grinned, prodding him in the ribs. 'Keep up.'

'Hey – no need to get personal,' he said. 'Or physical. Though I reckon I can forgive you this time. Hundreds of thousands of dollars though – are you serious?'

'Of course, at the very least. Your vocal line forms the basis of this kid's entire song.'

'Well, OK. But how on God's green earth do I get my hands on this loot that you cats reckon is out there?'

'We follow the trail,' said Hattie.

'What trail?'

'The paper trail. Revenue streams, royalty statements, publishing contracts. Ownership.'

'I wouldn't know where to start.'

'You don't need to.'

'That's why Hattie said "we",' said Dinah. 'Because she is a professional journalist blessed with that famous German efficiency we've all heard about—'

'—and *she* is a tenacious British bulldog that we've heard about too. And, more than anything we're fans of music,' said Hattie. 'Your music. Between us, I'm sure we could look into this for you.'

Dinah nodded. 'What's right is right.'

'And what's yours is yours.'

Not for the first time Bucky looked bewildered. He shook his head and put his knife and fork down again.

'Once again it's your lucky day,' said Dinah.

'Your lucky week,' replied Hattie.

'Lucky year, I'd say.'

Bucky looked out the window and onto the road, just as a truck trundled by. On its back a billboard declared: *The Circus Is Coming to Town!* Beyond it, down at the docks, seagulls hovered over a trawler as crew members hosed down its deck, the remains of fish guts and viscera sluiced back into the sea from which they came.

'Isn't it just,' he said.

★

He told folk he was with her when she died, but that was a lie to assuage his guilt and it failed to make him feel any better.

After sitting with her all night, her hand tiny in his, he had gone to the corner store at first light. Whisky was on his mind. Whisky was what he wanted, needed. Whisky and a moment. A chug of liquor and the sun on his face. Fresh air that didn't carry the wretched and desperate smell of encroaching death upon it. He was only gone five minutes. Ten, tops. When he shuffled wearily up the porch steps and guided his key into the lock, his hand heavy, everything heavy, and let himself in, Maybellene Margaret Bronco was dead in the chair. She was there, but her soul had gone elsewhere.

They must have said goodbye 500 times but still it was not enough. Still he felt he had been robbed, the victim of a grave error. And that in itself added another layer of guilt — that of the one who survives, the one who is left behind.

★

They took a taxi back to the Majestic so that Bucky could put on his one pressed shirt. He had Dinah and Hattie wait in the lobby, in the bucket seats by the fruit machines. His nerves were getting the better of him once more, and those nerves needed an outlet, a bathroom, a quiet moment.

The seagull was back. It was marching in circles around its nest as if it were on military procedures; all it was missing, Bucky thought, was jackboots and a miniscule moustache. As he looked down upon it, it screeched and squawked at such volume as to be intolerable. He banged on the window, waved his arms, hissed, pulled a face and made his presence aggressively known, but to no avail. The seagull simply stared with those insolent black eyes that sent a shiver right through him. The message was made clear: the vicious bird lived there, but he was just passing through.

He withdrew and sat on the edge of the bed. It sagged beneath him and he felt ill, sick, fearful, insatiable, numb, raw, reluctant, energised and excited yet exhausted, and quite alone. He was still experiencing cravings, but for what he could not quite pinpoint.

Bucky buttoned up his shirt, slipped a tie around his neck and fumbled with the knot, all fat fingers – he never could get those things right; it always took his wife to make him presentable. Maybell had made sure he was turned out right, whatever the occasion. Shoes buffed, shirts ironed. Fashion is fleeting, she often said, but style is timeless.

He brushed his teeth, swilled and spat. He took the elevator and stumbled as it jolted between the second and first floors. Dinah and Hattie were awaiting him, both scrolling on their phones.

'What time am I on again?' he asked.

'Early,' said Dinah. '9 p.m. They like to announce the winners of the dance-off afterwards and then the DJs do a final set for as long as their licence allows.'

'Uh-huh. And what time is it now?'

'Close to five.'

'I know what you're thinking, Bucky,' she said.

'I'm fairly certain you don't.'

'Sure I do. You're thinking: there is still time to flag a taxi to the airport and be up at thirty thousand feet by showtime.'

'There you go,' said Bucky. 'You did it again. You really can read my mind.'

'I told you, it's just one of my many thousands of hidden talents. Another is getting the drinks in. Lots of them if necessary.'

'Hell, line them up.'

'Not here – at the venue. Let's go.'

★

They entered through a side door.

A large hospitality room was given over to Bucky. Windowless, it was tucked far away from the main ballroom and had the faded, musty feel of an old theatrical hideaway buried in the bowels of the building; all that was missing was the smell of greasepaint, the gentle clinking of champagne flutes, the quiet laughter of exhilarated air-kissing thespians hastily changing costumes between scenes.

Dinah had made sure there was beer, wine and especially whisky and brandy – good whisky and brandy, better than the raw, mass-market rotgut firewater that he was accustomed to swilling. There were snacks too, towels, even a white robe, which Bucky pulled around him as the cold aches and shakes had returned.

'Bucky's withdrawing from his meds,' Dinah explained matter-of-factly to Hattie. 'Opioids. It's a long-term addiction.'

'Sheesh, Dinah, why don't you tell it how it really is?'

'It's OK,' said Hattie. 'I thought as much.'

'You did?' Bucky replied, exasperated.

'Sure. I've seen similar in several people back home.'

'Really? Hell, I wish you'd said. Here's me trying to hide my cold clucking from everyone.'

'There's no shame in it, Bucky. It's the twenty-first century, everyone is, or has been, addicted to something.'

'That's what I said,' chimed Dinah, as she popped a mint into her mouth. 'I told him that. Didn't I tell you that?'

'I don't suppose there's much point in me asking if you're holding anything?' he said, making sure not to sound too desperate.

'Nothing that the power of music and an encouraging crowd can't give you,' said Hattie.

'Oh, you're sure about that?'

'She's right,' said Dinah. 'You can do this without it, I believe in you. We both do. I bet you'll soon be over the hump of it. Anyway, you're going to need a clear head when you tell Hattie your story.'

'I thought I already did.'

'The full story.'

'I don't follow.'

'We thought she could write your biography,' said Dinah. 'I mean, it's just all too perfect.'

'Biography?'

'A book. About your life.'

'Or documentary,' said Hattie. 'Or both. I'm undecided.'

'You two are crazy.'

'Probably, but as Dinah said, it's perfect. From obscurity to—'

'—Scarborough, England?'

'I was going to say "greatness".'

'You better break the seal on one of those bottles, sweetie. I think I'm going to need a big glug.'

★

Sess took them on a fishing trip once. It was his first summer back from college, and perhaps it was this widening of his world or brotherly instinct that compelled him to take Bucky out of the neighbourhood, out of the city, away from everything he knew, and introduce him to another America that existed away from the streets and the asphalt, the heat and the chaos. Whatever the reason, perhaps he simply fancied himself some fishing – it's possible that down the years Bucky had overthought his brother's motivations in light of everything that followed – he announced one day that they were going to take a road trip that weekend.

Who knew how he laid his hands on a tent, fishing rods and tackle, and everything else that two men need to camp out in the woods, which wasn't much, but Sess always was organised. So off they went, good and early on a cloudless, sticky Saturday morning, driving their way out of the dawn, and thank goodness his big brother knew where it was they were headed, because beyond the confines of the city, Bucky felt entirely hopeless and helpless. Here, indeed, was another country, green and spacious and utterly alien.

They set up camp somewhere deep in the woods, perched on a hill above a slow gliding river that Sess said he heard was 'stacked with salmon' – to which Bucky almost certainly made a crack about watching out for the cans floating downstream.

He remembered the flies and how they were both tormented by them; how haloes of them span across the water and around their hot heads. And the smell too, the smell of the river, like a big wet dog that had been rolling around in rotten things unseen.

At night they built a fire, heated beans, drank some beers – did the things that men in the woods do. Of the fishing, he remembered very little other than continually snagging his line on branches and in the undergrowth, and having to spend most of the time untangling tricky knots, and also the threading of squirming earthworms onto the hook, and the awful liquid that came out of them, and how it all seemed so much effort and so gratuitous. Barbaric, really. They fished a feeder creek too, fished it all day long, though he had no recollection of either of them catching so much as a cold, never mind a muscular salmon. But as his brother commented at the time: 'Fishing is about many things other than catching fish, little brother.'

'Oh yes?' Bucky had laughed, wondering when they could pack up and return to the city. 'Like what?'

'Like mastering the art of patience,' replied Sess in that warm, steady tone of his. 'Like communing with one's surroundings. Like learning that there is more to the world than fire hydrants and bus queues and apartment-block stoops. Like breathing in the fresh air and appreciating the trees and the birdsong and the way the river's moods and colours change throughout the day. Like spending time with your brother out here, beneath canvas, beneath the stars.'

These were the moments to treasure but only later – the next April to be exact, or in fact every time after that when he saw flies circling in that curious way, or if a summer's day was particularly sticky, or he heard mention of Detroit or prison or young men being choked to death in the street by policemen – did Bucky come to appreciate the value of such treasure.

Only later, much later, decades later when he was now an old man, did he finally appreciate just how wise beyond his years Sess had really been, and the generous gift that he had bestowed upon his younger brother that weekend.

★

Above the distant muffled noise of the music that was held at bay behind a closed door, and which came across the lobby, along a thickly carpeted corridor, down a stairwell and along another, narrower hallway, Bucky could hear the nearby ticking of a wall-mounted clock. It instantly elevated his anxiety, made him feel like a death-row prisoner whose final stay of execution had just been denied. The last meal had been eaten and now all that waited between him and the electric chair was a long walk and the slow passing of time – that and the second, more unpredictable, half of a bottle of brandy that he clutched with both hands.

As he saw it however, the only executioner was himself. It was all down to him now. Any sabotaging that might take place would be a sabotage of the self, which he knew he was more than capable of. That was the problem.

The door swung open and Dinah burst into the room. Her cheeks were incandescent with the glow of exertion and damp strands of her dark auburn hair clung to her brow. In that moment she appeared to Bucky as not only striking but handsome – a word which when applied to a woman, to a lady, some might judge to be inferior to, for example, pretty. But Bucky did not see it this way. Handsome was desirable. Pretty was ornamental, aesthetic, but handsome suggested strength, wisdom and so much more. Prettiness faded, prettiness cracked and aged, creased and sagged, but handsome ran deeper. Handsome was in the bone structure, in the eyes; it was imperial, it was regal.

'Hellfire, Bucky, there's a right bloody good turnout tonight. There's a full house up there. I've never seen it so busy. And it's all down to you.'

Behind Dinah there was a rabble of voices and bodies barrelling down the hallway towards them, but when she recognised the sozzled tones of her feckless husband Russell in amongst them, she swiftly closed the door and bolted it shut. A moment later there was the sound of soft fists hammering on the old oak panelling and then of several people asking to be let in. Then things fell silent as they retreated. There in the dressing room it was still. Without natural light, there was no indication as to the time of day, just the clock ticking loudly on the wall and the taste of good brandy burning at the back of Bucky's throat.

'I've had a word with Graham,' said Dinah. 'He's all set with the backing tracks. He knows the running order. He will have everything cued up. You have nothing to worry about – at least not on the production front.'

'How long?'

'How long what?'

'Until I'm on.'

'Oh, about fifteen or twenty minutes. Do you need to do some warm-ups?'

'Warm-ups? Like burpees, you mean?'

'Yeah, you know, for your vocals. And your body too.'

With the brandy bottle wedged in his armpit, Bucky held out his hands, palms down. They were both trembling.

'You know I've never done this before, honey. I'm at a loss here.'

'Why don't you come upstairs, just for a minute. We can watch a little bit of the dance-off from the wings. It's quite a sight.'

He fixed her with a look that she could not quite read. 'Dinah.'

She looked at him slumped in his chair. Already his top button was loose and his tie was askew. A shoelace on his trainers was undone and trailing behind him.

'Yes, Bucky?'

'Thanks for keeping those people out of here just now.'

'It's my pleasure. I mean, it genuinely is – one of them was my husband, though probably not for much longer.'

'And thanks for everything you've done for me this weekend.'

'Oh, I've done nothing except kept you fed and watered.'

'That's not true. You've done more than you know. Hell, you're an angel, a true saint. Just like my Maybellene was an angel and a saint. I mean, you'd have to be to put up with this sad sack.'

'A sad sack that's full of soul music just bursting to get out, I'd say.'

They fell silent for a moment.

'I like your shirt,' he said. 'And that skirt.'

Dinah twirled, and though it was intended in jest, she felt Bucky's eyes upon her.

'Why, thank you.'

'You really think I can make it through, huh?'

'Of course. I believe in you. But let's get your tie straightened and your laces tied, and then head upstairs so you can pop your head round the curtain so to speak, and at least get a flavour for the room. It'll help with the nerves, I'm sure.'

He slowly eased himself out of his chair. His feet ached, his knees ached, his hips howled. There was pain everywhere, and especially in his heart − his heart more than anything, a pain beyond the merely physical.

'Sweetie, I think I'm having a heart attack.'

Dinah looked at him for a moment. She studied his face.

'Maybe. But probably not. So if you could just delay it by half an hour, that would be most appreciated.'

★

When Maybell was diagnosed, it was Bucky who broke down. Broke like a dropped vase. Shattered. He sobbed as loudly as a newborn torn from its mother's teat.

His wife was taken aback by what she witnessed. She had never seen him like this: not when his mother died or when his father followed six weeks later; not when their apartment was robbed of all of their possessions in the late eighties − furniture, carpet, clothes, their unwashed underwear, *everything*; not when the Cubs racked up over one hundred losses in their worst franchise season since '66, and not even when they dramatically defeated Cleveland to break their century-long championship cold spell. She never saw him cry on the various anniversaries of Sess's passing (though the exact date would always remain uncertain), nor even when their beloved cat Rico ran off under a sky shattered by Thanksgiving fireworks, never to be seen again − though such was Bucky's despondency on that occasion that he was half-drunk and near-mute for weeks afterwards.

And here she was, still alive, vertical and, despite the diagnosis, still in decent health. There was the diabetes and the arthritis, and increasingly frequent migraines of course, but tablets took care of all that – the marvels of modern medicine – just as they took care of her husband's hip problems. But this reaction was like none she had ever seen in him. It was like something was unleashed, an outpouring of several decades of masculine emotions repressed. Male tears, especially salty.

Such was the extremity and suddenness of his falling-apart that Maybell found that it was *she* who was consoling *him*. And usually he was so stoic, so traditionally silent in his handling of life's many obstacles. But this time he just seemed too damned tired, too defeated by it all. Only when he had cried himself dry, and the strangulated gulps and exhausted sighs turned to laughter at the sheer snotty absurdity of his display, and she had slipped some music on the stereo – a little bit of Stevie followed by a little bit more of Sly, music that it was literally impossible to cry to – only then was Maybellene Bronco able to get her husband up onto his feet and shuffling on the carpet with her. They sang their way out of misery that night, danced away from death, just as they always did, just as he would now.

And though this time he was flying solo, she was still there with him, right behind his shoulder, out of sight, but very much in his mind.

★

They watched from the wings, Bucky and Dinah. She was standing close to him so that they could both look out across the ballroom. He could detect the smell of sweat coming from her, a funk that he found quite agreeable. It dislodged something inside of him, reminded him of the primal power of human scent. Her elbow brushed against his. The dancers were diminishing in numbers as a judge circled, tapping on the shoulders of those he was choosing to eliminate from the competition. Finally three dancers remained: a dandy-looking man in his fifties, who side-stepped and spun with the casual aloofness of someone who had been dancing to the Northern all of his life; another man around forty, who had the muscle tone and movements of a professional dancer well trained in several disciplines; and a much younger woman dancing with wild and joyful abandon.

One song turned into another. This one was more familiar. Bucky recognised it. It was 'You Shut the Door on Love (Didn't You)' by Pee-Wee Prentice. He leaned into Dinah.

'I think I sang backup on this.'

Dinah cupped a hand to her ear.

'What?'

He shook his head. Saved his voice. 'It doesn't matter.'

Bucky scanned the crowd that lined the dance floor. Many people were clapping and shouting encouragement, while others, taken by the music, were simply unable to cease dancing and continued their own routines – some of them well rehearsed, and some improvising in the heat of the moment, but each exiled on their own private islands of music.

He saw a figure awkwardly milling alone at the edge of the crowd. His eyesight was getting worse; he squinted. It was Shabana. She was sipping at a glass of Coke through a straw and surveying the room, looking just about as nervous as he felt. When her eyes came his way, he waved and signalled to her. She smiled and walked over. He welcomed her into the wings.

'You made it,' he shouted over the music. 'That's great.'

'Oh, my God and Jesus Christ, Bucky. There are so many people here.'

'Yes, there are. Don't remind me.'

Shabana leaned into him, one hand clamped over an ear.

'Are they really all here to see you sing?'

'Well, not entirely. But I guess some of them must be, yes.'

'I didn't realise that you were famous.'

'Hell, I'm not famous.'

'Of course you are. First you have a big hip-hop hit and now this. I should be asking you for your autograph.'

'Yeah, he's famous,' said Dinah. 'Bucky, accept it, you're famous – at least this evening you are. And irritatingly modest with me too. Hi, I'm Dinah.'

'Oh, pardon me,' said Bucky. 'My bad. Shabana, please meet my friend Dinah. Dinah, Shabana.'

They smiled and shook hands. Bucky pulled out the brandy from his back pocket and offered to tip some into Shabana's drink, but she shook her head.

'Sorry,' said Bucky. 'I forgot.'

'When do you sing?' she asked.

Dinah answered for him. 'Ten minutes.'

'It's so exciting.'

'Yeah,' said Bucky, distracted. 'Exciting. Ten minutes just about equals two more drinks. Shall we?'

★

To see a coffin lowered into the ground like that. The rough ropes running through the loosened hands of the cemetery workers as they gently placed it down on the damp clay bed, deep in the long shadows of the eternal earth. So lonely.

He shed no tears that day, at least not publicly. He felt angry, but tired too. Exhausted by it all. Being in such close proximity to death was debilitating; that was something they never told you. Death was a drain on the living too.

It was a small affair, no bigger than their wedding. A few far-flung family members who were still around, and a handful of faces from the neighbourhood. So many people had already gone – too many before their time. Those that remained and were in attendance were no spring chickens. And that was one of the worst things about growing old – the feeling of being left behind, one of the last to leave the party, or perhaps a sense of having overstayed one's welcome. The people you know disappearing until the circle becomes smaller. 'Growing old' was a strange way of putting it too. Aren't we really growing all that time, Bucky wondered, like a solitary tree still standing after all those around it have been uprooted by storms or fallen to the chainsaw? Or were we simply stagnating like the lonely pond that is no longer being refreshed by rain, and is simply sitting in the sun, losing all its oxygen; all of the life forms that it harbours slowly suffocating, the fetid stench of decay hanging over the unmoving body of browning water.

These were the questions that kept Bucky awake at night in the weeks that followed the funeral; these were the questions that had him reaching for the pills and the whisky, and which saw him getting his repeat prescriptions renewed more frequently than ever. Soon Raymond's face was the one he saw most often, the drug store, along with the liquor store and the supermarket the only places he visited for many months. Maybellene's plot was too much to bear. Several times he bought fresh flowers, yet could not bring himself to take them to the empty jam jar that sat six feet above where she lay. For some, the natural impulse is to gravitate towards the one they have lost – elephants, he had read, buried their dead and were capable of grieving, while chimpanzees had been observed standing sentry over their deceased and were known to gather in groups to hug one another in collective periods of mourning – but for Bucky it was quite the opposite. He did not want to think about her laid down there, so entirely alone in the deep, dark soil. It was too horrific. What was gone was gone, and what was left was left: him, Earlon Bronco, alone too, but alone in life rather than death, which was a different experience entirely.

And it was then, right in the pit of it, that he received the unexpected invitation to sing again.

★

Bucky crumpled. Back in the relative safety of the warm womb-like dressing room, tucked away up flights of stairs and down long, empty corridors, his legs buckled and he slumped into a chair, dropping his bottle of brandy as he did so. It landed on the soft carpet. His pulse was racing, his heart a jackhammer.

It felt safe down in that subterranean space, as if no one could possibly reach him. The idea of getting on stage and singing still felt beyond him, so completely hypothetical that it was as if he were watching a movie from the inside; he was trapped in a strange film that no one else but him was seeing. Everyone was living their lives in the real world, but he was right in the centre of it all, watching this strange drama unfold, completely helpless.

Dinah appeared with a glass of iced water.

'Here. Drink some of this.'

'Brandy,' said Bucky.

'No, no brandy. Water. Drink some. And suck on an ice cube – you look overheated.'

Bucky did as he was instructed. The cold water slipped down his throat. He felt it move through him like silk. He crunched on a cube.

'Now, big breath.'

Bucky lifted his head up. 'Huh?'

'Take a big, deep breath. In through the nose and out through the mouth. Come on – I'll do it with you.'

Again, he did as he was told. Together Bucky and Dinah slowed their breathing. In through the nose – 'Hold it for a moment' – and then out through the mouth. They did this ten times until Bucky became aware that the blind panic was subsiding – slowly, but subsiding nevertheless.

'Good?'

'Not good, no,' said Bucky, 'but better.'

'You're on in five minutes,' said Dinah. 'Well, four actually, but I don't suppose it matters.'

He looked up at her from his chair.

'I can't do this, Dinah.'

'I think you can.'

'I don't know. Your faith feels misplaced.'

'That's a bit patronising. You don't know anything about my faith.'

'Sorry, sweetie.'

'You don't need to apologise. But I know I believe in you, in Earlon Bucky Bronco, the man who cut "All the Way Through to the Morning". You're still that same person.'

'Doesn't feel like it.'

'Maybe not. But nevertheless you are still you. Always were, always will be. At least until the wheels finally come off, anyway.'

'It feels like a world away.'

'I'm sure it does. But, again, it's the same world, Bucky, and you're still in it. Maybe you were only put on this earth to sing your few songs. Nothing more. Just to sing for a while, and bring a little joy.'

'What if I mess up?'

'No one cares. They're on your side. Just to have you there in front of them is a big deal. You've made the effort. You came all the way from Chicago to here, to our little Northern town on the coast. You've already won them over.'

Bucky wearily shook his heavy head.

'I don't know, man.'

'What don't you know?'

'This whole damn thing. This Northern thing.'

'Well, what about it?'

'I mean – is it me?'

'Well, the thing is, it's not even really about you, Bucky. For us hardcore acolytes, a Weekender is as much about the experience as it is the music or the individuals singing the songs. It's about the swapping of records, style tips and gossip; that might sound superficial, but it's about the lasting friendships that are formed – real, lifelong friendships, sometimes. It's communal. Bodies perspiring together is not something that can be experienced at home, no matter how much we try to replicate it. All of this offers a safe sense of familiarity and stability in what feels like an unstable world – a world that if you study it too closely is likely to send you insane with despair. At least that's what I get from it anyway. Surely you're not so old you don't remember that need to cut loose once in a while?'

'Right, so you're talking about nostalgia?'

'Maybe. It certainly plays its part. To retreat into a recent past, one whose music is grounded in the expression of pure emotion, is a comfort for some and utterly essential for others. And if temporarily it's taking us back to better, simpler times ... well, is that really such a crime? Nostalgia is only bad if it eats away at someone and turns their present day sour. Same with sentimentality, I guess. It's not just this type of music that supplies this, of course. Other people get it from other pursuits. For some of us though – for *me* – soul music builds a bridge to that past, even if it only lasts as long as the song that is being sung. Three minutes of joy is better than no minutes of joy. I'll give you time to think about that for a moment.'

Bucky reached for the bottle of brandy. He stood up and unscrewed the cap, hesitated, then slowly put it back into place with the palm of his hand. Instead he drank more water, took more breaths. He started humming to himself, and then the hum turned into a melody, and then the melody picked up words along the way and it became a voice. He was singing, Bucky was singing for the first time in a long while. Longer than could remember.

He stopped when the door opened. It was Dinah again.
'OK?'
He nodded.
'Ready?'
'I mean, no. But I guess also, yes?'
'Come here for a moment.' Dinah beckoned him to the doorway. He walked towards her. 'Listen. Can you hear that?'

Bucky cocked an ear. Music was thumping from up above. It was the opening piano chords of 'Come on Train' by Don Thomas. Dinah put a hand on her hip, then took his arm and linked it through hers.

'Lock on,' she said. 'I'll get you where you're going.'

As they walked up the stairs towards the ballroom's wings, the music got louder and Bucky was suddenly flooded with memories of Maybellene, the song opening the floodgates. It was as if his life was flashing before him, but not in the way that people said you experience when approaching death. This felt more uplifting – a celebration of the good times they had shared together. A celebration of their love. No regrets, no grief, no mourning now. Just love. Dinah felt engulfed by the music too. She had heard the song 10,000 times, but tonight her reaction was one she had never experienced before. Tonight the message of the song, and the way in which Bucky had spoken about it in relation to what he had had with Maybellene – that 'something special, something eternal' – merely illuminated the utter desolate emptiness of her own marriage to her dead loss of a husband.

The signs were right there in front of her, and had been all along: soul music also entirely built around the notion that men are bad, and women know them to be bad, yet somehow can't bring themselves to leave them? Deep down she knew this all along – of course she did; soul's authority on all matter of love and lust and heartbreak had always been part of the music's appeal right back to her early teenage years – but only now could she acknowledge it with complete clarity, while finally recognising the course of action that needed to be taken.

She suddenly experienced a parting of the mental clouds, a wonderful sense of lightness of being. The shift that she had sensed earlier was real. Her marriage was dead and needed to be definitively declared so. Soul music had given her this realisation, this *gift*, just as it also held within it – for Bucky at least – a sense of gratitude for the enduring love that he held for his late wife.

Dinah felt that one door was slamming shut. But perhaps, just perhaps, another was opening.

From the side of the stage, Bucky watched a floor full of people dancing and smiling. Down at the barrier, several rows of faces were already in place. Front and centre he saw a young couple, smiling and kissing – really smooching – and then smiling again. They too were in love.

Dinah leaned into Bucky. 'Are you ready?'

He put a finger in one ear and leaned closer towards her. 'What?'

'I said, are you ready? You looked miles away there.'

'I was just thinking about something.'

'What were you thinking?'

'I was thinking about something you said.'

'What was that?'

'Grief is the price of love, that's what you said.'

'I did, didn't I?'

'Yes. And I was also thinking how it's just about the only thing that anyone has said to me these last twelve months that's made any sense at all. That and the fact that maybe it's not so bad to live partly in the past, now and again. God knows, I've tried to avoid going there for so long.'

189

Bucky took a swig of brandy. He swallowed it down and looked at Dinah and she looked at him, and did a small, smiling shrug of excitement, of anticipation. She gripped his hand. She squeezed it. He squeezed it back.

The song ended to applause, then from somewhere up above and all around there came a voice. It was as if God himself were speaking.

'Ladies and gentleman, the moment you've all been waiting for, the man you've all been waiting for, the greatest soul singer of his time…'

★

Naturally built for it and not being the fearful sort, Bucky was always better at fighting than his brother. Sess was always buried in one book or another. Their dad used to joke that Cecil would read anything that was put in front of him. Novel, newspaper, magazine, instruction manual, recipe book, map, cereal packet – it didn't matter what, so long as it was the written word Sess was sure to be interested.

Bucky, back then however, was more of the physical type. He could hold his own on the football field or the basketball court, though he was always more seduced by music and girls. And when it came to fighting – and it came to fighting often – Bucky was more naturally inclined to give and take punishment than his big brother. Only once did Cecil put the gloves on when they were down at the neighbourhood gym, and swiftly received a bloody pummelling while sparring with one of the kids his age. Never again.

Bucky, though, was bigger and stronger and refused to take a step back in any confrontation. This was why what happened was such a tragedy; if anyone had dared to predict, it was surely young Earlon who was the more likely candidate to end up incarcerated for a dumb offence and Cecil Bronco who would go on to be a lawyer or a senator or, who knows, maybe even president, because everyone knew he had the knowledge and the application.

Not that Bucky was inclined to violence; it was just that he had a low tolerance for injustice and was often to be seen sporting a black eye. In their neighbourhood, at that time, such attributes were way more valued than being able to recite poetry, explain a scientific equation or recall the minutiae of an obscure piece of state legislature. Sess Bronco would go far – if he made it out the neighbourhood in one piece. But his kid brother's survival was never in question. He never started a street fight, but he often ended it. And even if he lost, he always lost in style, and with his head held high. Plus, young Earlon could *sing*, and if a man could sing in harmony on a doo-wop track, replicate a hit-parade soul cut or lead on a gospel standard in church on a Sunday, then he was king. Sess couldn't sing for toffee. Couldn't even whistle.

If he could have, maybe it would have been him sitting here in Scarborough, England, today instead of Bucky. Or maybe it could have even been the two of them? Maybe the both of them might have made it through as 'The Legendary Bronco Brothers' or some such. Because with his street smarts and Cecil's book smarts – and both of them fine-looking men with good manners too – they could and should have conquered the world together.

So as well as being for his beloved Maybell, this moment was for Cecil Bronco too, forever frozen in time as a young man on the cusp. It had to be. This was the funeral Bucky never got to attend. The elegy he never got to read or the lament he never got to sing.

This, finally, was for the future his brother never had.

★

Bucky let his legs do the walking. They took him out there onto the stage; he was quite beyond their control. They led him to the microphone stand, and the spotlight, and the song.

The applause died down and a prolonged moment seemed to stretch out all around Bucky, a void of sorts, in which anything – or nothing at all – might happen. This is exactly what crossed his mind: *I wonder what will happen now?* It was as if he were seeing the stage from the floor, the wings, the gods, and was curious and nervous with anticipation as any audience member might be. *I wonder what will happen now?*

But then an opening crack of a snare drum rang out and ricocheted around the Spring Gardens's ballroom as the backing track began. It was far louder than he expected, so loud that for the briefest nano-second he thought perhaps someone had fired off a bullet into the ceiling, and instinct almost sent him down to the floor to take cover – almost – but then the music plunged straight into the lush string-laden intro bars of 'Until the Wheels Fall Off'. Bucky took a step forward and as he slipped the microphone from its holder on top of the stand, he suddenly remembered the advice he had been given by an engineer whose name he had long forgotten, and that was to let the vocal melody follow the warm, rubbery bass line rather than the 4/4 drum pattern being hammered out on the snare drum with metronomic precision in order to achieve consistency, melodic purity and stamina. The tip came rushing back as if it were being shared for the first time, and then suddenly, even more buried memories of being seventeen years old were unearthed to engulf him: drunken late night feeds at the Gold Coin or the Pine Lodge or Bamboo City – better known as Fatback Freddie's – the lingering smell of clove smoke and the scent of the hair pomade he used back then – what was it called? Was it King or Prince or something like that? Duke? Yes, Duke, that was it: *Women love that Duke look!* – long sobering walks back from the city, arriving home with the dawn chorus – a sweeter sound than any when the night had been blessed with good company, hearing – and seeing – Clarence 'The Frogman' Henry and Jamo Thomas and Sam and Dave for the first time on *The !!!! Beat* TV show, and *Bonanza* too, he never missed *Bonanza*, even though Sess said it was just dumb revisionist history, and getting high on rooftops, smoking himself silly and digging The Doors and *Are You Experienced?* too, and 'Reach Out' by the Four Tops playing from every damn radio that summer, and the memories of other girls he thought he had long-forgotten – Tina and Deborah and Kimberley – oh, hell, how long had it been since he thought of sweet Kimberley? – and that old boneshaker bike he had to ride when doing deliveries for the bakery that hot-as-hell summer, and beer, lots of foaming beer from ice-cold bottles, and laughter, and song, and a record contract, and the new suits, the new shoes, and meeting Maybell for the first time, everything laid out ahead of him.

Bucky wrapped the lead around and to keep his other hand occupied, he whipped the trailing cable so that it leapt up, snapping across the stage from one side to the other with a dramatic flourish. It was like a snake rearing up – venomous. The crowd roared their approval, and he looked out across the packed hall, but all he could see were the blinding white lights and the upturned faces of those down the front who were pressed up tight against the stage. He saw the young couple, teenagers maybe, with their arms around one another, emanating pure undiluted love towards one another, and towards him too. Several others around them were smiling and whooping and one or two of them had their eyes pressed tightly shut and what first appeared to Bucky to be looks of anguish on their faces, were in fact, he realised, displays of unrestrained emotion; one woman, he saw, had tears streaming down her cheeks and one arm raised as if in reverence, adulation, deliverance, even. It was the countenance of the ecstatic, the truly beatific.

The collective energy of the crowd, along with the driving thrust of the song, a song that for over fifty years had signified nothing for its singer/composer but bad memories and ill feelings of regret, disappointment, exploitation, gave Bucky an adrenalised charge, a tangible shifting sensation up his spine that was both thrilling and sensual, as if the breath of a stranger were at his neck, whispering in his ear. Real shivers. Again he looked out down to the front rows and it struck him that the cherubic faces that he saw, pale in the pulsing flare of the stage lights, were akin to those of angels ascending a stairway towards the heavenly light.

A sharp salvo of horns signalled the first verse was just a moment away, the piercing, stabbing sound of trumpets, trombones and saxophones from so far back in his life as to sound as if they were being delivered from a past age, an alternative realm, but recorded in just minutes by Sweet Chariot's regular session guys all those years ago, and it felt to Bucky now as if, like Rip Van Winkle, he was waking from a deep half-century slumber, the brassy clarion call of the horn section all that he needed to bounce him back fully into the moment. That music, that song. It was like touching electricity.

Bucky took two neat steps sideways. He cleared his throat, closed his ears and tilted his head way back as he brought the microphone to his mouth and began to sing.

He felt no pain.

★

Wasn't it church were they first met?

Bucky knew that he once recalled the very minutiae of that first meeting – the conversations they had, the weather that day and even what they were wearing. He had held these details firm in his mind for decades, but now the memory had become translucent. Light shone through it, and made him question everything.

No – now he remembered. It was indeed the church where he first laid eyes upon Maybellene, which was long before they ever conversed. It came back to him now as he sang, that first image of a gap-toothed girl, two years younger than him, which at sixteen can seem significant. They were queuing to give thanks, to shake Pastor Presley's hand. She was up front and turned back to look at him, just a glance, and then the turning away of a blushing face of someone feeling the first flush of adolescent emotion.

Their first proper meeting didn't come until later, several years later, when Bucky was a hard-bitten young man, an only child now, and Maybell was a care worker. It developed from there, with milkshakes and hand-holding, double bills at the cinema and the slow reintroduction of laughter back into his life.

She had clung to the idea of Jesus longer than him, much longer. Though Maybell would stop attending church not long after they had married, he suspected she had secretly held onto her belief for the rest of her days; he had lost his faith in God, goodness and justice one night in Detroit whereas for his beloved wife, religion had remained a private concern. Such belief is a hard thing to shake off when it is bred into a person at a young age, especially when you had no good cause to do so.

Instead it had been music in which they placed their faith and found an altar at which to worship: the church of the dance hall, the disco and the radio dial. The shrine of the turntable and the living room rug. Small circles of plastic held the only gospel Bucky and Maybellene Bronco liked to preach as life moved forward with an unstoppable momentum. It was a personal communion, faith through feeling.

Music filled the spaces that had been left behind.

★

The dressing room was busy with the excited chatter and clinking bottles of everyone who had crammed into the small, windowless basement room. Hattie was there, and Shabana, and Graham Carmichael, and the disc jockeys Kath Bullard and Brian Waller, alongside several of the regulars, including the men and the woman who had made it to the dance-off's last three, and a handful of the Weekender's younger attendees. Russell Lake had been turned away at the door, and after banging on it petulantly, he had barrelled away into the night, in search of a more welcoming party.

A photographer was taking photos, the bright flashbulb of his camera briefly illuminating the room and lending an added layer of glamour and sense of occasion to the triumphant mood.

Bucky was sitting in a chair in the corner and leaning forward with his forearms resting on his thighs, a towel hanging loosely around his neck. Dinah came over with two bottles of beer and passed him one. He raised it to her and winked and she reciprocated. They each drank without saying anything, until Dinah broke the moment with a long, deep baritone belch. She sat down next to him.

'Well then.'

'Well, indeed.'

'So?'

'So … what?'

'How do you feel?'

'I don't know.'

'Of course you do, you daft plank,' said Dinah.

Bucky pulled a face of mock displeasure.

'Well, Dinah, by my reckoning you've called me a lummox, a doughnut, a turnip and a plank these past three days. Anything else?'

'Oh, definitely. The weekend's far from over yet. You should take it as a compliment: I only reserve my best put-downs for the best people. Anyway, don't swerve the subject. You can't tell me that after that performance you feel nothing. You tore the place apart, Bucky. You blew the roof off the whole bloody building, you great big bloody…'

Dinah's eyes searched the far distance for the right word.

'You great big bloody *ballbag*.'

She nudged him with her shoulder and he smiled in return.

'I did though, didn't I?'

A joint appeared in Bucky's hand, and he took a hit. He coughed and gave it to Dinah, who blew on the end so that it glowed and then she inhaled on it, passed it on.

'So, how do you feel? Come on, man, it's not like you Americans to by shy in sharing.'

'OK, well, I guess, more than anything – greater than the sense of relief and satisfaction, and being a little drunk and high too – is that I feel *awake*. I feel awake for the first time in a long time, sweet pea. This morning I was as tired as I've ever been. Dog-tired. And two hours ago I felt like I'd rather be down there in the dirt, buried with just the worms for company. I've been sleepwalking for months. A whole year or more. But now? Right now, in this very moment, I feel awake. Beautifully, gloriously, *violently* awake.'

'Excellent,' said Dinah, as Hattie and Shabana crossed the room to join them, and someone played a soul mix through a portable speaker. 'I'm glad you're not entirely spent, because I've just had a rather good idea.'

★

The night was still alive with slurred voices, slopped drinks and illicit smoke. Conversation filled its corners. The mood was one of victory and disbelief. For the dozen or so people in the dressing room, and those up above who were spilling out onto the town's seafront, a small slice of history had been made. Earlon 'Bucky' Bronco had returned with an electric performance that was nothing less than a resurrection, the essence of American soul music laid bare on an old stage, in an old building, in a once-grand town, in an ailing nation. Because although England was an island adrift in troubled waters of its own making, tonight, for now at least, all the worries and debts and doubts and deficiencies and disappointments of those who had witnessed one man sing from the very depths of his own healing heart, were temporarily forgotten. Magic had occurred and not a single person who had borne witness would forget it.

Shabana's face was aglow as she stood before Bucky.

'Oh, my goodness,' she said. 'You really can sing, man.'

Bucky pulled a face of mock indignation.

'You mean you doubted me, Shabana?'

'I mean, yes. Perhaps I did just a little bit. It's just – you know – you didn't look like you had it in you.'

'Oh, some of us knew he had it in him,' said Hattie, as she joined them. 'Keep the faith, right?'

'What is this "keep the faith" business anyway?' Bucky asked.

'It's just something northern soul fans say,' said Dinah. 'It's like a motto or a mantra maybe…'

Bucky nodded. 'Right on.'

'So what happens next?' Shabana asked.

'What do you mean?'

'I mean, when is your next performance? You only did twenty minutes.'

'Twenty minutes is about all I've got in the tank.'

'Perhaps if you learn a few more songs, work on your – what's the word? Stamina? Then maybe—'

'She's right, you know,' Dinah said. 'Shabana's right.'

Hattie nodded in agreement.

'Maybe what?' said Bucky.

'Maybe you can do more shows. Longer sets. More money. All of that.'

'You three are some crazy cats,' said Bucky. 'This has been fun, but come on.'

'Hey, that thing you mentioned about the sample,' Hattie said.

'He told you about that?' asked Shabana.

'He certainly did. I sent a couple of emails off before the show. I've got a friend in Berlin who works in music copyright. He's a lawyer and thinks it's a case worth looking into.'

'Hell, I can't afford no lawyer,' said Bucky.

'You don't need to. He'll look into it for me. For you. For all of us. Like I said, he can follow the trail to the end of the rainbow. And if there's money – and Berthold thinks there could be – then you can pay him. And did you know that song was used in a Marvel movie?'

'Which song? "All the Way Through"?'

'No, the one that sampled it. "Honey Trap"? So there's a potential cut of licensing fees too. The point is: someone somewhere is making money off you. And that's not right.'

'You should listen to Hattie,' said Dinah. 'And Shabana. They've got your back. We all have. But you could tour. You *should* tour. Go international.'

'International? I already am international – I'm in England, aren't I?'

'National then. I bet we could book some dates, no problem. You need to parlay this momentum and I know loads of people on the soul circuit. Doncaster. Carlisle. Grantham. Ipswich. Crawley. Margate. All the hot spots. England is your oyster, Bucky. Scotland, Ireland and Wales too.'

'But I'm meant to be flying back tomorrow. Or today, even.'

'It's an open ticket, Bucky. It's not a problem. What's waiting for you back there?'

He considered the question.

'You really think this thing has legs?'

'Have you not learned by now that I'm always right?'

'I think the message is getting through, sweetie, yes.'

'Well then. If you've done it tonight, then you can do it again. And you can get paid.'

'That would be nice. How much are we talking here? I mean, what's the going rate?'

'I'd have to ask around. I'm sure Graham and Hattie and others can help out on that front, but given there's only one Bucky Bronco making his comeback, I'd think a couple of grand per show would be reasonable.'

'Two large?'

'I don't see why not.'

Hattie nodded in agreement. 'Definitely. Then there's Germany, the rest of Europe.'

'But I've only got three songs.'

'It's four, strictly speaking,' said Dinah. 'But given they're twice as good as anyone else's, I reckon they count as eight. Drop in a few choice covers for the old faithful and you'll have nice tight set. Half hour is enough. Forty minutes, tops. You just need to get in shape and go hard like you did tonight, blast them out, then leave immediately. We could have a car waiting, Elvis-style, and you could be back in your bed, wherever that may be, within minutes.'

'Maybe you could write one or two new ones too,' said Hattie. 'I know so many musicians who would want to chop off their right arm to record with you.'

'Seems drastic, especially for the trumpeters. What would I write about?'

'What *wouldn't* you write about?' Dinah replied. 'Life and everything in it. Love, lust, loss, the whole shebang. I've even got a title for a song for you.'

'Oh, yeah?'

'"Grief Is the Price of Love".'

Bucky nodded, mulling the suggestion over.

'Yes, you should definitely listen to these ladies, Bucky,' Shabana said. 'I don't know much about the business of music, but I know that you can sing, and if you can sing, none of the rest matters.'

Bucky looked from Shabana to Dinah to Hattie. He thought of Maybell. He thought of his late dear mother, who had stood by him and Sess throughout their troubles, who loved her husband, held a family together and had encouraged them in everything they ever did, but never recovered from the heartbreak of the ultimate loss – the unjust theft of her firstborn. He thought of grief. He thought of the price of love. And he realised that, despite everything, it was all still worth it.

'Truly, angels sent from heaven,' he said. 'You must be. Hell, there's just no other explanation for it.'

★

The night was deflating and the backstage dressing room had thinned out, the excited chatter of those that remained now fallen to a sozzled but satisfied murmur.

'What was this other idea of yours anyway?'

Dinah looked at the clock on the wall.

'It's pretty late.'

'It is.'

'It's very late.'

'It is.'

'And neither of us seems too tired.'

'Wired, more like.'

'So you're not in a huge hurry to get back to your room?'

'For once I'm not,' said Bucky, an open bottle of brandy held in one hand and a plastic cup in the other. 'No. Who knows what madness awaits me up there. I'll not forget the Majestic in a while, that's for sure.'

'And I'm definitely in no hurry to get back home,' said Dinah.

'OK.'

'And it's not even that long until the sun comes up.'

'That's surely one of life's certainties, sweetie. But I'm afraid I don't quite follow.'

'Well, I thought, seeing as it is so late – or so early, depending upon which angle you view it from – we could maybe go and have a little dawn dip.'

'Dawn dip?'

'Yes, a swim.'

'Oh, *hell*, no.'

'Why not, Bucky? A swim in the sea is nothing compared to performing in front of a well-oiled crowd of soul fans. It's nothing compared to singing in public for the first time.'

'Honey, I'm drunk and I'm a little high, but I'm not sure I'm that drunk and that high to go native just yet.'

'When you've had a swim you'll be neither. And really there's no time like the present.'

'Sometimes there is. Sometimes a preferable time is later or, even better, never.'

'What's the matter, don't you trust me?'

'Sure, I trust you, but cold water is cold water, and while you're a very capable person, I'm pretty sure there's nothing much you can do about that, Dinah. Besides, isn't it dangerous.'

'Dangerous how?'

'I mean, a guy could drown out there, couldn't he? Or – excuse me – a woman.'

'Not if you stand up, you won't. If you're feeling worried, you just put your feet down and stand up. It's simple. You just stay in the shallows where you feel comfortable. Plus, the sharks and alligators will be asleep now. You'll feel better afterwards.'

'I feel pretty good now. Not quite brand new, but definitely the best I've felt in a long time.'

'You'll feel even more awake then. All those aches and pains? You won't even notice them.'

'I didn't feel them back there, on stage. For those twenty minutes I forgot all about them. What time is dawn anyway?'

'Around seven or so. But we could freshen up a little, then get down there beforehand, and be in the water for when the sun comes up.'

'I thought the swim was the freshening up?'

'Oh, you know what I mean.'

'But don't we need gear for this? All the right clothes and some such?'

'It sounds to me like you're making excuses now, fella. All I need is a swimming costume, and I have one with me at all times for these exact occasions, and all you need is your shorts. Unless you favour the natural approach, of course.'

Bucky's eyed her sideways and frowned.

'Butt-ass naked, you mean?'

She smiled.

'Oh, now I know you're tripping, Dinah.'

'Well, look. I'm going for a swim. You don't have to come in the water. But you could at least hold the towel and the brandy for me.'

'Sweetie, you have got yourself a deal.'

★

It was not yet light but down on the beach, out beyond where the waves were gently lapping at the shore, the sea was like setting jelly. It appeared still but held within it an ebbing energy and fantastic flowing power, a sense of settling into itself forever.

Beneath a towel gripped tightly around her, Dinah changed into her swimsuit with a deftness that was impressive. It took her mere seconds.

Bucky looked at her askance again and raised a sceptical eyebrow as to whether she really intended to enter that big body of water.

Dinah hopped from one foot to the other, then wrapped her arms around herself and rubbed her goosebumped skin.

'Having doubts?' he asked.

'Not at all. I'm just waiting for you.'

'Don't you at least feel a little bit of fear, or reluctance at the very least?'

'Of course, of course. It would be unnatural not to.'

'Yet still you do it.'

'I seem to recall you feeling the fear five minutes before you went on that stage.'

'Fear might be an understatement.'

'And what happened?'

'What happened? I went onstage and did what I did. Did what I could.'

'And you were brilliant. Really, really brilliant.'

For once Bucky took the compliment. He let it in.

'So the moral of the story is,' she continued, 'conquering that reluctance, that fear, that *sheer bloody terror*, is half the fun. Satisfaction can be found in the doing. And here endeth the lesson.'

He sighed and smiled, then shook his head. It had been a weekend of disbelief, but now he was intent on suspending it. He felt he owed it to himself.

It was cold enough even with his clothes on, yet the last dash of brandy, the weed, the tablets and the post-performance adrenaline that were still coursing through his system emboldened him, and not for the first time this night, Bucky found his body taking over where his mind did not dare to go. Before he knew it he was slowly unbuttoning his shirt, loosening his belt and stooping to untie the laces of his trainers. And there he was standing in his shorts.

Shivering slightly, he felt unmasked, vulnerable, but oddly emancipated, as if nothing mattered anymore and that embarrassment was beyond him. Even death seemed a good distance away, and certainly nothing to fret about. Bucky reached for the remains of the brandy and took a swig. He smacked his lips then silently passed it to Dinah, who did the same. She did not comment on him joining her just in case the verbalisation of the act – the recognition of its inevitability – made him decide to back out.

The sand was soft and cold as his feet pressed themselves into it. It slipped between his toes and though unfamiliar it was not unpleasurable. He took a step backwards and watched as the footprint before him slowly erased itself. Within seconds it appeared as if he had never stood there at all.

Dinah took a few long, deep breaths.

'It helps,' she said, so Bucky followed suit. 'Also, the longer you leave it, the harder it is to get in. So let's get in.'

Before Bucky could say anything, she dropped her towel and ran straight at the water. Dinah didn't stop when it rose over her feet and ankles, nor when it was up to her knees, her waist. She waded a few feet further and then dropped down into the water, all the way under. For a moment she disappeared, but then a moment later she resurfaced further out. She flung her wet hair back.

Bucky breathed deeply. In through the nose, out through the mouth. America lay behind him, he felt it at his back. It was part of something that was already fading from view now – the past. The past never went anywhere; it simply diminished then disappeared, just like his footprint. The old invisible ink trick. But the future – that was different. Suddenly the future had possibility, it had potential. It was no longer a void or a vortex. Existence was not simply to be endured or survived. It didn't have to be that way. This thought hit Bucky like a revelation that was as a rare as that thundersnow he'd seen on one or two occasions during cruel Illinois winters.

From the sea, Dinah gestured to him. She waved from the water.

'Oh hell,' he said, 'I must be out of my fuc—'

But before he could finish the sentence, he found himself running towards the still sea too, properly running, for the first time in years. The dense lumber of his body rolled from side to side to accommodate this sudden burst of activity and his hips howled in protest, but it was a protest that for once went unheard as mind and body seemed to be entirely separated now, and Bucky was propelled forward in a motion that felt as if a hidden motor was driving him onwards. The action was entirely beyond his control. The North Sea was approaching and he was about to enter it, and that was that: no argument, no discussion, no analysis. Then he was in the water, and the water was cold – of course it was cold – but something compelled him to kick off from the bottom and let the salty sea take him, hold him aloft and temporarily defeat gravity. He was swimming. He was swimming in the sea.

'I'm swimming,' he said with glee. 'I'm swimming in the sea.'

'Yes, you are,' laughed Dinah. 'How does it feel?'

'It feels…' he struggled to reach for the right word. 'It feels like…'

Dinah waited, she did not dare to interrupt this revelatory moment that he was experiencing.

'It feels like flight,' he said, as the water lapped at his open mouth. 'It feels like music.'

★

A dawn mist twirled low across the water, as light as the candy-floss spun onto sticks along the many amusement arcades that would soon be opening up for another day. Bucky too felt a lightness he had not experienced in so long. Decades. Not just a physical lightness, but a mental weightlessness too, a buoyancy and an unburdening

They swam further out, and he let the tidal pull move through him. He was at its mercy, but it was not unpleasant. Some water splashed into his mouth and he tasted salt, sand and thousands of years of decay and decomposition of all the once-living things that now flavoured this sea.

High above, a seagull dipped and circled. It flew lower, closer, but then it banked away on the breeze, silently reverent in that moment when night became day. For once it let Bucky be.

Dinah turned onto her back. There was an ethereal glow about her face, a soft pinkness, and with her wet hair swept back, Bucky again saw the full strength and beauty of her. He too turned onto his back. His wrinkled toes poked out from the murky water, small, shrivelled and curling, like uncooked shrimp.

'You did it, Bucky. You did it. It's not so cold, is it?'

'I mean – yes, it is. At first anyway. But now, somehow, it doesn't feel quite so bad. It's almost like I'm warming up. Like my mind is convincing my body otherwise.'

'I'm proud of you,' she said. 'And I'm proud to have met you too.'

'Hell, Dinah,' he said, as if he were making a big announcement. He caught himself for a moment, and then he continued, 'I'm proud to know you too. You're the type of woman a man might lose his mind over. You're a different kind of woman, a rare one. An individual. And I'm individual too. But we get on, don't we? Hell, we get on.'

'Like two sides of a single. A-side and B-side.'

'Amen.'

They floated for a full minute, and already the day was becoming lighter, the first glimpse of sun now visible, weak but strengthening with each passing moment.

'So what are you thinking about going home?'

Bucky splashed water over his face, his head. He smiled.

'I'm not.'

'Look,' said Dinah. 'Behind you.'

Bucky turned around.

'What in the hell?'

Not far away, about thirty feet or so, was the black shape of a creature that had risen from the water and was now staring intently at them.

'What is that – a dog?'

'A seal, you daftie.'

'What's it doing here?'

'What do you think it's doing? Same as us, probably – though with a bit more grace and dignity. They're often here of a morning. They're quite used to people.'

The seal flared its nostrils. Bucky smiled and gave a little wave. Droplets hung from its stiff whiskers and its black eyes suggested a sense of bemused puzzlement; it was not afraid. Behind Dinah there was a snorting sound as a second seal rose from the murk.

'Oh, hello,' she said.

Dinah and Bucky treaded water as the seals did the same. Soon a hot syrupy sun would be rising. Out in the offing, the curve of its crown was peeking over the skyline, warming the water and heralding a new day.

Bucky's blood was pumping.

He heard his heart.

Acknowledgements

For her advice, acumen and friendship I would like thank my agent Jessica Woollard. Thanks also to Clare Israel, Emmanuel Omodeinde and everyone at David Higham Associates. At Bloomsbury: thank you to my excellent editor Allegra Le Fanu for her invaluable contribution and to Greg Heinemann for his artwork. Thanks also to Paul Baggaley and Ben McCluskey.

For their input and early encouragement with this novel: Geoff and Dorothy Myers. David Atkinson. Elliot Rashman. Rowan Aust. Nickie Sault. Zaffar Kunial. Thanks, as ever, to Carol Gorner and the Gordon Burn Trust, who let me write in their house, and to Richard and Helen Myers, who did the same. And to Kathryn Myers, all-round organiser.

Special thanks to my wife Adelle Stripe, the human Swiss army knife, not only for her musical input here, but also her endless support.

A Note on the Author

Benjamin Myers was born in Durham in 1976. He is the author
of ten books, including *The Offing*, which was an international
bestseller and selected for the Radio 2 Book Club; *The Gallows
Pole*, which won the Walter Scott Prize for historical fiction and
was adapted for a BBC series by Shane Meadows with A24;
Beastings, which was awarded the Portico Prize for Literature; *Pig
Iron,* which won the inaugural Gordon Burn Prize; and *Cuddy*,
which was awarded the Goldsmiths Prize. He has also published
non-fiction, poetry and crime novels and his journalism has
appeared in publications including the *Guardian, New Statesman,
TLS, Caught by the River* and many more. He lives in the Upper
Calder Valley, West Yorkshire.

benjaminmyerswriter.com / @BenMyers1

A Note on the Type

The text of this book is set in Bembo, which was first used in 1495 by the Venetian printer Aldus Manutius for Cardinal Bembo's *De Aetna*. The original types were cut for Manutius by Francesco Griffo. Bembo was one of the types used by Claude Garamond (1480–1561) as a model for his Romain de l'Université, and so it was a forerunner of what became the standard European type for the following two centuries. Its modern form follows the original types and was designed for Monotype in 1929.

Generative Phonology

This book offers an accessible and integrated overview of generative phonology as it is practised today. Bringing together the various strands that have developed since the appearance of SPE a quarter of a century ago, Iggy Roca supplies the basic terminology and conceptual tools to allow the non-specialist reader to penetrate current problems and debates.

He looks at major developments in mainstream generative phonology as well as work carried out under the umbrella of 'particle', 'dependency', and 'government and charm' phonology. All arguments and theoretical constructs are backed up with empirical illustrations drawn from a variety of languages, along with pointers for future research.

Setting out to overcome the apparent fragmentation of the field, the author draws out and integrates genuine advances and innovations to provide both the phonologist and the non-specialist with a coherent model of phonology.

Iggy Roca teaches phonology at the University of Essex. He is the co-author of *Foundations of General Linguistics* and the editor of *Logical Issues in Language Acquisition* and *Thematic Structure: Its Role in Grammar*.

Linguistic Theory Guides
General editor Dick Hudson

Relational Grammar
Barry Blake

Current Morphology
Andrew Carstairs-McCarthy

Functional Grammar
Anna Siewierska

Categorial Grammars
Mary McGee Wood